Other Books
by Ainsley St Claire

If you loved Venture Capitalist: Temptation, you may enjoy the other sensual, sexy and romantic stories and books she has published.

In a Perfect World

Venture Capitalist: Forbidden Love

Venture Capitalist: Promise

Venture Capitalist: Desire

Venture Capitalist: Obsession
(March 1, 2019)

Venture Capitalist: Longing
(June 1, 2019)

Ainsley St Claire

VENTURE CAPITALIST

Book 4

Temptation

A Novel

Venture Capitalist: Temptation/Ainsley St Claire—1st edition

CONTENTS

Chapter One — 1

Chapter Two — 15

Chapter Three — 22

Chapter Four — 30

Chapter Five — 39

Chapter Six — 44

Chapter Seven — 47

Chapter Eight — 55

Chapter Nine — 69

Chapter Ten — 75

Chapter Eleven — 80

Chapter Twelve — 92

Chapter Thirteen — 106

Chapter Fourteen — 111

Chapter Fifteen — 132

Chapter Sixteen — 147

Chapter Seventeen   150

Chapter Eighteen   155

Chapter Nineteen   161

Chapter Twenty   165

Chapter Twenty-one   170

Chapter Twenty-two   173

Chapter Twenty-three   183

Chapter Twenty-four   188

Chapter Twenty-five   207

Chapter Twenty-six   213

Chapter Twenty-seven   221

Chapter Twenty-eight   228

Chapter Twenty-nine   234

Chapter Thirty   247

Chapter Thirty-one   255

Chapter Thirty-two   263

Chapter Thirty-three   266

A few words...   269

How to find Ainsley   273

About Ainsley   275

GREER

*E*XITING MY FLIGHT AT JFK, I see a placard with my name on it. *CeCe, you didn't have to do this.* I'm quite fine taking a ride share into the city. I walk up and introduce myself. "Hello, I'm Greer Ford."

"Good morning, Ms. Ford. My name is Carleton. Ms. Arnault sent me and asked that I give you a ride to your hotel and be available to you this afternoon for shopping or whatever you may want to do today. May I take your bag?"

Reluctantly, I hand him my bag. I was only expecting to come in for Fashion Week a few days early to see my cousin and support CeCe, one of my best friends. I wasn't expecting her to be worrying about me instead of preparing for the biggest event in her professional career to date.

For everyone, family dynamics are stressful for a multitude of reasons, but my family is more difficult than most. My cousin Vanessa is my age and understands all the challenges I face. Our mothers are sisters and equally crazy, so we've always had one another to lean on in difficult and stressful times. She also works in public relations and owns a small company that caters to designers and companies in the beauty industry here in New York City. Fashion Week is her twice-a-year crazy time.

Carleton opens the passenger door of the Mercedes for me.

"Did CeCe tell you where I'm staying?"

"She mentioned you were at The Whitby Hotel on West 56th Avenue. Is that correct?"

I sit back in my seat and try to relax. "Yes, that's the place."

I look through my e-mails, but nothing is happening that I need to deal with, so I fire off a text to CeCe.

> Me: **You didn't have to send a driver. I'm quite able to get a car and meet Vanessa later today. You have enough to worry about this week. The girls and I are good and here to help you, not the other way around.**
>
> CeCe: **I know that. Don't worry about it. It took two seconds to tell Carleton to get you, and he was grateful not to be here waiting all morning.**
>
> Me: **Somehow I doubt that. I bet he'd much prefer watching models get ready for Fashion Week.**
>
> CeCe: **He'd have been stuck in the car downstairs. Go. Have a great time. Love you, and have fun with Vanessa. She's been amazing to work with this week.**
>
> Me: **How are things going?**
>
> CeCe: **Great. A few things to get done, but we're almost ready.**
>
> CeCe: **Come by the suite at the Four Seasons when you can and let's figure something out.**

Watching the landscape change as we drive in from the airport to Midtown Manhattan, my excitement grows. This week I'll have everyone I care about most all together.

The Whitby is close to Central Park and shopping on 5th Avenue. I've stayed here for many years and love it. As we arrive at the hotel, Carleton jumps out of the car to open my door, and the doorman greets me. "Good to see you again, Ms. Ford."

"Thank you, Tom. How are your wife and the twins?"

"Excellent. I have pictures I can show you later, if you're interested."

"Without a doubt."

He ushers me into the lobby, and the front desk clerk looks up. "Why hello, Ms. Ford. Welcome back to The Whitby Hotel. It's so nice to see you again."

"Thank you."

She clicks a few times on her computer, takes my credit card and prepares the keys. "Here is your room key for the suite. May we send up a bottle of champagne?"

I glance at her name tag. "Thank you, Monica. Maybe later. I'm off to meet my cousin shortly, and the champagne will put me to sleep after the red-eye from San Francisco."

"Please let us know if you need anything. The bellman will bring up your luggage. Would you like a houseman to unpack your bags?"

"No, I can manage that, but thank you."

I take my room key and head up to my usual suite with a beautiful terrace and two bedrooms. I'm staying alone tonight, but when everyone arrives from San Francisco tomorrow, we'll add the room next door and it'll become a three-bedroom suite.

When I was growing up, Vanessa and I would spend days here, just the two of us. Our mothers both have some mental health issues, and we would run away to get a break from our home lives. Our dads would set us up here with unlimited room service, and we'd have a great time eating junk food and watching television all night. We didn't go to clubs and weren't very wild; we had wild at home. We came to The Whitby to escape and get some peace and calm.

My cell phone pings.

Vanessa: **Hello, my beautiful cousin. Are you too jet-lagged to meet me for coffee at the Met?**

Me: **I can't wait. 20 min.?**

Vanessa: **I'll be the one who has giant raccoon eyes and knuckles dragging on the ground.**

I know that may be how she feels, but I've never seen her look like that—ever. Vanessa loves the crazy pace that Fashion Week provides, and she's so good at what she does.

Me: **That'd be a first. See you soon!**

My luggage arrives, and after tipping the bellman, I pull a freshly pressed silk pantsuit from my suitcase. I know there's snow on the road, but I won't be walking on the streets for long and can head to the Met to enjoy brunch. Knowing the two of us, it'll be coffee; this time of year, I swear Vanessa doesn't sleep and just mainlines caffeine.

I call Carleton to let him know I'll be right down, then make my way out of the hotel. My blood must be awfully thin, because although the temperatures may be just below freezing, even with the heat roaring I can't get warm. I'm a San Francisco native to the bone.

Carleton drives me to *Flora Cafe*. Located at the Met, it's a perfect place to sit and chat away from the hustle and bustle of New York City.

Taking a seat in the back corner, I can't help but grin from ear to ear when Vanessa walks in. Wearing a full-length fox fur coat, she's absolutely beautiful.

"GiGi!" She calls me by my childhood nickname and opens her arms wide for a sisterly hug.

"Vannie, you look well rested and ready for the week."

"Oh, you have no idea. I have a model who's working four

shows and is on TubeIt saying defamatory things about minorities. What a mess. I wish she'd shut her mouth already. I have a designer who's so wasted he can't work. And forget the drama in getting the gift bag people to stay within their contract with Metro Composition Cosmetics." Her job in public relations is significantly more challenging than mine, since she's dealing with artists whereas I'm dealing with practical technology people. I don't envy her job in fashion in the least.

I watch her light up when she talks about her work. She's made for this.

When she finally takes a breath, I reach for her and say, "You know you love this."

She looks around to make sure no one is listening. "I do, but don't tell anyone," she whispers at me and winks. "How are things going with your corporate espionage at SHN?"

How *is* it going? I'm so grateful that Vanessa signed SHN's nondisclosure, as she's helped me with the New York press and has been great to discuss issues with. She's someone whom I know will keep it on the downlow.

There's a mole in our company who's been sharing our confidential information with clients and the industry. It seemed like they were sharing with just one company at first, though we recently learned that wasn't the case.

"Well, it's taken a strange twist. The company that's been benefitting from the mole has been struggling because we floated bad information, but we learned the mole is also feeding our information to other competitors. It's a mess, but business is good, and I love my job. No high drama usually."

"Oh my God! How do you tackle the unknown in PR when you don't know whom you're combatting?"

She understands. That's part of why I love my cousin so much.

Not only does she appreciate my mess with my mom, but she works in my field, so she's a constant source of encouragement. "Exactly. We're doing the best we can. We're putting the word out that we're financially sound and just trying to be more proactive than reactive. I hate this."

"You're good at it though," she sympathizes.

Coming from Vanessa, I know this is a true compliment. She'd call me on it if she thought I was dropping the ball or not doing my job well. "Not as good as you are. I wish you'd leave this drama of models, photographers, and crap and come to San Francisco and work with me. We could start our own company together and rule the town. " I miss her. We used to talk every day, but now we only manage to catch up when we can.

"You know I'd love to, but you'd never leave SHN, and what would Angus do?"

Angus is Vanessa's husband, and they're perfect for one another. They both love their jobs and are very focused on that. "He's an investment banker. He could run his fund from San Francisco. There's a large finance community, and he even knows them all."

Even as I suggest it, I know Vanessa would never consider leaving New York City. She loves the fast pace, great restaurants, and the craziness that comes with living here.

"Speaking of Angus, how are you doing?" The grip on my hand tightens as she implores, "It's been almost eight months since Mark left. Are you ready to date?"

Trying to hold back the tears, I share, "Not really. He married his assistant a few months ago. He should be announcing his candidacy for Congress before too long."

"Wow, just like your dad. I'm so sorry." She stands and moves around the table to sit next to me on the bench, then puts her arm around my shoulders and pulls me in for a tight hug. Mark decimated me, but only CeCe and Vanessa know how deeply it cut.

"Thanks. Her father has money, and he made the papers recently for donating a bunch of money to Mark's campaign. Plus, there's no Eve in her life." I don't want to dwell on this; I've already spent too much time rehashing it in my mind and with my friends. Shifting the conversation away from me, I say, "I've missed you so much. How's Gillian doing?" Eve and Gillian are our mothers. We started calling them by their first names when we were in our early teens as a way to separate the extreme behavior that comes with their issues.

"Crazy as ever. And Eve?"

I've been taking a break from Eve recently. As an only child, I'm often the one who's called in to manage her erratic behavior. She lives north of me up in Napa Valley, and I check in on her every few days, but she rarely answers my phone calls or texts. "Still crazy. She tries."

"I hear you. Gillian has her moments. How are you doing?"

"I'm trying. I worry every day that I'm going to turn into my mother. But I have a job that keeps me busy and out of trouble and amazing friends who help keep me sane."

She grins. "You do have amazing friends."

"CeCe has been a beacon. She's so happy with all you've done to help get her here this week." Vanessa's the one who spearheaded the push for CeCe's company, Metro Composition, to be part of Fashion Week. It's really hard for an independent makeup company to get noticed and participate in the event, so if it goes well, Metro Composition may see many more Fashion Weeks. And because of Vanessa and her guidance, I have all the confidence they will.

Vanessa looks at me and holds my hand. "Caroline absolutely

adores you."

"Why do you call her Caroline and not CeCe?"

"Because professionally she's Caroline. CeCe is reserved for friends and family, and we have a business relationship."

I look down at my empty cup and debate a fourth round of coffee, but I may never sleep if I do.

Vanessa's phone keeps lighting up, but she isn't paying attention to it as I begin to gather my things. Together we stand to walk out.

"Well without you, CeCe wouldn't be here this week. Thanks for helping to make it happen," I tell her sincerely.

"We've been working on this for a while. This year we had success, and we're participating in three different designers' shows. Metro Composition's going to be a hit. I need to get over to the suite and check to see how it's coming along. Do you want to join Angus and me for dinner tonight? We'll eat about eight. I know we can squeeze you and Caroline in if you'd like to join."

"I'll check with her, but I bet she won't have time."

To sweeten the idea of joining her for dinner, Vanessa shares, "Well, there are a few men who work for Angus who would trip over themselves to meet you both. Very casual. Promise."

I release a deep laugh. Everyone is ready for me to move on, but I'm not there yet. "You and CeCe are always the matchmakers."

"We need to move Mark firmly to your rearview mirror."

I know she's right, but I'll get myself there in my own time. "Come on. Let's get over to the suite."

I tighten the coat's tie at my waist, and push through the door. The cold winter air hits me square in the face, and it's miserable. I can't stand this weather, and I don't know how anyone does.

As we take our seats in the car, Vanessa turns her phone's

ringer back on and it immediately rings. It's nonstop calls all the way to the Four Seasons. I listen as she directs one call and then another, counting eight different ones in less than five minutes.

Walking in, she gives her coat to the hotel coat check and we head upstairs, where CeCe spots me before I see her.

"Greer! You made it." She gives me a sisterly hug and I return it just as enthusiastically, so happy to be here. Not just because I love clothes and all things fashion, but also because Fashion Week has been on my bucket list for years.

I put my arm around CeCe. "Well, having Carleton at my beck and call makes a difference." Looking around the suite, I see boxes and, truly, a controlled chaos. People are actively setting up what looks like high-end beauty chairs facing large mirrors around cabinets that an electrician is trying to light. There's a team of eight people dressed in black stretch pants and black T-shirts, standing over what must be twenty rows with easily fifty gift bags in each one. Every team member has an armful of Metro Composition products they're dropping into the bags. I see a few of the new spring colors that haven't hit the market. *I wouldn't mind one of the gift bags.*

Beginning Thursday in the hotel's penthouse lounge, the makeup artists from Metro Composition will host a nightly "beauty therapy bar," where guests can sample products and have their brows shaped for free. Looking around, I see all sorts of makeup samples scattered everywhere. I know they sent samples for each Fashion Week ticket holder's goodie bag, but those who come to the suite will be very lucky. There's some pretty impressive stuff here.

CeCe is perfectly coiffed in black palazzo pants and a beautiful blue silk blouse. She's calm and not crazy, but everyone around her looks like they've had six cups of coffee too many. She doesn't seem frazzled, but I know that over the years in the public eye, CeCe has learned to hide it well.

"You don't look stressed at all," I comment. "In fact, you look amazing."

She hugs me again and kisses my cheek. "Aren't you sweet. And no, I'm not stressed. I pay all these people to be stressed and get it done for me. They'll make it on time. I know they will." Looking over my shoulder, she spots Vanessa. "Hey. You just missed the reporter from *Women's Wear Daily*."

"How did it go?"

"I think pretty well. She didn't ask too many tough questions. If you find out, can you let me know? If not, it'll be in the *Fashion Week Daily* tomorrow. I can always read it then."

"Caroline, you're the last one I worry about. You've been managing press your entire life."

She's right. CeCe is from an old-money family, and her parents are the founders of Sandy Systems, a Fortune 10 company her brother currently runs. She's been in the limelight since she was born.

"What can I do to help?" I ask.

"You can join me for a late lunch. Have you eaten?"

I just look at her. She knows me well enough to know I start every morning with coffee. Some people think that's why I'm so thin, but the reality is my taste buds are so acute that I struggle with how strong I taste things. For some reason, eating breakfast out seems to bother me. "I'll go wherever you want to go." I look around the room, taking it all in. "Everything looks fantastic. You've been here a week. How are things going?"

"We've hit a few snags, but nothing earth-shattering." She reaches for my hand and gives me a tour of the suite. There are so many things going on at once, and it's impressive. CeCe's amazing assistant, Ginger, is like a traffic cop as she jumps from call to call, directing people both on the phone and in the suite. "I'm so excited you're here. Do you want to get together tonight?"

Vanessa cuts in. "My husband, Angus, and I are entertaining two investment bankers from his firm. Would you both care to join us at Musso's for steaks tonight? We have reservations at eight."

CeCe looks at me expectantly. "If you want to eat that late, I can do it." She turns to Vanessa. "Are you sure you can add two people to a reservation this late?"

"Without a doubt. You'll enjoy Todd and Steffen. They both run different funds for Angus, and are incredibly handsome and *very* eligible."

I look over at CeCe. "That means they're players, so look out. We'd be fresh meat."

Vanessa laughs. "Well yes, they might date a lot of women, but I do know they wouldn't mind settling down if they met the right one."

CeCe holds up her hands and says, "I think we should go. You need to meet someone who doesn't have political aspirations or is a giant social climbing creep."

Vanessa nods. "See? What was I just saying? Mark needs to be an afterthought."

WE SIT IN THE HOTEL RESTAURANT, and while CeCe orders herself a big sandwich, I choose a salad and another cup of coffee to get warm. After this much coffee, I may never sleep again. It's overrated anyway.

CeCe catches me up on some of the drama Vanessa alluded to about her gift bags. She's glowing and having a great time.

"I'm so happy for you, Ce. You deserve all of this and more."

CeCe's parents started the largest computer networking

company in the world, Sandy Systems. When her mother decided she wanted to make a change in women's lives, she started Metro Composition Cosmetics. Her parents retired a few years ago, and her brother took over Sandy Systems while she took over Metro Composition, having worked for the company during the summers and after school since it was founded. They donate 10 percent of their profits back to women's issues, and the family motto is to remain an independent. This is very challenging in the cosmetics industry, because the big companies keep eating up the small ones and it becomes more challenging to get cosmetic counter space in the big department stores.

When we're done with our meals, CeCe heads back to the suite to continue her preparation for Fashion Week, and I go back to my hotel.

Turning the television on to a mindless rerun of a police drama for a bit of background noise, I set the alarm on my phone to help me manage the time, then set myself up at the dining room table to check on my work e-mails. I have an out-of-office message auto-replying to everyone, but I like to keep my finger on the pulse of what the wires are saying.

As I read through the mountains of articles on our competitors and clients, my eyes get heavy. I'm jet-lagged, and despite all the coffee I've drunk, I'm tired. There's a large overstuffed couch, and I decide to lie down to just rest my eyes for a moment.

As I listen to the show on TV, I must drift off because suddenly the alarm on my phone is ringing. I'm disoriented when I wake, forgetting where I am or what I'm doing here. I can't believe I actually slept—I just don't sleep well anymore. Now I have just enough time to get ready before CeCe arrives to pick me up.

At 7:00 p.m. exactly, the doorbell to my suite rings. CeCe is always on time.

Opening the door, I ask, "How's it possible that you look even better than this afternoon and you worked all day?"

She giggles as she walks past me. "I left at four and took a power nap."

I don't believe her, but I learned a long time ago that it isn't worth arguing. CeCe is one of those people who can sustain herself on four to five hours of sleep, and I hate her for it. I could get so much more done if I could do that. I may not sleep well, but I can keep going with only a short burst of it now and then.

She hands me a bouquet of flowers and a beautiful box of my favorite hard candies from Europe.

"These are lovely. What are they for?"

"For all the mental support you bring with you, and really for recommending Vanessa. She's been amazing through all of this. We'll give her a nice bonus when we pay her bill."

"I know she's thrilled with the work."

"You have no idea how much she's done. Honestly, I never thought I would see anyone as talented as you are in public relations, but she comes a pretty close second."

I laugh. "She wipes the floor with me. Who are you trying to kid?"

"No way. You deal with the unknown. She knows all the players and works them well."

I'm here to support my friend just as she's supported me time and time again. It doesn't require any kind of thank-you gift, and particularly one so generous, but I know it's useless to refuse. "I'll enjoy the candies. Thank you."

She links her arm in mine and conspiratorially asks, "Now, what do you know about these two guys she's playing matchmaker with?"

"Well, Todd is Angus's number two and runs the biggest fund

for Angus's company. Steffen is a German guy who's some kind of numbers wunderkind. I still think they're players and only looking to get laid."

"You're probably right. I still can't believe she tamed Angus."

"I don't know if he's tame, but she keeps him on a tight leash. No funny business for him. I don't think he cares though. He only has eyes for Vanessa."

We gather our coats and head downstairs. I'm excited to have my two best friends together—Vanessa and CeCe. The added mix of the fix-up will either make dinner something to laugh about later or be a fun way to pass the time.

TWO

ANDY

OOKING OUT MY WINDOW, I see twelve years of hard work. And it *has* been hard—California droughts, cold summers, flooding rains, hail damage, California fires, parasites and everything else that's hit us. It's been worth it though. We finally started to get out bottles of the red last year, and it's like a light switched. We're firmly in the black these days, and it's really a relief.

Moving to Napa Valley from Italy, I oversee our US operations. I knew as a young boy that I'd be sent abroad to build the family brand and prepared for this my entire life. I've never minded the hard work and push for success. My family is very supportive, and together we run vineyards across the world. I've built a great wine that represents the family vineyard, but also a bit of my personality—serious yet unpretentious.

Looking over the day's receipts, I'm excited by the numbers. Each month, our revenues climb. They haven't gone up the same as months before though, so I need to prepare for our eventual plateau. We're making just enough to keep our creditors at bay, but we've gone from a well-known winemaker in Europe to expanding across the world over the last twenty years. We're small by many of the big brand's standards, but having a presence on almost every continent brings many different flavors and standing within the high-end wine community.

Taking a deep breath before I enter the tasting room, I close my eyes and calm myself. I try to avoid the tasting room these days. It seems I've become the *man du jour* for the wealthy women of Napa Valley. When I was younger, I loved all the superficial attention, but if I'm being honest with myself, even then I probably still hated it. I know the only reason I'm so popular with the ladies these days is because some women see me as a conquest that no one's had. Ever since my divorce became final a few years ago, I haven't felt the need to date, or even get laid, honestly. I'm tired of the game I thought I would never play again.

I see her across the room. She's beautiful by most standards. I can't remember her name, even though she told me just last week when she was here. If I remember correctly, her husband left for a younger version of her, and Napa is her Tuscan getaway.

She sees me and lights up, waving me over. She's sitting with a group of women of similar age—late fifties and all chasing the younger versions of themselves.

"Andrew! Please meet my friends Jennifer, Eve, and Lisa Marie."

I bend slightly and without trying to be obvious that she doesn't know my name—Andreas, not Andrew. I pull out my heavy Italian accent and say, "Nice to meet you, ladies. Please call me Andy. I hope you're enjoying your wine."

They all nod enthusiastically as she continues, "Andrew, can you sit down and join us?" She pats the seat next to her.

I try hard not to correct her. I don't have any interest in spending time with her and her friends. This is my job, not a social hour for me. Instead, I paint a smile on my face and pretend that her calling me by the wrong name doesn't bug me. "That's so kind of you lovely ladies for the invitation. Unfortunately, duty calls. Enjoy your drinks."

Excusing myself, I work my way over to Sophia. "How's it going?"

"Well, the ladies who flagged you down have been sitting here for over an hour waiting for you."

I roll my eyes, making a mental note to watch myself. I know if I spurn one of these women, it could affect the business. Wine and their fans can be fickle.

"Thanks for the heads-up." Despite all the opportunity that comes my way, I'm a one-woman man who prizes genuineness and thoughtful conversation above lipstick and high heels.

I hear my name being called, coming from the table of women. I paint a smile on my face before I turn around. "Yes, ladies? What can I do for you?"

Eve speaks up. "Marnie thought you might be interested in joining us for dinner tonight." She raises her brows and puffs her large breasts out at me.

"I certainly wish I could. Unfortunately, I have—"

She holds her hand up to stop me. "Before you say no, hear us out. We have a table at French Laundry." She runs her fingers along the neck of her very low-cut sweater and licks her lips in a seductive way. "And we all promise to entertain you fully."

Trying to keep my eyes from bugging out of my head, I try to grasp that she could be inviting me to a sex party with all four of them. "Wow. That's very kind of you to think I could keep up with you minks, really, but I already have plans I can't break." It may be a microwave meal and a soccer game, but it's still plans.

The woman named Lisa Marie looks like she may cry. She runs her hand up the inseam of my pants and I step back, both startled and surprised by her audacity.

"You ladies have a fantastic time. I've never had a bad meal there." I quickly walk away, making an escape before I have to be more direct in my refusal.

Sophie gives me "the look" and a nod at the four young women who just walked in and are sitting at a corner table. She doesn't want to be the bad guy and is going to let me kick them out for being underage. "Welcome, ladies."

They giggle, and the leader of the pack says, "We'd each like a flight of the red." She looks me up and down before breathlessly adding, "Please."

"Of course. But first I need to check everyone's IDs."

All of a sudden, they're nervous. The leader winks at me, "We're all over the drinking age."

"I have no doubt you're over the drinking age in some countries, but I need to be sure you're of age in *this* country."

They all guffaw and murmur excuses.

The leader whines, "It really doesn't matter, does it?"

"Unfortunately it does. Because we're in the wine business and we have a liquor license we don't want to lose, I need to check." I lean in close and point to a strange man sitting at the bar. "See that man over there? He's with the California Alcoholic Beverage Control, and if I serve minors, I'll lose both my liquor license and my vineyard."

A shared look of panic crosses their faces, and the leader says, "Well, I guess we should be heading out, then."

I nod. "Enjoy your night, girls."

I watch them walk out to ensure they actually do. We get far too many young people who think they can drink alcohol without being of age, but the rules for vineyard tasting rooms are much stricter than a bar or liquor store. We got a ticket for serving a minor shortly after we opened. The ID was a close match to the girl, and Sophia made an honest mistake, but it was an expensive $10,000 mistake we'll never make again.

I walk over to the guy I pointed out to the girls. "Hey, Tim."

"Did I hear you say I was with ABC?" he asks with a giant grin on his face.

"Yep. I won't risk my vineyard on a bunch of young girls."

"You have too many ethics for this town."

"Not at all. How's my favorite bottle salesman?"

"Doing great. I just met with Sophia, and we walked through your needs for the crush. We should be in good shape."

"Great. Care for a glass of wine?"

"No, thanks. No drinking and driving for me. A quick way to become unemployed."

"I understand. Let me know if there's anything you need from me."

He waves as he leaves.

There are a few couples, and I see another table of women who keep making googly eyes at me.

Good grief. I'm sure there's something better I can be doing than being treated like a piece of meat.

AT SEVEN, WE CLOSE and lock the outside gates, then shut off all the lights in the tasting room. I send my sister Sophia home to her husband before heading up to the office to go through today's bills. It never stops.

Before I realize it, it's nine, and I can call my mom in Italy for our almost daily check-in before I give in for the night. It's 7:00 a.m. in Tuscany, but she'll already be up and busy. She fields calls from my brothers and sisters from all over the world all day long and loves every minute of it. My parents are the only people in the family who really don't speak any English, but it's a good way for me to keep up with my Italian. Sophia and I tend to only speak to one another in English unless we're having a heated discussion.

The phone only rings once before my mother answers. *"Pronto."*

"Mama!"

In Italian, she says, "My American son has called." My father joins the call, and we have a quick meeting to update everyone on what's going on here, including the daily numbers from the tasting room.

We often talk about the differences between winemaking in the States as compared to Italy. Napa is a tourist destination unlike any other country we operate in, so we see a decent income from tastings. It helps that Sophia and I grew up on our family's wines and learned the process and what makes a good wine long before acquiring a taste for the fermented grape. Sophia primarily runs the tasting room and helps me with the books.

I'm the tenth of fifteen kids, the oldest of the last five. My siblings and I have spanned the globe, starting vineyards and trying to make the family brand, Bellissima, the wine of the world.

"We'd like everyone to come home next month for a group meeting," my father says. We meet every quarter for a week at home. Someone always has something going on that becomes the focus of the meetings; it's never a good thing to have eight brothers and our father focused on your vineyard.

"Please bring your American girlfriend so I can meet her," my mother adds.

"Mama, there's no American woman in my life." Ever since I divorced, she's been after me to meet someone. She worries I'm alone. I promise her that I'm happy, but she doesn't buy it.

"You have time. I have a good feeling you will find one and bring her home. One I will like, of course." My parents are notorious for not liking anyone's future spouse when they brought them home. My oldest brother married a French woman from an old champagne-producing family, and even that was difficult for them.

It's hopeless to argue with her. "I'll try. Talk to you tomorrow."

We hang up, and I make my way to my apartment above the tasting room. Exhausted, I strip down and crawl into bed with only my underwear on.

Though I try not to, I keep rehashing the end of our conversation. My mother's usually a bit subtler, so it's surprising that she's pushing so hard for me to bring someone home.

My head hits the pillow, and I'm out.

GREER

$\mathcal{L}$YING IN BED, I can't help but think about our dinner tonight. Steffen was nice. He's interested and has already texted me—**Good night, beautiful**—but I don't know. He was tall and very handsome, and the German accent is a little sexy. I can see why Vanessa would think he's a good catch for me, but he's a little too attentive, and he didn't wow me. Not many people seem to wow me anyway. I'm still licking my wounds. Mark was my world for many years, and I used to be his. Then one day I wasn't.

Losing him was worse than anything I've ever been through. We'd made so many plans for our future. I helped him get elected to San Francisco's City Council. Together we found issues that he and his constituents could be passionate about. He's charismatic and well-liked by everyone.

Then one day he met me for lunch and told me I was a liability to his political career. Me? No, it really wasn't me. My mother was the liability, and because of that, he cut me loose. No regrets. He walked away, and I haven't received one phone call, text, or e-mail since.

I wake to my cell phone alarm, still tired and hungover. Too little sleep makes my head pound like a jackhammer chewing up a concrete city sidewalk.

Emerson, Sara, and Hadlee arrive today. It'll be nice to have all of my friends together for a fun weekend without the boys in tow.

I glance at my phone and see a text from Steffen. **Good morning, beautiful. Can we meet tonight? I'd love to see you.** Ugh. That's two texts within twenty-four hours, and I never responded to the first one. He's laying it on a little too thick for my taste. It's too much.

Instead, I text Vanessa.

Me: **Hey, thanks for arranging dinner last night. It was great to see you and Angus.**

Vanessa: **Steffen seems pretty smitten.**

Crap. I'm so not interested.

Me: **He's texted me twice. Once to say "Good night" and then this morning to ask me out for tonight.**

Vanessa: **Uh-oh. Do you want me to explain to him what "take it slow" means?**

As much as I'd like to just ignore him, or let her tell him, I need to own this. I didn't give him any signals I was interested in him last night. I swear, sometimes men are like cats; if you ignore them, they seem to circle.

Me: **No, that's okay. I'll try to figure out how to politely let him know.**

Vanessa: **When do the girls arrive?**

I roll over and do some quick math.

Me: **Three hours and eighteen minutes. But who's counting?**

Me: **That would be me! All of my favorite females in New York at the same time. Makes me so happy.**

Vanessa: **Are we still doing a sleepover tonight at your hotel?**

Me: **Yes!!! But I totally understand if work pulls you away.**

Vanessa: **I have it all under control. See you girls at the Metro Composition suite in four or so hours.**

Me: **Love you!**

Vanessa: **Back atcha!**

I get into my running clothes, put on a wool hat and a pair of mittens, and head downstairs toward Central Park. I've done this run a thousand times, and I enjoy it no matter the season.

I love running. The first half mile is always miserable, and I always want to stop at that point, but once I push beyond that feeling, I start to get that runner's high. I started on this route when I was in high school to manage the stress of school and everything going on at home. Now I run because my job is very stressful. The endorphins kick in after a while, and I figure out how to fix problems plaguing me at work or at home, and start to feel like I can do anything. It's really helped me manage the breakup with Mark, keeping me from falling into a bottle, sleeping with anyone with a pulse, or taking a long walk off a short pier.

It's a three-mile run, and I do it in seventeen minutes. It isn't super-fast, but it works for me.

I cool down quickly in this weather, then head up to my room and wander to the bathroom to start the shower. Jet lag kills me, but a nice hot shower and a carafe of coffee after my run will make me human again.

As I prepare to step into the shower, I hear my cell phone ping. I'm sure it's Vanessa again, or maybe the girls, who are on today's red-eye from San Francisco.

Steffen: **I got reservations at The Gilded Lily—hardest place in town to get into—for us tonight at 10. I'll have a car pick you up at your hotel.**

I never told this guy I was available. Do women in New York jump like this?

I want to text him back, but instead I call. He answers before it even finishes the first ring.

"Hey, beautiful. You haven't left my mind since we met last night. You were even in my dreams. You have no idea how much fun we had. I may have even taken care of myself last night and again this morning thinking of you."

Wow. That's a bit too much information from a guy I only met less than twelve hours ago. "Steffen, I appreciate the offer of heading out with you tonight, but I can't go. I have friends coming into town."

"They can't get along without you?" he whines.

"No, I'm not that kind of friend. When I commit, I commit. It was very nice meeting you last night."

"I know if Vanessa knew you were passing up The Gilded Lily, she'd be pretty upset."

"She might be, but she also knows I'm here to visit her and support one of my best friends at Fashion Week." I can almost hear him thinking of a comeback, but before he can dig himself any deeper, I tell him, "I'm sure a man as handsome and accomplished as you are will be able to find someone to accompany you to The Gilded Lily tonight. Thank you so much for thinking of me."

"Promise me you'll call me the next time you're in New York."

Not a chance in hell, but it isn't worth being rude. "Of course. Goodbye, Steffen."

"Goodbye."

I shake my head in disbelief. I've never had anyone pursue me this aggressively before. It's not a turn-on at all. I'm pretty sure I dodged a stalker with that one.

My cell phone pings again. I almost hate to look, figuring it's Steffen and he isn't giving up after all. Instead it's my friends.

Emerson: **We're in the car and on our way. The driver tells us we should see you in less than an hour.**

I bounce like a schoolgirl in my seat and silently clap my

hands together as my excitement bubbles to the surface.

Yeah, my friends are here! May the girls' weekend begin.

Me: **I'll alert the media and let them know we're complete and to look out!**

Emerson: **Sara just snorted her water. See you soon.**

I text CeCe to fill her in.

Me: **The girls are on their way. Should be here at my hotel in about an hour. Would you like us to come to the suite to meet you?**

CeCe doesn't immediately text me back, but I know it's crazy busy for her this week, so I'm fine with that. If I don't hear from her, we can decide as a group what to do.

As I'm putting the finishing touches on my lip gloss, I hear the ping from my cell phone.

CeCe: **Come here when they're ready. I have dinner reservations tonight, and my plan is to relax.**

Me: **Great. Are you ready for tomorrow?**

CeCe: **We just finished. Vanessa is a godsend. She's joining us tonight, right?**

Me: **Of course, but she has to stop calling you Caroline. I keep thinking she's Sister Catherine at Convent of the Sacred Heart.**

Sister Catherine was our only teacher who insisted on calling her Caroline. We know when people approach CeCe and use her given name, they don't actually know her.

CeCe: **I've asked a dozen times. We'll work on her.**

Me: **See you in a few.**

Moments later, the doorbell to my suite rings and I'm thrilled to see my other three best friends in the whole world. There's a lot of screaming, laughing, and hugging. To strangers, you'd think we didn't live in the same city and see each other regularly, but this is more a celebration of being together—and of course, we're here at Fashion Week.

"Hadlee! I thought you couldn't get out of hospital stuff?" Hadlee is a pediatrician, and sometimes it's a challenge for her to get time off.

"I got someone to cover, and Cameron would've chartered a flight to make sure I was here for CeCe."

"Isn't that sweet." Cameron and Hadlee recently got engaged. They really do bring out the best in one another, and I'm so happy for her.

She's been friends with CeCe since kindergarten, I joined them in high school, and Emerson was CeCe's college roommate. Needless to say, we've been friends for a long time. Sarah works with Emerson and me and is CeCe's soon to be sister-in-law. We've become quite the group.

"How long do you need to get ready to meet CeCe?"

Sara volunteers, "I just have to pee."

"This is the beautiful people. I should do something with this mop of red mess on my head." Hadlee announces, though she already looks amazing. Her auburn hair cascades down her tight black turtleneck sweater, which she paired with skinny jeans and knee-high stiletto lace-up boots.

"You look fantastic, but I totally get the pressure. I look at all the lithe models and want to go have a pizza and show them what it's like to enjoy themselves."

At that, Emerson suggests, "I'm up for pizza whenever you are." We all smile.

Twenty minutes later, we're caught up on last night and their flight out. We alert Carleton that we're on our way down, and he's waiting for us at the door in a warm car to drive us to the Four Seasons.

As we continue to chat and laugh, I lead everyone into the suite where CeCe's talking to someone with a camera around their neck. She waves us over and introduces us to Nicky.

She turns to CeCe. "Are they wearing your makeup?"

"They'd better be," CeCe says without a second thought.

We all nod, because of course we are. We'd pay for the makeup if she'd let us, but most of the time she supplies us with everything so we're always sporting the latest colors.

Turning to us, Nicky asks, "May I photograph all of you? I think you're a perfect representation of Metro Cosmetics."

What a compliment!

She brings in the models and does all sorts of poses, mixing us in with them as well as taking photos of just us. She makes it a lot of fun.

As we all pose together with CeCe in the middle, she says, "I hope you'll share that group photo of us."

We finish forty minutes later, our group standing in a daze.

"How did that happen?" Emerson asks.

"She's with *Women's Wear Daily*," CeCe explains, "and they're doing another highlight of our line in tomorrow's *Fashion Week Daily*."

"That's fun," Hadlee shares.

"This is all due to Vanessa's hard work. We really do appreciate all she's done to get us here and make sure we're a success," CeCe gushes, giving me a hip bump. "And she never would've taken us on as a client without you asking her to, so I owe you big, lady."

I laugh. "We aren't even close to even. I owe you so much more. But this isn't a contest. I'm just glad to see Metro get all it deserves. When does your mom arrive?"

"We're doing a big founders event on the last night, so she'll come in for that."

"She's so proud of you," Sara assures her.

"She's driving me crazy right now. I put her calls on silent. That way I don't have to ignore them outright." Looking around, she continues, "If she wanted to have input, she should've come earlier and been part of the planning for the week."

Hadlee gives her a big hug. "This is all fantastic. What can we do to help?"

"I need retail therapy," CeCe exclaims. "Let's get out of here before someone else wants something else from me."

GREER

STEPPING ONTO MY FLIGHT HOME, I'm exhausted. I have an eye cover, a seat that will recline completely, and I plan on sleeping the entire flight home and all day tomorrow.

I can't say my vacation was a vacation, but I had a great time at Fashion Week helping one of my best friends pull off a successful event. This week was so much fun. Between the parties, fashion shows, hanging out in the suite, and helping where they would let us, I got hardly any sleep, but it was worth it. CeCe had a great time, and I loved spending so much time with my friends.

I think my favorite was the Versace show, which kept CeCe super busy. It was typically Versace unique and very sparkly. Personally, the highlight of the New York shows would definitely have to be the Monica Adams collection. From the inspiration behind the garments to the execution of the show, every element was spot on. Being able to distinctively witness the sneaker-inspired dresses, pants, tops, and bags was very comical for me. But I did the most damage to my bank account when I added several items from up-and-coming designer Julia Seaman. Her clothes are my style—professional, tailored and made for my itty-bitty-titty figure.

A car picks me up for my ride home, driving me from the airport into the stop-and-go traffic. I push my sunglasses farther up my nose and read the San Francisco Chronicle.

Opening up the Local section, I see a big picture of my ex-fiancé. Mark is announcing his bid for Congress. By his side is his wife and she's huge. No fucking way she's pregnant. We just broke up eight months ago. My heart skips a few beats as I read the article through the sting of bitter tears. She has the life I wanted with the man I thought was my soul mate. I can't help but be sad at the same time. This is the life we planned for us.

Looking out the window, I watch the cars in the neighboring lanes inch along and think about our conversations about why he didn't want children. He didn't plan on being around. His star was rising, and they would slow him down. It was perfect because I didn't want children either. Now she's pregnant, and it seems everything he ever said to me was a lie.

My disappointment moves from sad to angry very quickly. I wasted too much time on him. He was only interested in my money. My friends and I knew that with growing up as part of the 1 percent, we needed to be cautious and on the lookout for those people who were only using us for something, but he played me so well that I chased him. *Fuck him!*

Finally home, I drop my bags just inside the front door and walk to my bedroom, the exhaustion pressing down on me as I'm feeling overwhelmed all at once. I crawl between the sheets and sniff the orange blossom scent the housekeeper uses in the dryer, letting it relax me as I drift into a restless sleep.

I WAKE TO MY PHONE RINGING. It's after three in the afternoon, and the sun is at its warmest of the day. CeCe's calling, but I don't even have the energy to be happy for her success at Fashion Week, so I ignore her call. I'm a terrible friend, but I don't want to deal with anything or anyone.

Putting my phone on silent, I walk into the kitchen to find something to eat. Opening the fridge, everything I have seems to be growing legs and ready to walk out of my fridge on its own. *Mental note: Have the housekeeper clean out my fridge. Yuck!*

Moving through my apartment, I walk into my living room and pour myself a deep glass of Johnnie Walker Blue neat. I want to numb my feelings.

Sitting in my garden patio, I watch the sun begin to set behind the Golden Gate Bridge. *Time to put my big-girl panties on and stop crying over Mark.* When he first left me, I took all of the things he left at my house and donated them to a homeless shelter. Then when I found out he'd cheated on me with Sydney, I took all the jewelry he gave me to a jeweler I knew and sold it, then donated that money to a food bank. I was hurt then, but now I'm angry.

I'm wallowing in my own self-pity, and if I'm not careful, it'll become a black hole I'll struggle to get out of. I need to stop feeling sorry for myself and see what CeCe needed. Maybe I can talk someone into going out to dinner with me. Picking up my phone, I see twelve missed calls and a dozen text messages.

CeCe: **I just saw the news. Are you OK?**

CeCe: **I'm getting on my flight with my mom. Do you want to have dinner with us tonight at my parents'?**

CeCe is a true best friend. She's just coming off two weeks of constant work and no sleep, and now she's worried about me.

Hadlee: **Cameron and I are thinking of you. Do you want to meet us for dinner?**

Emerson: **Hey. Fuck Mark. Do you want to grab something to eat?**

CeCe: **I'm thinking of you. I also donated $5,000 to his opponent, Jennifer Chang. I know nothing about her except that she's running opposite of him. Mom and Dad each donated to Jennifer's campaign, too. He's going down!**

Trey: **Hey. He's a loser. Don't let him get to you. Sara and I will also be donating to Jennifer Chang per CeCe's orders. :)**

Sara: **I echo everything Trey has said. You're such a class act. Fuck Mark.**

CeCe: **Sydney's a cow. She can't hold a candle to you.**

I adore my friends. They stick with me regardless and have for years.

Before everyone comes to my door, I send a group text to the partners from work and my friends.

Me: **I'm fine. Mark is an asshole. Please come to my house this evening and bring whatever you want to throw on the barbecue. I have wine and Johnnie Walker Blue, so if you want something other than that, bring it. Come whenever you can.**

I then set out to decide what to put on the grill to prepare for my impromptu dinner party. I haven't even finished when Trey and Sara ring my doorbell, arms laden with grocery bags. They live just a few blocks away, so it makes sense that they made it so quickly.

"We were coming whether you invited us or not," Trey announces.

Sara hugs me and hands me a beautiful bouquet of flowers. "We were at the grocery store when we got your text. Perfect timing."

I'm beside myself at the generosity of my friends, fighting back a couple tears that are threatening.

My doorbell rings again a moment later, and I open the door to Cynthia. "I heard there was a party, so I ditched a bad date and picked up some wine."

"Thank you. We'll use any excuse to get together." I chuckle at how something I thought was such a disaster really isn't. I'm so lucky to have so many wonderful friends to make sure I get past this.

Cynthia hugs me and kisses my cheek. "My date was a little too self-absorbed. I'm so grateful for the excuse to leave. I just have a bad picker."

Sara walks up just then. "What's a bad picker?" she asks.

Without skipping a beat, Cynthia explains, "Well, if there's a player, married man, or overall self-centered asshole, then he's attracted to me."

I chuckle. "I must have a bad picker, too." Turning to Sara, I say, "Can you fill her in on the details of my bad picker and why we ended up here while I show Trey to the grill and make sure he can get it going? And you can tell her everything. No use having any secrets with my friends."

Sara gives me a big hug. "Cynthia, our good friend Greer here had her heart broken by a monster jerk..."

I miss the end of the conversation, but with all my friends circling, I feel like a million bucks. Trey and I wander outside to the garden terrace and my outdoor kitchen. My home is a penthouse that used to belong to CeCe's godmother. She sold it to me a little over two years ago, and I couldn't wait to move in after some slight remodeling. We used to come here as little girls, enjoying a view of the Golden Gate, Alcatraz, Marin, and the East Bay. But what I love most are the English gardens. I learned quickly that I needed a gardener to manage them, though; I'd rather be out with friends than digging in the dirt.

"Hopefully you can make this grill work."

Trey looks me over carefully. "I know I've been saying this ever since I met him, but you were too good for him. It's truly his loss."

"Thank you."

Pulling me in for a brotherly hug, he murmurs, "Remember, we all meet our soul mates at different times. Yours is out there, he just needs to find you."

"Thank you," I repeat, biting back tears.

I hear the voices increasing inside before Dillon says, "Save a hug for Emerson and me."

They envelop me into a big hug, and my heart grows with my friends and the love they give me. They may not be the family I was born with, but they're the family I've chosen. I'm so lucky to have them in my life. I'm not sure where I'd be without them.

Emerson announces, "We brought kebabs for the grill. Lamb, chicken, and beef."

"Sounds delicious." I give her another welcome hug.

Cameron and Hadlee arrive, producing several cuts of steak, chicken, and pork. No one is going hungry tonight.

I'm quickly surrounded by all my good friends, CeCe and her parents arriving as I walk back inside. My dining room table is full of salads and side dishes.

"For an impromptu dinner gathering, we're going to eat well," I announce.

CeCe's father, Charles, dryly says, "Well you did offer Johnnie Walker Blue." Everyone laughs as he takes a bottle out of a bag.

Mason and Annabel are the last to arrive. Annabel stands at Mason's side, and no one really seems to greet her. It's too bad that none of us seem to like her. She worked as the receptionist when I started at SHN, then became Sara's legal assistant, but she recently left the company because she and Mason moved in together.

She just doesn't seem to fit into our group, not because she's younger than all of us, but I think she tries too hard. But as CeCe says, "She must be able to suck a golf ball through a garden hose," because Mason's positively whipped.

We have a corporate spy feeding our confidential information to our competitors, and Annabel's eagerness and constant hovering has her high on most people's lists as the spy. Recently she moved in with Mason, but he required her to find another job. My understanding is that she isn't working, just living with him and waiting for an engagement ring. I'm not sure she's our mole, but I do think my mother is right with her "She's a gold-digger" assessment.

The guys are standing around the grill outside, probably talking about sports. The girls are inside rehashing our week in New York.

Standing around my home, we have the comfort of a family. We can tease and be fun loving. Having grown up an only child with half-siblings, I was often alone. Looking out at the pockets of friends, I hear conversations about wedding planning, trips being planned far away, trips being taken locally, gossip about our jobs and friends, and the sharing of our lives. I notice several people are without drinks, which means I'm shirking my hostess duties.

"So, what are we drinking?" I ask the group

"Emerson brought a pitcher of lemonade," Annabel volunteers with a broad and plastic smile.

I'm surprised by that, as usually Emerson is our amateur bartender and has fun, creative drinks.

She laughs and tells us, "It's *adult* lemonade." I'm not sure what that means, but before I can ask, she hands me a glass with a sugared rim. "It's equal parts lemon juice, limoncello, vodka, and sugar."

I take a small tentative sip. Wow. A nice pucker and a little sweet, but it hides the liquor well. This is good. "That'll knock me on my ass if I'm not careful."

"Thankfully we all live close and can either walk or take a Lyft home."

CeCe holds her glass up. "To Greer, for always being a lady when she rightfully should be a bitch."

"Here, here," everyone echoes.

CeCe leans in and asks, "What can we do to make Mark regret using our good friend to bolster his political career and then leaving her for a mouse?"

I smile and hold back the tears. "You all are wonderful and incredible friends. Thank you. I can't lie, it hurt to see Mark and his pregnant wife, but having all of you here this evening means the world. I can't tell you how much I appreciate having each of you in my life. Now, let's eat."

We enjoy a fun dinner, and I forget about Mark for a little while.

CeCe is the last one, sitting on the couch opposite me after we've said goodbye to our other friends. "Okay, hon, I've known you since we were eight years old. I know this hurts, but don't let your brain go into overdrive. You aren't your mom. You're smarter and much more adept at managing this."

"I know." I fight back the tears that are pushing to come out. "I want to blame her for this, but I know it's her illness."

"Exactly. He was looking for an excuse. He may have had the charisma, good looks, and charm, but he doesn't understand his constituents, and you were the one behind him making him look like a rock star. He'll die a terrible political death, and quickly."

I nod, knowing if I say anything, I'll crack and the tears will come nonstop. I just sit and watch the lights on the sailboats along the bay.

"Do you want me to stay tonight?"

"No, I'll be fine. You just got home after being gone for a month. Go. Sleep in your own bed and get caught up on your life."

CeCe stands and I join her. Giving me a big hug, she whispers in my ear, "You're beautiful, smart and fucking awesome in every. Single. Way. You don't need any man to validate you. Just remember that."

"Thank you." We walk to the front door, and she squeezes my hand before she leaves.

I look around at my house and think of what my friends did for me tonight.

CeCe is right. I've given Mark too much of my time and energy. I'm ready for a change.

ANDY

$\mathcal{I}$ HEAR THE DOOR from the tasting room open. "Sophia? Can you help me with this issue in QuickBooks?"

"I'm on my way. We have a little over $3,000 in sales today. Not too bad for a Tuesday."

"I'm balancing the books, and I'm stuck with this $5,240 check. What is it for?"

"Why are you balancing the books? That's my job."

"I need to send the P&L to Dad and Giovanni for the quarterly financial meeting." Looking at the screen again, I ask, "So, what is this check for?"

She looks down at her hands and studies them as if she's never seen them before. I wait patiently for her to answer.

Looking up at me through the hair that's fallen in her face, she finally mutters, "Me."

"What for?"

She whispers, "A bonus."

I'm stunned. "Sophia, we can't afford any bonuses right now. We're hiring like crazy to prepare for the crush. I need interns, pickers, drivers, pruners, and the water bill is sky high. We need that money back. You know half of this business belongs to you, but we can't take anything out of it right now."

"I really needed it."

"Sophia." My blood pressure is skyrocketing. "I haven't had a paycheck in several months. You make a very good living. You need to repay that tonight."

"I can't. I spent it." In rapid Italian, her voice becomes angry and bitter. "You get $3,000 a month and have no expenses because you live here rent free."

We go through this argument every few years, where she feels that things aren't equal. "Yes, and you earn $50,000 a year, and you *could* live here rent free, but you and Luke choose to live in town."

"You and Luke don't get along," she pouts.

"He stays home and smokes pot all day. You work. Forgive me for wanting him to pull his own weight." I'm tired of this fight, and I'm still pissed that she just wrote herself a check. She's never done anything like this before. When we argue, it's usually about when I'll sign the vineyard over to her, but the bank owns over 90 percent right now, and it's in Bellissima Holdings with me as the guarantor. There's no value to this yet.

I know Napa Valley is expensive, but had she talked to me, I would've lent her the money from my own account. She's right. I don't have many expenses, and I would've given her a loan. But now I have to figure out how to make it work in the books, and she has to know that surprising me isn't the way to make a smooth transition with my father and brother. "I'll bring it up with Papa and Giovanni. They're going to be more upset than I am."

She's becoming upset by the conversation. "Too bad. I work myself to the bone for this vineyard, and everyone treats me like I'm a hired hand and my opinion doesn't count."

"What are you talking about? I value you and your opinion. You know why I can't sign it over today. It's against the terms of Bellissima Holdings. It isn't you specifically—it goes back to our great-grandfather and his wanting to be sure the wine remained in our family. This affects all of our sisters. We all agree that when Giovanni takes over for Papa, he'll change that provision. Plus, you and I make all of our decisions together knowing this is half your vineyard."

"Not on paper where it counts."

"What the hell is Luke feeding you? You know the moment the holding company allows us to make you a full partner, I'll do it."

"I'll believe it when I see it." Sophia walks out and slams the door. We have this fight more often when Luke isn't working. I hate that she's stuck supporting his lazy ass. He sits home all day watching sports television and getting high.

She can have the money. She works hard, and I'd be lost without her. But how do I explain this to my dad and Giovanni? If my brother hadn't gone to business school, I wouldn't have to worry about it, but he's the unofficial chief financial officer of Bellissima Holdings, Ltd., our parent company, and he'll immediately know something's off.

My monthly meeting with Giovanni and my father is over Skype and in rapid Italian. The conversation does not go particularly well. I know they meet with all seven of the vineyards over a few days, but it's a lengthy meeting, and sometimes I feel like we go through every expense and have to explain each one. Bellissima Valle has been the most expensive undertaking of all the vineyards we've started, and there are a lot of eyes on every expenditure. It's a crown jewel—or at least it will be once we're fully producing. Currently, we're barely in the black.

"She wrote herself a check?" Giovanni asks incredulously. I swear I can see a vein pulsing in his neck through the computer screen.

"Yes." I pinch the bridge of my nose.

My father is turning red with anger and is hardly understandable, but I can make out "Then she doesn't get a paycheck until she pays it back, and we take all check signing abilities away from her. We can't trust her."

"Papa, this is Sophia. We can trust her, but I can't hold her check. Luke isn't working. They need the money," I implore.

"Tell them to move home," my father answers simply.

"Papa, it isn't that easy."

"Yes it is. I want her off the checking account, and if she can't pay her bills, she moves back to the villa, either there or here."

If only it were that easy. I end up agreeing to put her on a payment plan, though I know I'll be the one who really pays it back. She truly works hard for the company, and maybe I don't appreciate her as well as I should. Times are rough, and when things get better, she can pay me back.

After the call, I lean back in my chair and stare at the ceiling. Sometimes I wish the vineyard was all mine and I could just gift her part of it.

Sophia walks in. "What did they say?"

"They're very angry with you."

"I don't care." She shrugs, pretending it doesn't matter, but I know it does.

"I'm going to cover the money this time, but if it happens again, Papa is going to require you to move home. And I don't mean here, I mean Bellissima Grande."

She snorts. "That'll never happen."

"I love you, baby sister. Don't take money from the accounts again unless we discuss it first. I'll lend you the money this time, and you will pay me back when you have it."

Turning to look at me, her eyes are pooling. "I only took what I needed. I won't do it again. Everything is just so hard with Luke not working right now." Before she leaves, she hugs me. "Thank you, big brother. Luke has a job starting next week. We'll be fine."

GREER

$\mathcal{S}$TRETCHING AS I LIE IN BED, I think about last night. For the first night in how many months, I didn't think of Mark, nor did I dream of him. A wave of happiness envelops me at the thought.

It's still early, but I want to go for a run before the heat of the day makes it too oppressive. I dress and head downstairs, nodding at my neighbor who must be thinking the same. After we stretch in the front portico, I follow him, trying to keep up with his grueling pace without complaint. He has a good eight inches on me, and for every stride he takes, I cover about two-thirds the distance.

The suffocating humidity of the warm morning weighs down on me, making me sticky. My clothes and hair, slick with perspiration, cling to my skin, sweat rolling down my body in thick, salty beads as my heart throbs inside my chest at four times its normal pace. My skin feels the heat of the morning sun like it's roasting. I bounce slightly as I jog in place at the red lights, which wears me out quickly. I eventually settle to stumbling along behind my neighbor as fast as I can. I'm vaguely aware of a burning in my legs and lungs.

Reaching the waterfront at the Marina, I go to the public drinking fountain and gulp down deep pulls of refreshingly cool water, trying to catch my breath. My lungs feel like they'll burst and my throat is so dry. With my hands on my head, I walk slowly in circles until my breathing becomes regular once more.

As my breathing slows, I smell the salted air of the bay and the thick scent of coffee from a stand nearby. It's a siren's call—I love the taste, the smell, and sound coffee makes when it hits the bottom of a paper cup. This spot is out of the way for tourists, and the line forms early and persists until the beans have run out. We chase our need for a caffeine fix as a city.

Taking a sip of my coffee, I pick up a newspaper and walk out onto the pier, loving the way the sun warms my skin. I find a quiet spot to let my legs dangle off the edge and start reading the paper. I spot a different article about Mark and his bid for Congress, and his dagger turns in my gut again.

I'm not vindictive, but I plot. I've always considered revenge to be a much-belied concept. Knowing I've always served people what they've truly earned kept me happy and serene. They can play their passive-aggressive bullshit games, and I'll smile, nod and give every impression that I'm the gracious loser of the skirmish.

I'm not going to go after him directly. Don't get me wrong, I'll contribute and volunteer for his opponent, but my revenge is pretty simple—I'm going to live my life and be happy without him. I'll love again, and my next boyfriend isn't going to be a narcissist who's only concerned for himself. I want a nice guy who will appreciate me for me and wants to live a quiet life.

I lift my arms into the air and stretch. It's almost seven, and I need to get to work. Dumping my empty cup and the newspaper in the recycle bin, I begin my moderate jogging pace home. The exercise allows me to clear my head and think through everything, helping me figure out what I need to do at work and my personal life.

I need to help come up with a plan to help catch our mole. Every time we get close, I feel they slip through our fingers. As I jog back, I work through the challenges of my day and how I'll work through the problems. I don't have all the answers, but I do come up with some.

I'm going to go out on a few dates, though I'm not looking for Mr. Right, maybe just Mr. Right Now. I want to have fun and have someone to enjoy my time with. It doesn't need to lead to anything more than that.

After a quick shower and choosing an outfit for work, I apply my makeup. I'm almost presentable. My brain wanders to my schedule as I paint my lips with lipstick; they're a shade darker than my flushed cheeks when I decide that's enough. I like the soft contrast of my face against my dark hair and eyes. Slipping on my dress, it fits like it was tailored for my curves. It makes my hips round, my breasts seem larger and my waist small.

My calendar is full of activities today, and I'm ready.

Today I'm going to be happy. Today is going to be a good day.

chapter

SEVEN

ANDY

SURROUNDED BY ACRES OF VINES, I'm talking to my harvest
interns, explaining to them what I need from them today
when the walkie-talkie sounds. "Andy, can you come to the tasting room? We have a guest I need some help with."

Crap. That means there's a drunk and disorderly guest. I'm
frustrated that someone in the tasting room would serve someone
enough to get drunk. That could affect our liquor license. But on
the flipside, we have to be careful that we don't push the guest out
and they make a scene. We have a good rate with a cab service,
and the ride shares are always close by, so that helps when we
don't realize some guests have had too much.

After directing the interns to the warehouse to clean out some
of the bins as we prepare for harvest, I climb in the golf cart with
my waterproof boots and mud-covered jeans and head to the
tasting room.

I can hear her before I enter, and I can tell she isn't drunk.
There's no slur; she's just talking fast and loud. I open the doors
and let my eyes adjust to the dim surroundings.

"There he is!" A woman who looks familiar places her hands
around my neck and rubs herself against me. She's certainly
disheveled. She has smudges of dirt on her face and her dress, her

hair is a matted mess, and her feet are filthy in her sandals. "Hi there, handsome. You up for a good time?"

Pulling myself from her grasp, I pull back and get a look at her. Her name is at the tip of my tongue, but I'm so taken off guard by both her appearance and her aggressiveness, I can't pull her name out of the recesses of my memory. "So good to see you—"

"Andy, my love. How about we go back to your place and do a bit of the naked tango."

I think I remember her name. "Err, Eve, right?"

"Yes. Yes." She grabs for my crotch, and I step back. "Don't be so shy. Rumor has it you aren't gettin' any, and I'm here to change that for you. I'm a goddess when it comes to sex."

"I'm sure you're right, but today's not a good day. Did you drive here?"

Eve is talking fast, and she's not completely coherent, like she's in overdrive. "Oh, you know my husband left me for a younger woman, and it was really hard. I had to raise my daughter on my own. He started a new family and left us behind. Don't get me wrong, I was far from broke, but she was difficult, to say the least. She's close to her father, but she's the reason he left me. She's in her early thirties now. Do I look old enough to have a daughter that old? No, I don't. I was a child bride. But you know, I've had a tiny bit of work done. Not as much as the other girls, of course. I have great skin. You should see. I love sex. The longest I've ever been without sex is a week. I'm good at it, too. I can show you. Wouldn't you like to have the time of your life?" As she bounced from question to question, I don't think she took a breath.

I'm starting to get concerned. "Eve, are you here alone?"

"Why? Are you looking for a third to join us? I did that a few times. Nothing like showing a man what real pleasure is. I'm up for anything, but I must warn you, I don't suck if you don't lick. I mean, oral sex is amazing, and I'm able to cream all over your tongue. I've been told my cum tastes like candy." She grabs my hand and tries to move it to her chest. "And honey, these babies are real. And they don't point down—"

"Eve, hold on a moment." I take her hand and look her in the eye. "Eve, how did you get here?"

"I walked. I'm very fit. I can walk miles." Turning, she points to her backside. "See this ass? It's in perfect shape. I spend sixty minutes every day on a stair climber. Feel it. It's firm." Leaning in, she says, "I like back door, too, if you want to do that."

"Okay, Eve. Do you have the phone number of someone I can call who can come get you?"

"Why do I need someone to come get me? I haven't had anything to drink. I'm perfectly capable of walking home. If you don't want some of this"—she waves her hand around herself—"then you know, you *are* missing out." Raising her voice, she yells across the tasting room. "You are missing out big-time! I'm amazing in bed. I'm a MILF. I may be older, but I know how to give a very good time."

With that, she turns and is out the door, leaving my head spinning. I take a moment to speak with Sophia, both a little stunned by what just happened.

"Do you think we should call someone?" she asks.

"Yes, but I don't know who. I don't have the number of any of her friends. Do you?"

She shakes her head. "Do we call the police or the hospital?"

"I'm not exactly sure." I have so much to do. *Shit. I hate this.* I walk to the office upstairs and look out the windows for her while the phone connects to the non-emergency line at the St. Helena police station. I explain to them what happened and ask if there's anything I should do or someone I should call.

"Did you see where she went?"

"Honestly, I didn't. I was a little surprised by it, and it happened so fast. She can't have gone far."

"Okay, we'll send someone down the highway. We can call the right person if we find her."

"I'll look, too, see if I can't find a family member's name." I hang up, looking at the pile of paperwork on my desk and all the work that needs to be done. Instead I'm looking for an unstable woman who wandered into my tasting room.

Walking down to the golf cart, I drive out to the road, looking both left and right down the desolate street, I don't see anyone walking. Knowing my luck, she drove off.

I see the police cruiser approach, the officer rolling down his window. "Hey, Andy," he greets me.

"Jeremy. I'm glad it's you."

"I didn't see anyone on the road. Did you catch the woman's name?"

"I met her with friends. Her first name's Eve, but that's all I know. And she said she walked, but she may very well have driven. I didn't follow her right out the door. We were a bit surprised by her."

"What happened?"

I walk him through her appearance and rambling speech in the tasting room.

"Sounds like she's had some sort of break. If she comes back, call us. We'll take her to the hospital or jail, whichever seems most appropriate."

"We're pretty positive she isn't drunk, but it seemed like she might need a hospital."

"All right then. Let us know if she comes back."

I wave him goodbye and go in search of my interns. We're only a few months off from the crush and life will get very crazy around here. We have a lot to do to get ready.

I work nonstop all afternoon—with a farm, there's always something to do. As I pull the golf cart into the garage and prepare to do the paperwork I need to get done, I look forward to eating a frozen microwave meal and watching a soccer match.

The radio at my hip crackles. "Andy?"

"Yes, Jose?"

"I'm out in the cab vines, and I know this may sound crazy, but I swear I just saw a woman out here."

Fuck! That's the other side of the property. How the hell did she get out there? "Dark hair? A yellow dress with big pink flowers?"

"Dark hair, yes, but I think she's naked. I can't be sure. She saw me and hid, and I'm not seeing her, but I can hear her talking, though I can't make out what's she saying. I swear I'm not crazy."

"Don't worry, Jose. I don't think you're crazy. She was in the tasting room this afternoon. I'm on my way."

Driving in a small truck through the acres of grapes, I see Jose at the top of a crest and head over.

"I can hear her, but I can't see her."

I stand still for a moment and pick up a singsong lilt just above the rustle of the leaves on the vines. I yell, "Eve! It's Andy. Where are you?"

A head suddenly pops up about a hundred yards away and a few rows over. "Andy? Is that you?"

"Yes, Eve. It's me. Come on over here. Let's get you home."

She walks over, wearing just her bra and a single sandal.

"Eve, honey, do you know where your pretty dress is?"

She shakes her head. "It's freer to be naked, and I have a perfect body."

"Okay. Let's go back to the villa."

Nodding, she walks to the truck. Her eyes are alert, and they dart around like a caged animal who's been cornered and looking for a way out.

Noting her demeanor, I speak very soothingly to her. "Eve, have you been out here wandering around the vines?"

She nods. "I got turned around. But that man scared me. He took my clothes."

Jose holds his hands up and shakes his head. I know he didn't take her clothes, and who even knows where they are. "All right, let's get you back to the villa. We'll get you cleaned up and maybe call someone to come get you."

She's silent and still looks like she's ready to run.

I call ahead on the radio, asking in rapid Italian, "Sophia? Can you meet me around back with a blanket?"

"A blanket?"

"Yes. Now, please. Eve and I are approaching the back."

"Eve?"

"A blanket, Sophia."

"I'm on my way."

As we pull up to the back, Sophia exits the building and approaches with the blanket. She's as shocked as I am at the state of Eve. "Let's get her upstairs to the apartment and get her in the shower." Turning to Eve, I ask, "Eve? Who can I call to come get you?"

Her shoulders slump, and she sounds like a little girl. "Call my daughter, Greer." She rattles off a phone number.

"I'll do that while you get cleaned up."

Sophia nods at me, and I head into the tasting room. Thankfully we're closed, and Sophia was only cleaning up.

Picking up the phone, I dial the number, though I'm not 100 percent sure what to say. She picks up after the second ring. "Hello?"

"Hello, Greer? I own Bellissima Valle Vineyard in St. Helena. Eve Ford gave me your number. I was wondering what I should do. She was in our tasting room earlier in the day and left abruptly, then was later found wandering the vines nearly naked. Should I call an ambulance, or can you come and get her?"

"Andreas? This is Greer Ford. We've met. I'm close friends with CeCe Arnault?"

"Oh yes. I had no idea. Is she your mother?"

"Yes. Everything you've described sounds just like her. I'm in my office in downtown San Francisco, and I'll need to run home and pick up a few things so I can stay with her tonight. It may take an hour to an hour and a half to get to you. Is that okay?"

"Of course. Sophia is here with her trying to get her cleaned up. I should warn you she was partially naked. She may need some clothes, too."

I hear a breath of irritation over the phone. It sounds like she's struggling not to cry. "Thank you for telling me. I'll bring something. I'll call her doctor, and he'll tell me where I should take her." There are a few seconds of silence, and she finally says, "Thank you, Andreas. I appreciate you calling me rather than the hospital. I'll be there as soon as I can. If she gets too difficult, please call me. This is my cell phone, so you can reach me anytime."

Hanging up the phone, I can't believe Eve's Greer is the same one I met several months ago and have dreamed about since. I've wanted to call her so many times, but my life is chaos trying to get my vineyard up and running, and I didn't think it would be fair to start something and then be unavailable. So many things about her left me intrigued, and I'd only scratched the surface.

Maybe someone is trying to tell me something.

GREER

ISCONNECTING, I can't believe Andreas just called me. Since we met, I had hoped he was going to call. I only wished it was for something other than a problem caused by Eve.

My day had been wrapping up, and I was going to go out with Cynthia and CeCe for dinner. Now I need to run. I know they'll understand, but I wish I was canceling for something other than taking care of my mother.

I text CeCe.

Me: **My mom is having an episode at Bellissima of all places. I'm headed home and then to Napa.**

CeCe: **No worries. Bellissima? Do you need any help?**

Me: **No, but thanks. I need to call her doctor. I'll try to check in later tonight.**

CeCe: **Be safe. Call me if you need ANYTHING. Find Andreas and jump his bones while you're up there.**

Me: **I'll be safe, but Andreas won't be interested after experiencing a full episode with Eve. I have to bring clothes for her. She was naked and wandering the vineyard.**

CeCe: **I'm so sorry.**

I quickly run home and grab a few days' worth of clothes, then call Mason to let him know what's going on.

"Don't worry about a thing. Go take care of your mother."

"Thanks, Mason. I'll have my computer and cell phone. I may work from Napa for the rest of the week."

My mom is bipolar. Imagine the worst nightmare you've ever had, take a moment to recall it. Then imagine you were unable to wake up from it because you're already awake. All those bizarre ideas that make so much sense when you're asleep start to make sense with your eyes wide open. Eve will do well for months and then decide she doesn't want to take her medication. It's been this way ever since I can remember. I've managed this forever with Eve.

When I was young, she took CeCe, Hadlee, and me on a road trip. When we got to Los Angeles—five hours south of San Francisco—CeCe called her parents, and they had the police come to get us. While they took Eve to a hospital, we waited at the Hollywood police station. I've never been so scared in my life. Her family took me in and showed me what a normal—if there is such a thing—family looks like.

The last time I saw Andreas was at Hadlee's birthday party. We flirted mercilessly, but I watched him flirt with every woman there, so I wasn't exactly sure he was really into me. Hadlee told me he'd shared with her that he seemed disappointed when I was speaking with someone she went to medical school with and was visibly relieved when he found out the man was gay. He asked CeCe for my phone number but never called. I figured she had pressured him into it. I was certainly disappointed, but I didn't stay home waiting for him to call.

I drive like a madwoman to get to Napa. Tearing into the driveway of Bellissima Valle, I'm ready for what's ahead of me. I talked to the doctor, who suggested I take her directly to the hospital.

Andreas is opening the door before I can even get out of my car. "I'm sorry I had to call you about this."

I stop short and take in his deliciousness. He's wearing low-riding jeans and an old T-shirt, his feet bare as he leans against the doorframe. I could just eat him up. "You have nothing to be sorry about."

He gives me an embrace that makes me want to melt in his arms, then holds my hand as we ascend the stairs to where he has my mother. "She's asleep on the couch."

I stop short when I see her. She looks so peaceful, like a sleeping baby, and I know when she wakes we'll either be in a manic episode or a depressive one. "I'm really sorry she's disrupted your day. Do I owe you any money for anything she might've ruined? Please tell me when she was wandering the vineyard she didn't do anything to your vines."

"No, she was fine. Really. I was worried about her."

I'm relieved she didn't do anything to his grapes. I'm a wine enthusiast, and I've learned how delicate the vines can be, especially right now as they prepare for blooms that will lead to grapes. "I've talked to her doctor. I'm going to drive her to the hospital in Calistoga."

"Whatever you need to do."

I go over to the couch and rock her gently. "Mom? Wake up. We need to go see Dr. Phillips."

She wakes up, and the look in her eyes tells me a manic moment is coming at me. "What are you doing here? I'm here with my boyfriend. I don't need you here. You ruin everything. You ruined my relationship with your father and now with Andy. Get away. Go home. You're embarrassing me, Greer. You need to leave now."

Andreas speaks up. "Eve, I called Greer. I was worried about you."

She pulls the blanket tight around her body. "Is there some

aspect of me that worries you? Oh, I get it. You're one of those who insist on me taking my medicine. Well you can't make me. You think I might give you what I've got or drive you crazy, that me trying to 'wake up' means I have to go mad first? Hmm. Well I won't lie to you, that's what it means for some people, but that's only if they aren't with me. I can 'wake up' without the need for psychosis. Anyway, once you have some kind of awakening, you realize the pills they force you to take leave your brain in an ugly fog. You don't want that, trust me. All the pills they've made me take can ruin your life for years, and sometimes you don't really recover. You can lose people close to you, people you love. I don't recommend it, not for anyone, and least of all you. You're so nice. I think you're adorable! But we need some ground rules. I need to know when you're coming, for a start."

This is her argument every time this happens. It used to make me cry, but these days I just listen and rub her arm to comfort her as she rides the manic mood. It doesn't take long, and I'm able to talk her into getting into my car.

When Eve insists Andy join us, I turn to face him. "I hate to inconvenience you any more than we already have."

"It's not a problem. I really don't mind."

We drive the thirty minutes to the hospital and take her in together. I'm grateful Andy is here, as she walks in with her head high.

Her doctor comes out and speaks to me. I have Andreas share what happened this afternoon, and then I tell him, "I stopped by her apartment. It's a complete wreck and looks like it has been for some time. I have a feeling she's been off her meds for a few weeks."

"We'll do a work-up and see what we can find."

I nod. "Thank you. I'll stick around her house for a few days and work from here. I can be here in less than twenty minutes."

"How are you doing, besides this?" My mother's doctor is well aware that since bipolar disorder is genetic, I could develop symptoms, which is my biggest fear. I hate what it does to my mother, and he knows it.

I'll always have to care for her, and these kinds of episodes are going to happen. She has no one else. My father couldn't take riding her moods, taking care of her and fighting with her to take her medications, so he left her for another woman. He's always worked hard to include me with his new family, but I'm really all my mom has. Her family's in New York, and they're all dealing with the same thing with Aunt Gillian—Vanessa's mom.

I look over at Andreas, wanting to be careful what I tell the doctor. "No signs yet."

"Greer, it isn't a death sentence. There are many people who live fulfilling lives with the disorder."

"Thank you. You have my number." I turn to Andreas. "I should get you home."

He looks up and asks, "Have you eaten? I'm starved."

"I could use something, but it's after ten. I'm not sure what's open this time of night out here in the boonies."

He gives me a beautiful smile that goes all the way to his chocolate brown eyes. I could just eat him up. "I know this isn't the crazy city, but there's an all-night diner not too far from here. Would that work?" He shakes his head and chuckles like I'm the country bumkin.

I'm touched by his generosity of not only today but seemingly wanting to make sure I'm okay. It's refreshing to say the very least. "Sounds perfect."

We drive in silence. I don't know how to explain what happened, so I just keep my thoughts to myself.

We walk into the diner, and it's busier than I expected. We're shown to our seats in a booth against the window. "I'm really sorry. I'm embarrassed, and I don't know what to say or how I can apologize to you."

"Why do you need to apologize?"

"She ruined your night. If we're lucky, that's all she did."

"Greer, you have nothing to be embarrassed about. Tell me about your mother's illness."

I'm grateful for his understanding, but the same happened with Mark in the beginning, so I'm not going to let my guard down too easily. Rather than tell him all the stories of my childhood disappointments, I attempt to change the subject. "How did she end up at Bellissima?"

"You know, I'm not sure. She came about two weeks ago with a few other women. They were a little friendly, but nothing out of the ordinary. But I promise you, your mother and I aren't dating. Not even close. Today was only the second time I saw her. She came on to me pretty heavily, and when she was rebuffed, she stormed out. I'm glad one of my vineyard workers found her. We water after dark and the temperature drops at night. It could've been a real problem for her had we not found her. She'd walked a considerable distance, and somewhere she lost her dress and her underwear."

"I love her, I really do, but she can be like a child when she goes through these cycles."

He pats my hand, and the waitress comes to take our order. She stares at Andy as if he's the last glass of water in a hot, dry desert, but he ignores her as we order, barely making eye contact. I get the cheeseburger and fries, and he orders a chicken sandwich and a salad. I feel guilty for eating junk, but I don't care. I'm tired both mentally and physically.

"Let's see. The last time I saw you, you were having a great time at Hadlee's birthday party. I haven't seen you at the winery since. Did you decide you didn't like my wine?"

"Are you kidding? It's amazing. It's been a busy few weeks at work, and CeCe took her company to Fashion Week and now this."

"Tell me about your work. What do you do? Besides love wine as much as I do."

I'm flattered by his compliment. I was worried when we met that I'd waxed on about wine and sounded pretentious. "I work in public relations for a venture capital fund."

"What does that mean?"

"Well, you met most of the team at Hadlee's birthday party. Mason, Dillon, and Cameron all went to college together at Stanford, and they eventually all went to work for start-ups that went really well. They started combining their money and investing in new companies or ideas, and eventually those companies exploded. Are you familiar with PeopleMover?"

"Of course. Aren't they the biggest social media platform these days?"

"They are. We're their only investors outside of the founders who created them."

He whistles. "That's huge, isn't it?"

"Yes, my job is to work with our investments and help break down the technology to sell it to Wall Street as they go public. And I deal with the PR nightmares that can come up at our own company and our investments."

"You have nightmares at your company?"

I debate for a half second on telling him about our chaos, then figure I can at least give him the generic view of our challenges.

"For the last three years, we've had someone wreaking havoc. It's created a tremendous amount of work because their goal was to put us out of business. We've had a top-notch security team on it, and we've dug into our computers and employee backgrounds, but we can't figure out who's the problem child."

"That must be really tough. You're obviously very good at your job. I watched how you managed your mom tonight. You were grace under fire."

"Thank you. I have more practice than I'd like when it comes to Eve." I'm uncomfortable with the compliment. I've faced so much criticism over the years because of my mom, and losing my fiancé over it was the icing on the cake.

"Do you like your work?"

"Most of the time."

Our meals arrive, and my burger looks delicious. Popping a french fry in my mouth, I'm ready to move the conversation away from me. "Now it's my turn. Tell me how you landed here in Napa with all the success your family's had in other parts of the world."

"I'm one of fifteen kids."

I almost choke on my cheeseburger. "Fifteen? Wow. Where are you in the birth order?"

"I'm the oldest of the last set of five."

My cheeseburger is stuck in my throat, so I take a long drink of water and attempt to gain my composure. Finally, I can talk. "Okay, but that doesn't tell me how you ended up here."

"We're the eighth generation to make wine in my family, and my father has taken the wine to international acclaim, but he wants our brand to grow. Since we can't get any bigger in Italy, he decided to grow more worldwide. He created Bellissima Holdings, and we've bought land in grape-rich areas across the world to add to our brand. We were all raised to go out and build vineyards around the globe. My older brothers were sent to Argentina, Africa, New Zealand, France, Greece, and Hungary, and many of my sisters have done like Sophia and partnered with some of us. When I was twelve, I started learning about grapes and how to make good wines. I spent my summers working and helping not only at home but abroad. Then I was sent to university here in the States, and we started buying land. Sophia and I planted our first grapes almost twelve years ago, and the rest you know."

"That sounds very mafia-esque," I laugh.

He laughs. "We aren't that organized." His eyes sparkle, and he reaches for my hand and holds it across the table as his fingers caress my knuckles.

My stomach flutters and my breathing quickens. I need to keep us on track or I might leap across this table and try to jump his bones. "Do you like the wine business?"

"Most days. I think it's like your job. Some days are fantastic, and others are grueling hard work." He looks me in the eye, his hand never leaving mine, and the sexual tension builds.

I nod. "That's a perfect comparison." I have an internal debate for a moment, but I can't hold my question back any longer. "Why didn't you call me after Hadlee's birthday party?" I sit back and bite my lip while picking at my nail under the table, waiting for him to answer.

"I can't tell you how many times I picked up the phone to call you. My life's crazy and often not my own. Trust me, I wanted to call you. You're smart and beautiful." I begin to blush. "I really liked you then, and I think fate brought us together now."

We spend the rest of our dinner talking. He's an incredibly handsome man, his body buff and in top condition. He looks like a middleweight champion, probably sports an eight-pack, and even when he wears something as simple as a T-shirt and jeans, his physique is still showcased. It's disgusting the way some wo-men—including my mother, unfortunately—scratch and claw at each other to garner his attention.

When we finish, I'm actually disappointed the night is ending. He insists on paying for my dinner, which tugs at my heartstrings. After all he's done for Eve, he's being a gentleman and treating me when I should be doing at least that for putting him out. As we walk to the car, his hand is at the small of my back, and it sends electrical jolts to my core. I don't think I've ever felt this physical chemistry with anyone before.

"Where are you staying tonight?" he casually asks.

"I was going to stay at my mother's, but when I stopped there on my way into town, I found it was unfortunately in pretty bad shape. I need to call around and find someone to get it cleaned. There's a bed-and-breakfast I've stayed at before, so I'll go there. They typically have room."

We walk to the car, our bodies close, an electrical current pass-ing between us that I'm sure everyone can see. "Would you like to stay at the villa?" he murmurs as he moves my hair from my face.

"I-I-I couldn't put you out like that. I've already taken advant-age of your kindness." My heart is beating so loud, I'm sure he can hear it.

"Please. Stay with me. I insist."

Before I can give him a reason why I shouldn't, he pulls me in close, his fingers gentle beneath my chin. He lifts my face to his, meeting my lips in a kiss of wanting and warmth. His tongue darts out to taste me, the movement filled with possession. As if emboldened by my flavor, he groans and pulls me closer with a hand behind my neck, his embrace crushing my arms against his chest. I can't move, but I feel the power I have over him. The ur-gency in his kiss, the hardness against my stomach, excites me.

"I really would love for you to stay." He kisses me again, more aggressive and urgent, our hands exploring. I want him. I want all of him. "Please, stay with me tonight," he groans.

I nod, and we climb in my car and drive back to the villa. My head's spinning and I'm nervous. I haven't been with anyone since Mark.

We're hardly through the back door when he pins me to the wall, his kisses become hot and feral. I find myself fisting the back of his T-shirt in my clenched hands.

"Greer, I've wanted this for so long." He looks at me, waiting for permission to continue.

I nod in response and his lips crash on mine again. His hands are wandering and aggressive. He's so good that I don't even notice he has my pants unzipped until they're halfway down my thighs.

His erection presses against my stomach, and flutters of desire take off deep within my core.

My body's still shaking from the aftermath of his heated kiss. He's managed to remove his shirt, and all the work he must do in the fields has his stomach just as I imagined, a tight eight-pack. God, he's beautiful.

He nibbles on my neck while his hands continue to explore me. "Shall we go upstairs?"

"Please," I whisper breathlessly. We're moving fast, but my pussy is doing all the thinking, and I'm not going to let my brain convince me it's a bad idea. How can it be?

Getting on his knees, he helps me out of my jeans, running his hands up and down my legs but never quite touching me in my most sensitive spots. He plants sensual kisses up my body as he stands, then pushes my legs apart with his knee. "You feel that, sweetheart? I wasn't joking when I said you turn me on," he breathes as he presses against me once more. "Your pussy's so wet."

Leading me by the hand, he pulls me farther into his apartment. I don't have the time to take in his space before his lips come crashing on mine. His tongue gently slips in and out between my lips, and I can no longer take the teasing, gentle kisses. I open my mouth wider and lift my head to forcefully take over the kiss in a blind passion. He groans as I work my tongue over his in long strokes. The electricity that sparks through my body from the taste of this virile man has made me lose all reason.

I want him. All of him.

We stumble to his bedroom. Frantically, trying not to break our kiss, we pull each other's clothes off, our hands exploring in our excitement. His chest is hard, and his nipples are a milk chocolate color. I can't help but want to lick them up. His hard cock poking me in the stomach begs for attention.

Pushing me to the bed, Andy breaks the kiss to open a bedside table, quickly sheathing his hard cock with a condom. I want to taste it. Heat spreads through my core, and God, how I want to feel him inside me. He enters me quickly and slides deep to the hilt. He's so big it stings a moment, but I adjust.

Moving his tongue against mine in tandem with his hips, the only sounds are the slickness and our bodies slapping together. He pins my arms to my side, which only adds to the erotic experience, and I soon feel something building inside me. I'm losing more and more control with each slip of his tongue and our bodies slamming into one another.

"Take it, baby, and just feel me," he groans against my lips.

He knows I'm growing desperate for a release when my own hips start grinding my drenched heat against him, begging for any friction to end my madness.

"Come for me, Greer." He deepens the kiss, and for the life of me, I can't tell where I am right now. He pinches my nipple hard and I scream out. What a perfect end to my current dry run.

"You look like an angel." He pulls his head back, stroking my cheek tenderly as he looks into my eyes with wonderment. Sweat beads have formed along his hairline, his chest lightly rising and falling as he catches his breath.

I want more. He's opened Pandora's box, and I crave erotic pleasure.

Pulling me into him with a tight embrace, he spoons my worn-out body against his. He feels so good, holding me tight. I doze in postcoital bliss and wake when he leaves me, feeling bereft and wanting of his warm body. He gets comfortable between my legs, and my nipples grow hard as his fingers explore me.

"Look at me. I want you to watch this," he gruffly commands.

I lift my head and look down to his eyes penetrating mine, swirling with heated passion. The erotic and vulnerable scene before me that this man has created takes my breath away. As he continues to work me with his fingers, he moves his mouth to my bundle of nerves, never breaking eye contact with me. I watch as he teases my clit by slowly tracing circles around it, still thrusting his fingers inside me. His wet, warm tongue feels deliciously sinful, and I instinctively lift my hips, seeking something more from him.

"Andreas... I need...."

He arches a brow and then opens his mouth to cover my clit in its entirety with his warm tongue. He works feverishly, flicking his tongue back and forth over my sensitive nub. My legs continue to shake against my will, and my toes literally curl. "Oh... my... God...."

Multiple sensations bombard me all at once, coursing through me, and watching him do this to my body becomes my undoing.

I've been so sexually pent-up for so long that I can't hold out any longer.

"Andreas, don't stop. Please... oh, I'm coming... oh God...."

I'm in free fall, embracing every second of these exquisite sensations crashing throughout my body.

My hips undulate with a mind of their own, grinding against his fingers and mouth as he suctions around my clit. It's all so intense, and I hear myself scream his name.

All too soon, it's over, and I lie on the bed out of breath in an obliterated mess. "That feeling doesn't last nearly long enough," I pant.

Our legs are entwined in a postcoital glow.

That was quite a way to break my imposed chastity. I want to do this again and again. He may have lit a fire that may take some time to burn out—if ever.

ANDY

HER SLENDER ARMS reach for me in her sleep, her body small and pale beneath the soft sheets. There's an electricity between us so strong it's as if it was harnessed from lightning in a storm. From the minute I met her months ago, I wanted this to happen, and she's occupied my dreams ever since. I never thought it was in the realm of any possibility. She lives in the city and has a high-powered career, and let's face it, I'm a farmer. I may only be a fling to her, but I'm determined to enjoy this as long as she allows it.

Her long dark lashes fan out beneath her sleeping eyes; she has prominent cheekbones, petite features, and beautiful raven-black hair that must reach to her shoulders spilling out over the pillow. Her skin is smooth and creamy white, not like some women her age who already have crow's feet at the corners of their eyes from too much sun. She's enchanting me, even in her sleep.

I can't help but reach for her, and she moans her appreciation. I love morning sex. My cock is hard and ready for more as I dip my head and take her nipple into my mouth, pulling and sucking gently at first. My fingers caress their way to her center and her legs open to allow me entry. She isn't fully awake and she's already wet.

Her beautiful blue eyes open and she smiles at me. Her hips are moving, searching for the friction in just the right place. Rolling me onto my back, she reaches for a condom and quickly covers my shaft. I'm ready to take her, but she climbs on top.

What a fantastic view.

"Make me come, Andy. Please. I need you to make this aching stop."

"Ride me, baby," I say, my voice hoarse. "Ride me hard."

She rises to her knees and takes me in her hand, wrapping her fingers around my girth. I lift her higher and align my aching cock with her entrance. The smell of sex in the air permeates everything.

I'm desperate and cede her the control she needs, even if that control is false.

"Fuck," I groan as she lowers herself onto me. She's tight, and I worry it may be too much for her. My fingers press into her hips so hard, she may have bruises tomorrow, but she just gives me that lazy smile as she watches every second of what she does to me.

Looking into my eyes, she takes me deeper. I blow out a heavy rush of air that I suck in as she glides up and down, allowing me to go even deeper. I have a big dick, and in this position, it must be almost painful for her.

She pushes through the pinch of pain I see on her brow, her pussy clenching my cock like a vise. Leaning back, her hands on my thighs behind her, she arches her spine. The position has her seated with her ass resting nearly on my balls.

"Christ. Slow down, Greer." The unspoken threat of what would happen if she continues at this pace hangs in the air, but she continues her assault, rocking her hips back and forth, round and round. The tension in my face drives her on while begging me to lose control. She rides me hard, her firm breasts bouncing up and down with each rise and fall. I want to reach for her erect nipples and play with them, but I hold on to her hips to control her pace. A sweat sheen covers her skin, and her thighs shake with anticipation as she positions so her clit has maximum contact. Wanting to help her come, I rub circles against her clit with my thumb, her hips following in unison. Her breathing comes in short, staccato bursts, and a moan escapes me as her orgasm grabs my cock. I can't take it much longer.

"Fuck." I grit my teeth. "I'm gonna come."

She lies down on me once we've finished, her ear to my heart. We don't talk, both panting heavily. She eventually rolls off me. "Good morning to you, too."

"You're amazing," I tell her as she caresses my chest hair. Finally, my breathing becomes close to normal. "Would you like some breakfast?"

Still struggling for her breath, she says, "Just coffee, please."

I get up and wander naked into my kitchen. The light's breaking and there's already activity outside; as my workers have arrived and are starting their grueling work for the day.

I hear the water in the shower start, and it takes all my energy and effort to not go in and help her soap up. *I can save that for another time.*

When she emerges from the bathroom, I can smell my soap on her. She's positively beautiful. Her hair is damp, she isn't wearing any makeup, and she's dressed in tight jeans and one of my shirts with the sleeves rolled up. She's absolutely sexy, and I'm completely mesmerized.

She takes a deep inhale of the coffee and thanks me for the piping-hot beverage. "I'd better get over to my mom's. My hope is to get it picked up enough that a housekeeper can come in and give it a good cleaning."

"Will you be staying again tonight?" I'm trying not to be too eager, but I want to see more of her. Forget this starting-my-vineyard excuse. I'm crazy about her, and I want to explore where we can take this.

"It depends on what the doctor tells me and how far I get with my mother's house."

"I'd like to see you again tonight—that's if you're up for it, of course."

"I think you're the one who needs to be 'up.'" She bites her bottom lip and flutters her eyes before she lets out the most beautiful laugh at her own double entendre.

I pull her into my arms and kiss her breathless as I press my hard cock into her stomach. "With you, it's never a problem to be up."

I see the conflict in her eyes of wanting another round before she takes in a deep breath and says, "I really would like to see you again tonight, but if the doctor tells me my mom will be a while, I'll head home. Unfortunately, I need to get back into The City for work."

"I understand. I have a lot to do myself." Before I can mumble some awkward goodbye, I pull her gently to me. My mouth opens in surprise as her warm lips press against mine, my hand closing around the back of her neck. The kiss is exploratory and soft, but it's also all-consuming and heavy. She lets out a little moan of pleasure, and my cock immediately responds, ready to go again. I'm into this kiss way more than is rational.

In an instant, her arms are around my neck, and I'm getting as good as I'm giving, finally coming up for air when she gracefully breaks us apart. Her breathing is ragged, her eyes glazed, giving me a little sense of satisfaction that the kiss rattled her as much as it did me.

"I'll see you soon," I tell her, my voice low and husky as I press a final chaste kiss to her lips before stepping away. "Thank you again for a fun night."

Running after her and begging her to stay crosses my mind. I haven't felt like this about any woman in a very long time.

Replaying our conversation in my mind and picturing the look of ecstasy when she came make my dick hard again. It was glorious, but I need to work and get my mind off her or I'll turn into a stalker.

It's BEEN THREE FUCKING DAYS since our night together. Why hasn't she reached out to set up another date? I've been out of the dating game for so long, I think I've forgotten how this works. I own a successful vineyard, I'm considered handsome, and I'm single. That combination made me, from what I understood, one hell of a catch, so why isn't Greer trying very hard to catch me?

I have to admit, as shallow as it is, I'm more than a little offended by her distance. So offended, in fact, that I send her another text. I sent her one yesterday morning letting her know I was thinking of her and hoped to see her soon. She sent back a thumbs-up emoji.

I want more from her. She occupies my mind, and I can't concentrate on my work.

Me: **When are you coming up to see your mom?**

Greer: **I've been swamped at work. I'm hoping for this week-
    end. Are you up for getting together?**

Hell yes. I want to hear her call my name as she comes.

Me: **I'm up whenever I think of you and our night together.**

Rereading my message, I may be laying it on too thick. Now she'll send me another thumbs-up emoji. Crap!

Greer: **Don't get me so excited.**

Oh thank God! She took it as flirting. I'm so out of practice with dating and texting. Just the thought of her excited gets my dick hard.

Me: **If it means you'll come visit me soon, I'll make sure your excitement is worth your while.**

Greer: **There are many things we haven't done.**

Holy crap! I can think of several, all of which I'd like to explore with her. I don't know if her on her knees in front of me is more titillating or just being buried deep in her pussy.

Me: **Yes, many things. First on your list?**

Greer: **Hmm... you very proficiently tasted me. I would like to do the same.**

Jesus. I think I just came in my pants at the thought of her mouth sucking me dry.

Me: **I like that idea, but only after you're completely satisfied.**

Greer: **I think if we're counting, I'm ahead.**

I'm not a selfish lover by any means. And I particularly like the way she says my given name when she climaxes. It's a total rush.

Me: **I don't think so. Even, maybe, but no such thing as you being ahead.**

Greer: **And what about you? What do you want to do?**

GREER

THIS KIND OF SEXTING is completely out of character for me, but he hasn't left my mind since I left him standing at his door. It took all my willpower to not turn around and go back to have a few more rounds. I didn't want to return to San Francisco and my work; it's been so long since I've had any fun. We definitely enjoyed ourselves, and our chemistry is sizzling hot.

Andy: **I want you to come on my tongue over and over again.**

Holy crap. His tongue is magic. What can I say that might get him as horny as he's making me?

Me: **What would you do if I dipped my nipples in wine?**

Andy: **I would lick them clean.**

My body unconsciously clenches. If I wasn't in an office with all glass windows, I'd call him up and have video sex.

Me: **Whipped cream and chocolate sauce?**

Andy: **A pussy sundae is a favorite.**

We've come back to his amazing tongue. Looking at my watch, I debate driving to Napa for the night, but I have a big day tomorrow and should be well rested.

Me: **How about from behind?**

Andy: **Yes.**

Me: **How about in the shower?**

Andy: **Yes.**

Me: **How about in my mouth?**

Andy: **Yes.**

Me: **Anything you don't like?**

Andy: **No. With you, I like everything and want to do everything.**

Greer: **I think I need to go take care of myself.**

I don't think. I know.

Andy: **Can I watch?**

Greer: **Maybe someday.**

Andy: **You should see how hard I am for you right now.**

Greer: **If I was there, I would take you in my mouth and make you very happy.**

Andy: **You always make me happy.**

Greer: **Have a good day. Can we talk tonight?**

Andy: **Call me tonight, and we can have some fun.**

I'd love to explore this further with him, but duty calls and I only have a few minutes before a partners meeting in Mason's office.

Wandering into the lunchroom, I grab a cup of coffee. I need a moment to cool down, and the small jolt of caffeine will help me make it through this meeting.

While the Nespresso machine pushes out the dark nectar of the gods, I glance around the pristine room. The leftover breakfast burritos from this morning are nicely plated and covered. They won't make it past lunch. Every snack you can think of lines the shelves on the wall, and the fridge is full of any drink an employee could want. I grab an apple and my coffee and run into Emerson on my way to the meeting.

"How's your mom?" she asks.

"She's doing okay. I got her set up at the hospital, and I should know how things are progressing this afternoon."

"Let me know if there's anything I can do. And don't be shy about taking time off to take care of her. We can lean heavily on the PR agency to cover for you. They're nowhere near as good, but they're fine if you need the time."

"Thanks. I'm good right now."

We take our usual seats and wait for Mason to start. Cameron is talking about his weekend away with Hadlee. They got engaged a few months ago. It was a short courtship, but they've known each other for a long time and belong together.

Cameron is probably my favorite person here. He's shy, smart as a whip and truly funny. He scares the hell out of most people with his 6'5" muscular body, and he has some significant tattoos hidden beneath his clothes, which I saw courtesy of his sporting a wifebeater on one occasion. Most of the time though, he wears an untucked dress shirt with the shirtsleeves rolled up, jeans, trendy shoes, and a baseball cap.

"Hadlee's face at the biker bar was priceless. They had no idea what was coming at them. This guy named Big cut himself, and she went into full doctor mode. I had to pull her out of there or she'd still be doctoring their wounds."

Everyone is chuckling when Mason walks in with Jim, our private investigator.

"Sorry we're late," Mason says. Both men take their seats, and Mason asks about various projects going on. Each of us is responsible for a few specific parts of the company, but ultimately Mason, Cameron, and Dillon run the show around here.

Mason turns to me. "How are things going at Visionaire?"

"They're on track. We're working through the profiles of the founders for the press packets. Tom Sutterland and his VP of Marketing of PeopleMover are heading to DC to testify on the Hill about social media impacts later this week, and I'm working on talking points with them."

"Do you need to go with them?" Dillon asks.

"No, I don't think so. Someone from the PR agency is going to run interference if needed. I can make it work if you think otherwise, but we have most of the questions that should be asked and aren't expecting any real bombshells."

Sara mutters, "Isn't that when they happen?"

"Yes, and we've watched the questions coming out of the hearings all week. PeopleMover may be the big social media gorilla, but Tom is very low profile, leaving his competitors to fight it out for second."

Mason stares at me a moment. "Have a go-bag ready just in case something goes sideways and you need to be on-site to manage the fallout."

"Of course."

"We have the interviews next week for the Emerging Markets partnership. We have one strong candidate who would buy into the partnership, and someone less experienced who would come in as a director. The decision comes down to who we think is a better match for our team. I've put time on everyone's calendars to meet the candidates. Please don't waste their time by canceling," Mason reminds us.

We go through almost an hour more of our meeting and looking at prospects of who we might bring into our fund.

Mason finally turns the meeting over to Jim so he can explain why he's joined us today. "Well, Perkins Klein will shutter and close this week."

Cameron is close to one of the founders, but he had a heart attack and is struggling with his health. "What's the plan?"

"They're selling what remains of their investments, mostly to Benchmark, and much of the staff is dispersing."

Turning to Emerson, Mason asks, "Are we hiring Quinn?"

Quinn was Mason's ex-girlfriend and broke his heart years ago, and he was adamant that he wouldn't hire her when it was considered long before my time.

Emerson clears her throat and says, "I'd like to. She'd be an asset to Dillon and Cynthia. But I understand that you've been against it in the past."

Everyone looks at Mason expectantly. "She was good to us in sharing about how Perkins Klein got our information, but never divulged anything confidential about them. I guess if everyone's okay with it, then I'm okay." He adds almost as an afterthought, "But only as a senior analyst. Not a partner." We all agree, and he asks, "Do we have anyone working for us who at one point worked at Benchmark?"

Sara speaks up. "I don't believe so. We've often shied away from hiring people from competitors since our business model's so different."

As the meeting continues, my mind drifts to Andy. I'd love to lie in his arms and enjoy a few days away, but his job is crazy and so is mine. Plus we live over ninety minutes away from one another when there isn't any traffic—and there's always traffic. I'm just going to have fun and enjoy this for now, no expectations.

ANDY

$\mathcal{T}$HIS INVENTORY COUNT isn't adding up. I know we're running out of storage space, but why can't we find these barrels? It's not as if they could've walked out on their own, so they must be here somewhere.

I run through the numbers again just to make sure, but we're definitely short forty-one barrels. This makes no sense.

My cell phone pings, and my heart beats faster. There's only one person who would text me at this hour.

Greer: **Hey there. Up for dinner tomorrow night? I know it's last minute.**

She's coming up. I was going to work late and try to find these missing barrels, but hanging out with Greer sounds like much more fun.

Me: **Ciao, bella mia. I'll cancel my plans to be with you.**

Greer: **Don't do that. I'll be back.**

This isn't a difficult decision. I'd much rather spend time with Greer than get grubby crawling around in the dark corners of the warehouse looking for the missing barrels.

Me: **My plans are to go through inventory. You're much more exciting than counting wine.**

Greer: **If you're sure. Where do you want to go?**

My cock stirs in my pants. I'd certainly prefer to see her in my bed and naked.

Me: **My place?**

Greer: **I'm sure at some point naked and begging will happen, but how about a restaurant?**

I'm already begging. I hate to be too obvious, but then again. I'm not surprised. Maybe a little bit disappointed.

Me: **Casual okay?**

Greer: **Casual is perfect.**

Me: **Come here and we can head out to this great place a friend owns. He runs a farm-to-table restaurant out of his barn. I'll see if he can make room for us tomorrow.**

Greer: **Perfect. I should be at the villa about 6.**

Me: **I'll make sure you come at least six times. Maybe more. Arrive when you can.**

Greer: **I'm meeting with my mother's doctor at 4 and will come by after.**

Me: **Can't wait.**

I need to call Philippe and see if he can make room for us to-morrow night. If not, I'll have to come up with a second-choice spot.

Greer: **Me either.**

Greer's never far from my mind. I'm excited to see her and want to know everything I can about her. She's a wonderful dis-traction, but I need to concentrate on why my numbers aren't adding up. I have less than a month before I go to Italy to figure this out. I've looked four separate times. Maybe if I give this to someone on my team, they can see where I'm going wrong?

Getting up from my desk, I stretch. My parents are hosting this quarter's meeting at Bellissima Grande, which is in the Tuscan valley. We'll come in from all over the world to discuss

Bellissima with the family. There's a lot of pressure on me and the US market, not to mention my mom's insistence for me to couple up.

My mother is really putting the pressure on me to bring someone home to the meeting. She's never been like this before, but now each time we talk, she wants to know if I asked her to come yet. How does my mother know about Greer?

Looking at the clock, I see it's late. I eat some dinner and then head out for a run, putting myself through a punishing workout of almost five miles at a sprint and then lifting weights to work through the stress and pressures of my day.

Finally, I collapse onto my bed and think of her.

I can't wait to see her, to taste her, to feel her, and to hear her call my name as she comes.

I'M NOT USUALLY A CLOCK WATCHER, but for some reason today I am. She was the centerpiece of my dreams last night and fills my mind today, which isn't typical for me by a long shot.

To distract me from the time that seems to be moving slower than normal, I head into the tasting room at several points to see if she's arrived. The disappointment fills me with dread every time I see she hasn't.

"There he is" comes the syrupy voice of a young woman I've met a few times. She's in her early thirties, if I had to guess, and is quite sweet, but she doesn't hold my interests in the least. I can't even remember her name. Meeting so many people in the business has its drawbacks when people think I remember meeting them. I try, and sometimes I'm good at it, but not today.

"Che piacere vederti!"

She stands and hugs me, kissing me on both cheeks. "Please let me introduce you to my friends. This is Hillary and Regina." Both girls are similar to her in age and grinning from ear to ear.

"*Benvenuti* to Bellissima Valle."

The one I think is Regina says, "Thank you so much for making this wine. It's super yummy." She bats her eyelashes but has lost my interest completely.

Yummy? What adult says a fine wine is yummy? Someone who doesn't know fine wine, that's who.

We chat for a short time, and I try to explain the notes in the wine and how to spot them, but they really aren't interested.

As I'm excusing myself, the woman whose name I can't remember reaches for me. "Oh, uh, um, the girls are headed back into San Francisco tonight. I was thinking about staying at the bed-and-breakfast up the street and was wondering if you'd care to join me for dinner tonight."

"You're extremely kind. Unfortunately, I already have plans this evening with my girlfriend." Okay, she isn't technically my girlfriend, but I'm hoping it softens the blow a little bit.

She nods, and I take her hand and kiss it. "There's a lucky man waiting for you, *bella mia.*"

I'm pulled to another table of local women, one of the threesome drawling, "Hey, handsome."

"Jeannine. What brings you to this part of the valley?" She works for one of the major local distributors and runs the operations. I don't believe she necessarily knows a lot about wine, but she's been by with friends before and does the rounds of all the tasting rooms.

"You, of course," she flirts.

"Well, I do have the best wines in this part of the valley." Her distributor buys up a lot of the grapes in the area and makes thousands of bottles that are sold all over the country and world. They're less an operation of fine art, which is what I consider Bellissima Valle, and more of a 'mix it up and send it out the minute it's ready' profit center.

"Only second to our wine."

"But of course. You're having the red flight, I assume?"

"It's quite good, actually. Very European." She winks at me.

I lean in and say quietly, "I hope you enjoy it. I'll ask Sophia to top off your glasses. Enjoy your afternoon."

"Feel free to stay. We don't have to talk wine if you'd like to relax and take a load off."

"You're very kind, but Sophia would kill me if I did that." I wave as I walk away.

I give Sophia the signal to top of their glass at no charge, and she nods and heads over with several bottles.

It's late in the day when I finally see her, and this time it's not my imagination. Her laugh is like music, her smile reaching her perfect eyes. She must have snuck in while I was sharing some of my enthusiasm for my process with a couple who are visiting the area and is talking to Sophia.

Walking over, I put my arm around her as a sign of possession. She hugs me back and kisses my cheek.

"Sorry I'm later than I expected. I spent some time with my mom."

"How did it go?"

"Okay, I suppose. She'll be in the hospital for a while. It looks like she hasn't been taking her meds for over a month, which is really hard on her body chemistry. They're having a hard time regulating her mood swings."

"I'm sorry about that, but selfishly I hope that means we'll get to see more of you."

"That's always a possibility."

"Would you like to take your things up to my apartment?"

"I wasn't sure I'd be staying, so I didn't bring much."

"You can stay as long as you'd like." I run my hand up her arm, causing goose bumps to rise on her skin.

"Would you like a glass of wine?" Sophia offers.

"I'd love one." She sits and enjoys her wine while Sophia and I talk a bit of business. We're both concerned about the missing barrels, but we don't want to make a big deal of it until we have the chance to do a full inventory.

"Go take Greer to dinner. She looks hungry," Sophia tells me.

I kiss my sister on the cheek and head for the door holding Greer's hand.

In the restaurant, I choose to sit next to her and continue holding her hand. My heart's racing and my palms are sweating; I'm giddy like a young schoolboy. *Good grief!*

We order a simple dinner and enjoy just being together. Something is definitely bothering her, and I hope I can get her to share what it is. "Tell me about what you did today."

"Today shouldn't have been this hard. I don't want to burden you with the mess that is my mother."

"Please, you can tell me. Has she always been sick?"

"Yes, long before I was born. I think my father loved her energy when she was manic, but as the years progressed, it got worse. When she's manic, she can be fun and exciting with so much energy, but when she's depressive, she threatens to kill herself and those around her. Her episodes can come and go quickly or they can stay for weeks. It's probably why I'm the only child of my parents' union, though I do have six half-siblings. My father liked to marry them young and marry often."

"What does that mean?"

"He likes them in their twenties. Then when they reach about my age—early thirties, usually—and they've had a few kids, he moves on to the next twentysomething. What about your parents?"

"Well, not nearly as exciting. My parents met when they were very young. My father was ten, and my mother was seven. They were partnered by the town matchmaker, and they always knew they would marry. They waited until my mother's sixteenth birthday. My father is the seventh-generation winemaker in the Tuscan valley, and they went on to have fifteen kids who are all winemakers, growing grapes and making wine all over the world. The US has been the most challenging market to break into, but it's quickly becoming the crown jewel—besides Italy and France, of course."

"That's just remarkable. Fifteen kids would mean you had a loud and rowdy family. As an only child, when my father left us, I felt guilty because without me, there was no one to take care of my mother. I've always envied people with big families."

"It was crazy. Constant chaos. I think that's why I love living here. I have my small apartment, and it's quiet. When I started Bellissima, it was the first time I had my own room. Even at university, I had a roommate."

"Really? Wow. Are you close in particular to any of your siblings?"

"Certainly Sophia. But she has a husband and a life outside of the vineyard."

"How often do you go home?"

"Funny you should ask. We tend to all go home about four times a year, I'll be going next month. Sometimes we'll meet when someone has the crush going on and all help out, but that's grueling work and my parents can't really do that anymore. My brother Giovanni's currently the chief financial officer, and my oldest sister Chiara runs the vineyard these days."

"I can only imagine. What happens when you go home? Super-secret winemaking meetings?" She laughs the most melodious sound, and my heart beats faster.

"No. We'll talk wine, of course, but it's really just an excuse for my parents to insist on seeing us all together."

"That actually sounds fun," she says almost wistfully.

"You should come with me." I don't know why I just said that. I hope it doesn't scare her off, but I'd really love to have her meet my family. They'd enjoy her passion for wine and her intelligence. Plus it's a chance to show her where I grew up.

"What? No."

"No, really. My mother wants me to bring someone home. She's big into symmetry and wants the balance at her table." *Good grief, why am I trying so hard?*

"So I'd only be there to make sure you had an even number during a meal?"

"Well, no. Certainly, I'd like to show you where I grew up and have you meet most of my family. I have a few brothers who drive me crazy, but they'd like you. I also think they'd love your ideas on public relations for the US market. It might even be worth trying them worldwide." *Now I really am trying too hard.*

"I don't know how to market wines. I just know what I like."

I need to face facts—I haven't liked anyone like this in a long time. "You're certainly sexy when you talk about wine."

She looks at me through her long beautiful eyelashes and her mouth curls. "Why, Mr. Giordano, are you flirting with me again?"

Being honest with her is my best bet if I want her to stay with me tonight. "I hope so."

"Well, you did promise me multiple orgasms—six, to be exact."

"I know I can accomplish that and more."

Her hand wanders to the bulge in my jeans, and she grins like the cat who caught a canary. "I guess we should go, then."

The short ride home is filled with electricity and tension, and it seems to take forever. I want her to drive faster, but these roads are steep and winding and, given the area, can often have drunk drivers at all times of the day.

We enter the apartment and it's awkward for a moment. I usually don't have guests here and don't know how to act with one. "Do you want a drink?"

She stares at me intently. "No."

Stepping in, I close the distance between us. Her breathing is ragged and fast as I kiss her softly on the lips, then trail mine down the slope of her neck. Lifting her dress, I break away only long enough to pull it over her head.

Licking my lips, I stare into her eyes and pull the soft silk of her bra aside, then dip my head to wrap my mouth around her taut nipple. I feast on her like I'm starved, sucking her nipple in deep. She cries out in response, but it's not from pain.

"You taste so damn good, my love." She moans as she arches her back, pushing her breast into my mouth.

Oh hell yes.

I move a hand to her other breast, mercilessly twisting and pulling her pebbled tip with my thumb and forefinger. I groan over the tip of her breast, stretching the nipple out with my teeth as I slightly pull back, giving her a sensation I know is shooting straight to her core. I trail my heated tongue across her chest to pay tribute to her other breast, and just before I wrap my mouth around her, I give it a quick nip.

My cock strains against the confines of my jeans, throbbing

and hot with my own need. I leave her breast and trail wet kisses up her neck, then turn her away from me so she can feel my throbbing cock pressed firmly into her back. I start twisting and thrusting my fingers inside her silk-lined pussy, curving them to rub her sweet spot.

"Oh God, Andreas!" she cries out with another traitorous howl. She pants wildly, bucking her hips against the palm of my hand. When I add a third finger, she breathes out a rough whisper. "Yes, Andreas. Please... don't stop."

"Oh, baby, I've got so much pleasure to give you." I thrust my fingers in a steady rhythm, plunging in and out of her wet folds. "Feel good, love? You like me rubbing against those tight walls of your pussy? I can feel your muscles quivering against my fingers." I lick and nip at the erotic place behind her ear as I breathe in her heady fragrance. I refrain from kissing her, wanting to hear my name from her lips as she comes for me for the first time.

I press my thumb firmly against her bundle of nerves and begin massaging it in small circles. Her legs shake uncontrollably against my thigh. "Come for me, sweet princess. Ride my fingers, work your hips and enjoy your pleasure."

Her pussy tightens and spasms around my fingers, and I growl as my dick throbs with need. Her labored breathing comes out in quick puffs between her lips. She coats my fingers with her luxurious juices, creating erotic wet sounds that have me almost spilling my load in my pants.

The moment she murmurs, "Don't stop," blood rushes to my cock.

"Mmm," she moans a little louder, pushing her ass back against my bulge.

"I've missed you. Can you tell?" I ask, my voice deep and gruff. Sliding my fingers in and out of her channel, I feel her delicate body shiver as I lightly caress from above her nipples to their hard peaks. "You're so damn beautiful. You want more?"

She moans again in agreement, turning her head toward me, searching for my lips. My cock begins throbbing with anticipation.

She seems to be emerging from her orgasmic haze when she looks at me and says, "I think it's your turn." Her standing in front of me naked makes my cock even harder. Her mouth is perfect as she drops to her knees, unbuttoning my pants so she can see the bulge in my underwear. "It's so big." She licks her lips and my cock throbs with anticipation.

Not wanting to come too quickly, I attempt to stop her. "Wa—"

"Shh, I need this. Please don't stop me," she murmurs, her fingers steadily pulling down my underwear and exposing the tip of my penis. Holding back the elastic band of my underwear with one hand, she tenderly removes my swollen cock from its confines using the other. She wraps her hand around my length, and I let out a low moan as my body shudders. There's a drop of precum on the tip, and she immediately snakes her tongue out to lap it up.

"Holy fuck, baby," I groan, making her grin. Using her tongue, she passes over the soft tip again, gentle and slow. Seductively, she peers up into my eyes one last time, giving me the option to stop her. Need swirls around me, and I don't utter a single word as I watch her enjoy feasting on me. All I can seem to do is pant heavily, hoping she won't stop now that she's started.

She tugs on either side of my underwear, bringing it to mid-thigh before she stops, freezing in her tracks. At the base of my cock, my balls look painfully engorged. She immediately engulfs my entire length with her wet, warm mouth, the tip of my cock touching the back of her throat, and it feels incredible. I gasp several times, trying to catch my breath as I thread my fingers roughly through her hair. "Oh shit, *cuore mio.*"

She puts everything she has into giving me pleasure, careful not to be too rough near the base of my cock as she wraps her hand around my shaft, stroking it gracefully up and down, her mouth following the rhythm her fist has set. I'm getting close. Her palm is soaked from her saliva, and as she begins to carefully knead and rub me, she slides my rock-hard erection between her lips, over her tongue, and to the back of her throat. She takes in a deep breath through her nose and lets out a long, low moan at the same time she squeezes my balls in a firm but tender grip.

Holy shit! My whole body tenses and I practically pull myself into a full crunch as I let out a feral howl. My hands shoot to the back of her head, threading through her hair to control her rhythm as she takes me deeper and deeper with each bob. I hold her head in place and pump my hips once… twice…. On the third thrust of my cock, I detonate as I continue to moan her name, shooting spurt after spurt of hot cum down her throat.

She eagerly laps up every drop, then continues bathing my still semi-hard cock with her mouth, making sure to get the little bit that lingers at the very tip.

After watching her worship my dick and then smile after swallowing my release, I'm in complete and utter awe of this woman—as if I weren't already.

GREER

$\mathcal{I}$ SLEPT OVER ALL NIGHT AGAIN. I haven't spent the night with a man since Mark. Andy feels right though. He spoons in behind me, and we fit well.

I tend to struggle to fall asleep, and then I struggle to stay asleep. It's insomnia in its truest form, and it's my curse. But tonight is different for some reason. I fall asleep and only wake when I hear people working outside in the vineyard.

I stretch and glance at the clock, noting it isn't even 6:00 a.m. yet. Who goes to work this *early?*

I roll over and see Andy lying there. His hair is tousled, and I want so much to run my fingers through it. I love the little tuft of hair he has in the middle of his chiseled chest, playing with it as I lean in and suck his nipples. He moves a bit, but his cock is what really stirs. I want it again this morning.

Taking a condom from the bedside table, I roll it on with my mouth while I massage his balls. I'd swear he was bigger this morning than he was last night.

"Good morning, *cuore mio.*"

He rolls me over and licks at my pussy, and I can't help but push farther into his mouth. As he's lapping up my juices, I pant, "How do you want me?"

"Roll over onto your hands and knees."

I quickly do as I'm told, needing him inside me. I would do anything he wants, all he has to do is ask.

He growls as he holds onto my hips, then slowly guides himself past my opening. The thickness of his cock stretches my core as he pushes himself in inch by slow inch from behind. My muscles exquisitely expand to accommodate the full length of his thickness as he fills me. We simultaneously moan in ecstasy as he pulls back out of me to start again.

My insatiable core fights to tighten and clench around his girth, not wanting him to pull out, going to any length necessary to keep him inside me. He pauses when the very tip of his cock rests just inside my opening. My greedy pussy tightens around him, beckoning for him to come back in. I sigh out in relief and savor the feeling when he slides his full length back into the depths of my warm center. His strokes are controlled and slow as he gives my body what it craves, letting out a satisfied groan each time he pushes back in.

His hands guide my hips, slowly rocking them back and forth over his hard cock, and I moan at the sensation.

Reaching down to my slick nub, I begin to work it in a frenzy, gliding over my center hard and fast. As my breathing quickens, I can't take it anymore and my orgasm hits me in waves. My pussy milks his cock and we collapse on the bed, both out of breath and euphoric.

I rest my cheek on his chest, snuggling my nose into his neck, breathing in his scent again. I could do this all day, but I know duty calls when you own a farm.

Andy strokes my hair and places his lips to my forehead, giving me a gentle kiss. All too soon, he breaks our intimate embrace, and I'm bereft of his warmth and comfort.

I hear the shower start, and I'm still breathing hard. Bracing myself with pillows, I sit up and scroll through my e-mail. Before I can dig in, Andy comes out wrapped only in a towel. I don't even realize I lick my lips until I see the hooded look in his eyes. My heartbeat pounds in my chest and my eyes fall to half-mast as I slip into a lustful trance. The moment grows stiflingly heavy and heated for a brief second as he looks upon my lips with desire.

"If you don't stop, I'll never get downstairs to get the crews off."

"I'm sorry. I can't help myself."

He crawls across the bed to me, taking my nipple in his mouth as he plays with my sensitive nub. I moan my appreciation. With his fingers probing my slick channel, he asks, "You're staying, aren't you?"

I'm almost there, and he continues working me. I can't speak, only nod.

He growls, "Come for me, *cuore mio*."

As if on cue, my body has an earth-shattering orgasm, my legs trembling in its wake. Sitting up, he licks his fingers. "You taste better than any breakfast sweet roll."

I watch him dress and am floored at his beauty. He looks at me and smiles. "There's coffee, and Sophia should be here by nine. I hope to be done by lunch, and then we can spend the day together." I nod in my post-sex high.

After he leaves, I can't concentrate. My breasts are sore from all the attention he's lavished upon them, and I can't believe what he did with just his fingers this morning. I've heard of women doing that, but holy cow, that pushed me off an amazing cliff of an orgasm that left me speechless.

I finally make my way to the kitchen and grab some coffee, taking a seat at the table to relax. With each passing moment, I move out of the fog of my climax, and my brain somehow begins to work. After my second cup, I take a shower. The bathroom is beautiful with granite countertops and a shower big enough for a few people, and I relish in its luxurious spray.

Climbing out and drying off, I dress quickly in a pair of jeans and a sweater, then park myself at his kitchen table with my laptop and begin working. It's a Saturday morning, but Mason, Dillon, and Cameron are early risers, and they're already busy talking in a partners chat.

Mason: **Benchmark quietly terminated four CEOs/founders of their investments yesterday.**

Emerson: **CEOs are a big deal to replace. How are they doing that? They don't even have an HR arm.**

I know a Benchmark client well, so I send her a text. **Hi, Suzie. If Benchmark was going to recruit CEOs, how would they do it?**

Suzie is quick to respond. **Caught that, did you? Benchmark was hoping that by doing it late on a Friday, it would go out with the trash and no one would notice.**

Me: **Well, I noticed. They don't have an HR arm inside, so how are they doing it?**

Suzie: **Jeannine has a girlfriend who recruits for them. They covet Emerson, but can't seem to find anyone they like. Rumor has it they've been interviewing her team, but no one's jumped yet.**

Holy fuck! Poaching. That's going to send the guys over the edge.

Me: **Thanks, Suzie. Sorry if I woke you.**

Suzie: **No problem. Let's meet for drinks soon. Lots to catch up on.**

Me: **I'd love to. Thursday?**

Suzie: **Perfect. 7 at Wine Bar?**

Me: **See you then.**

I lie back and carefully craft my message to the partners. **I've been watching the chat. I just spoke with someone who knows. Looks like Jeannine has a girlfriend who's recruiting for them. And rumor has it they're interviewing some folks from Emerson's team. My contact stressed no one has jumped as of now.**

Emerson: **Did they say who it was?**

Me: **They didn't. Just that they covet you—which we all do :)**

Mason: **Okay, we need to make sure our house is strong. And it's interesting they're using an outside source to recruit.**

Emerson: **It does allow them to do it under the radar. There's more anonymity using a third party.**

Me: **She also mentioned that they hoped by doing it on a Friday, it would go out with the trash and go unnoticed by us.**

Cameron: **So they've figured out we might be watching.**

Me: **Exactly.**

Sara: **What does "out with the trash" mean?**

Me: **Companies like to bury the ugly stuff on Fridays because people will miss it in the Saturday news. They may read the Sunday paper, but it's already over 24 hours old, so it's easily missed.**

Cynthia: **You PR folk are pretty crafty!**

Mason: **Can everyone make Charles's tomorrow night?**

Me: **I'm in Napa dealing with my mom's stuff, but I can try.**

Emerson: **You take care of what you need to. If you can't get down, we understand.**

They continue to chat, and I start thinking of all the things I need to get accomplished today. It's already after nine, so I pack up my bag and head downstairs.

Sophia sees me and seems surprised by my presence.

"Greer, how lovely to see you. Please tell me my brother has lifted his vow of chastity and finally done something delicious?"

I'm not really comfortable talking to Andy's sister about our sex life, so, with a good-natured laugh, I tell her, "Well, you'll have to ask him about that. I was going to wait for him, but do you mind telling him I'll be back in a few hours? I need to go take care of a few things at my mother's."

"Of course. You have a wonderful glow. I'm so excited for you both."

"Slow down, Sophia. I don't live here, and it isn't anything serious."

"You don't know my brother. He doesn't sleep around. He's serious. Now you need to get serious."

"Well, we'll see." I quickly walk out before the inquisition continues and I'm pressured to commit to something I don't want to.

As I think about what Sophia said, I have a bit of spring to my step. I've watched women trip all over him, and to know that despite obvious opportunity, he doesn't sleep around, I'm very excited that he slept with me and seems to want more.

Driving into St. Helena, I stop at Starbucks and grab a venti mocha frappuccino, then make my way to my mother's. The cleaning crew was supposed to get it picked up this week. They had called a few times and mentioned the bed was soiled and needed to be discarded. I agreed to have them take out whatever they felt wasn't salvageable.

When I walk in, my mother's condo is almost empty. My heart drops. *Shit. Mom, why did I miss it this time?* It smells of bleach and disinfectant. I can't help but be disappointed and angry with myself for not doing a better job of checking on her. This didn't happen overnight. We talked via text, and she'd tell me all about things she was doing with friends and the occasional date. Sometimes she didn't respond, but I figured she was out having fun.

I call Vanessa, the only person who truly understands. Her

phone goes to voice mail. "Vannie, it's me. Mom went on vacation from her meds long enough that she soiled essentially everything she owns. I feel like I'm a terrible daughter. Call me back."

Then I text Andy. **I'm at my mom's and am heading to the hospital to see her. I'll be back for dinner if that works? If you have other plans, don't cancel them. I completely understand.**

Andy: **You were my plans. Come back to the vineyard when you're ready.**

Me: **Can't wait.**

Andy: **Miss you already.**

I miss him, too, but I need to protect myself. Andy only got a onetime taste of Eve. From experience, I know men tend to run away once they get the full scope of how crazy my mom can be.

Me: **Miss you, too. I promise to make it up to you many times tonight.**

Andy: **I'm counting the minutes.**

Vanessa returns my call just as I read his reply. "Gigi, what happened?"

"I called and texted, but I didn't try that hard." I tell her the whole story of what happened with her current break, including the state of her condo, and about Andy's involvement in the whole mess.

"Sweetie, it isn't your responsibility. You can't make her take her medications. She's an adult. We just need to be grateful she didn't hurt herself or anyone else."

"Thank you for listening to me. I can't help but think a few more episodes of Eve and the other shoe will drop."

"I'm over the moon that you've met someone. Your mom is a secret matchmaker. You can't live your life waiting for a show—unless it's a great designer. I love you."

"I love you, too."

Wiping the tears away, I scoff. My mom a matchmaker? That'd be a first.

I force a smile and get in my car to drive to the hospital, stopping briefly to pick up flowers for Mom—her favorite yellow tulips. I call her doctor and get an answering service, so I leave a message that I'm heading over to visit her.

As I park, the doctor calls me back. "Hello, Greer. Your mom should be outside. She had a rough night. She was in a manic episode, and this morning it's moving to a depressive episode. Your visit might help level her, but just be patient. The staff will keep an eye on you both."

Great. Depressive episodes can range from her being tired to wanting to kill herself or me. I'm mad at myself. Had I been around more, I might've noticed she wasn't taking her meds. She's good at hiding them, but her state when we sent her here was the worst I've ever seen.

After I sign in, the caregiver walks me back. "Dr. Phillips told us you were coming, so we told Eve."

"How did she take it?"

"She was excited."

"Was it excited to hurt me or excited to keep her manic?"

He smiles at me, knowing what may sound like sarcasm is really my reality. "She isn't suicidal this morning. You know the sign if she starts behaving erratically. We'll be watching and will intervene."

"Thank you."

My mother's sitting on a bench under a tree by a pond watching the ducks. "Hi, Mom."

She doesn't move or acknowledge me as I sit next to her and hand her the flowers. She takes them but doesn't look at them or say anything. We watch the mother duck manage her babies. One keeps trying to get away, and she chases it.

Finally, she mumbles, "That's what it was like for me. My daughter would do the opposite of whatever I told her. If I asked her to hold my hand to cross the street, she'd run out into the traffic. If I asked her to stay by my side when we were shopping, she'd crawl into the clothes rack."

"Mom, I was young when I did those things."

Turning and looking at me, she finally recognizes me. "Greer, are you here to take me home?"

"I'm afraid not. They're still working on your medicines. Once they get them figured out, I'll take you home."

"I don't need any medicines. I wish they could understand that it makes my brain all foggy."

"I know, Mom, but they're important."

"How much medicine do you take?"

This is a fight we often have. Her mother was bipolar, as is her sister, and she thinks I'm bipolar, too. I'm scared I might be, but so far all indications are that I'm not.

I decide to change the subject, as much for me as for her. "How are your art classes coming?"

"Fine." She looks down at the bench and notices the flowers for the first time. "Oh look, my boyfriend, Andy, brought me flowers."

A big sigh escapes from my mouth. It isn't worth having the fight or correcting her. "They're beautiful and your favorite. Whoever gave them to you must love you a lot."

"Oh, he does. And boy, he's a real tiger between the sheets, if you know what I mean."

"That's really nice."

"Your father has a little penis. That's why he likes all those younger women. They don't know any different."

"Tell me about your music class. Are you singing or playing the piano?"

Our afternoon continues like that, talking in circles and her oversharing with me, mostly half-truths and lies. She hasn't said anything to me that I haven't heard before.

I can't take much more today. I'm ready to head back to Bellissima. "Okay, Mom, I need to get back. I have a friend waiting."

"Tell Mark he needs to come visit me again."

"He came out and visited you recently?"

"Just yesterday. He's quite the charmer. You're very lucky to have him."

"I'll tell him to come again soon."

I kiss her forehead and she gives me a half hug.

Walking away, I find Dr. Phillips to debrief him. "She mentioned my ex-fiancé visited her yesterday, and she talked about my current boyfriend being her lover."

"You've been her only visitor."

I share with him the final outcome of Eve's condo, and he takes notes without offering me much advice or guidance.

"Okay. I'll try to drive up again next week."

"Greer, I know this is hard. She appreciates your visits."

"Call me if you need me for any reason, day or night."

As I drive back to Bellissima, I want to cry. *Why can't my mother be normal?*

The tasting room is stuffed full of people when I enter. I watch Andy move from table to table, the women drooling all over him.

I take a seat at the bar and order a red flight, then sit back and enjoy the wines.

I still can't decide which is my favorite as a hand rests on my back. "*Cuore mio.* You've returned." When he kisses my cheek, I note the dirty looks women are giving me.

"You're going to lose your harem if you aren't careful."

"I don't care. They need to love my wine, not me."

If looks could kill, I'd be dead. A woman old enough to be my mother stops next to me. "You look a lot like my friend. Do you know Eve Ford?"

"Yes, she's my mother."

"I see." Turning to Andy, she says, "You met Eve a few weeks ago. She's as crazy as they get. She had dead cats in her condo. They had to throw out all of her belongings. It's hereditary, you know." Nodding at me, she continues, "She's just like her mom. You'd better watch out." She offers a sickening smile and reaches for Andy.

He gently moves her hand away and takes a moment to respond. He knows my mom is sick, and that she had a breakdown, but he doesn't know much more than that. I'm nervous that he's going to ask me to leave. That's what Mark essentially did after my mom had a difficult episode.

"Thank you, Marnie." I can see her eyes light up at him saying her name. "When you leave today, please don't come back. We don't tolerate insulting our visitors in our establishment. And, in particular, my girlfriend. I think you should leave now."

This is obviously not what she expected to hear. "You've just ruined yourself. You won't sell another bottle of wine to anyone in this community."

"Well, that's too bad. I suspect there are many others who will happily buy my wine."

She storms out with her friends at her heels.

Turning to me, Andy apologizes. "I'm so sorry you had to witness that."

Holding back tears, I give him a huge hug as my heart sinks. "Andy, this isn't the first time and won't be the last that someone goes out of their way to point out the obvious." I suppose it's time for me to walk away. "Nothing she said isn't true. My mom struggles with a disease. It's hereditary, and I don't know if I'll develop symptoms." I struggle to continue. It hurts my heart to tell him, but I need to do this now before it's too late. "I can't bring you into this mess. It'll only serve to ruin your business."

I walk upstairs, wiping the tears away as I go. Andy is quick to follow behind me. "Greer, I don't know what other kind of men you've dated in the past, but I don't care if your mother has mental health problems. You haven't met my mother yet. And as things happen with Eve, we'll figure out how to manage it together. Let's just take one day at a time, okay?"

I nod, too stunned for words. I've never had anyone offer to help me with my mother. "Together?" A tremendous weight lifts from my shoulders, the one that's been there since I was very young and learned my mother was sick. I crumble into his arms, and he holds me tight. I feel safe with him.

Pulling back, I look at him, staring into his eyes down to his soul, and then our lips come crashing together. I can't explain the feeling of relief, even if it's only momentary.

"You called me your girlfriend."

"Of course I did. What did you think I'd call you?"

I shrug. "We just haven't really talked about it."

"Do you want to talk about it? We can. Do you not think of me as your boyfriend?"

I lean in and place a soft kiss squarely on his lips. "I like being your girlfriend."

His eyes hood with desire and his cock is hard against my stomach.

Andy pulls me upstairs to the first room, which is filled with a desk, couch and a spectacular view of the vineyard. Our bodies repeatedly collide in urgent need, my jeans around my knees and his fingers exploring before I know it. He knows what he's doing, and he makes my body respond like no one ever has. He uses his tongue and fingers to tease and torment me, my climax building within me. I'm no longer aware of the hard wood of the desk beneath me, or the cool air on my ass, or the fact that less than half an hour ago, I was going to leave and never come back. All I know is the pleasure and sweet agony of the need to come.

I pull back, look into his eyes and moan, "Take me, please. I want you!"

Bending me over the desk and unbuttoning his pants, he puts one hand on my upper back to hold me down and runs the fingers of his other hand up the inside of my thigh to my sweet spot between my legs. I hear the foil wrapper of a condom and let out a low groan as his fingers gently rub against my clit. Then he slowly traces my core, slowly rubbing along the canal around my clit to my slick channel. He's teasing me, and my hips move involuntarily to feel him. I want him inside me. I *need* him inside me.

His fingers piston into my pussy and my body shudders as I let out a very loud groan of satisfaction. He starts pumping me with his fingers, slapping my ass with his palm. He continues to hold me in place with his other hand on my back as I wiggle and squirm underneath it. My pussy explodes as I cry out from one orgasm after another, moaning his name through it all.

Pulling his fingers out, he roughly grabs my hips and pulls me onto his thick and rigid shaft. He slams into me over and over as I grip the side of the desk to hold myself steady, my whole body bouncing uncontrollably back and forth. My nipples rub across the desk, and that coupled with the onslaught on my pussy is creating the most pleasurable sensation I've ever known. I'm dizzy as I cry out in an orgasmic intoxication, his pounding making me grunt with every thrust forward as he pushes into me over and over.

Having climaxed several times, my creamy fluids are running down my leg. I try to regain myself after each orgasm, but Andy won't let me. He doesn't allow me to come down, keeping me peaked and euphoric.

When he finally pulls out of me, I feel empty without him. Rolling on my back, I'm breathing heavily, my breasts heaving up and down, the hair around my face soaking wet with sweat. I feel as if I just had an out-of-body experience. Attempting to collect myself, I anxiously wait to see what more he would do, my body tense and ready on the desktop as my chest rises and falls in rhythm to my rapid breathing.

I gasp as he grabs my legs and hooks them over his shoulders, rubbing his cock in a slow dance against my clit. I can't take this teasing. I thrust my hips forward, causing his cock to penetrate me deeper. I've never felt this much stimulation in my whole life. He shoves his cock deep into my wet pussy as I cry out for more, pumping me harder and harder, burying himself to the hilt. My breasts bounce wildly in rhythm to his powerful lunges.

My orgasm is growing deep from within as his finger works my clit and my body clenches around his cock.

"Andreas," I moan at the same time he grits out, "Greer."

We're both spent, panting and seeing stars—at least I am.

I ease myself to the floor, both exhausted and exhilarated. I hear movement, but I'm still dazed from that round of orgasms.

Andy hands me a glass of water. "You do something to me that I've never felt before."

I look at him and smile. "I feel the same way."

THIRTEEN

ANDY

*L*YING AWAKE, I hear her rhythmic breathing next to me. I'm beginning to really like this. She was so upset last night after Marnie made her scene. What a bitch. Why would I care about her mother's illness? I don't mean that in an uncaring way, of course. But Greer seems so ready to run when someone makes a big deal of her mother's issues.

What have people done to this sweet woman?

I think of my own family. Wait until she meets Uncle Frederic. Most likely he'll pull his pants down and expose himself while telling her dirty jokes in Italian. He's my mother's youngest brother and suffered a head injury when he fell off a horse at a young age, leaving him stuck mentally at the age of thirteen but with the sexual urges of an adult male. He isn't dangerous, only a pervert, but we can't control what he does around others. In the same vein, she has no control over her mother's illness.

She stretches her arms above the sheets, exposing her breasts. "You're awake. Good morning."

Leaning down, I kiss her perfect forehead. *"Buongiorno, cuore mio.* Did you sleep well?"

Nodding vigorously, she says, "I did. It must be all the fresh air and quiet of the vineyard."

"Tell me about your home in San Francisco."

She rolls into me and I hold her closely, kissing the top of her head.

"It was a place I visited as a child with one of my best friends. The woman who owned it had it for many years, but she was ready to move over to Marin and leave the city behind, so she sold it to me for a steal."

"May I come visit you?"

She props herself up and places her hand on my chest. "You can come visit me any time. I thought you had commitments here at the vineyard, but I'd love to show you *my* San Francisco. The places I spent my time when I was growing up and the bars and restaurants I visit with my friends. Please come down often."

I smile internally. I want to see my Greer in her busy and natural habitat. "Then it's settled. I'll come up one evening this week."

She leans down and gives me a slow and lasting kiss.

Spending the morning reading the paper and enjoying nice strong Italian coffee, we seem to fit well together. She's warned me she has a partners meeting tonight south of The City, so she'll leave after lunch. I miss her already, and she hasn't left yet. I want to enjoy as much time as I can with her.

"Before you need to go, would you want to head to old town St. Helena and wander the stores? There's a great place we can get a light lunch, too."

"Sure. I don't have to be in Hillsboro until six."

Holding hands, we wander in and out of the handful of stores. We skip the shops that sell various wines, glass sets, decanters, and assorted wine-related stuff to tourist, finding the galleries the most enjoyable. There's an interesting watercolor painting of a vineyard that attracts her attention like no other. "Isn't it beautiful?"

I'm stunned. I didn't direct her to the piece, but it was painted by a friend of mine. "I know the artist. She interned for us, maybe two years ago? Painting was always her passion. We sell prints of the villa at Bellissima. This scene is actually our cab vines on the western side of the vineyard."

Her eyes fill with shock and wonder. "Are you pulling my leg?"

The gallery owner approaches. "Andy! So wonderful to see you." She kisses me on both cheeks, then says to Greer, "It really was painted out at Bellissima Valle. It's the original, and there are no prints. I tried to get the artist to do prints, but she insisted this be the only copy."

Greer is studying the large watercolor of rows of vines with a majestic patchwork of green and golds in the hills in the background.

"Sharon, this is my girlfriend Greer." Turning to Greer, I tell her, "Greer, this is Sharon the owner of this fine establishment."

Sharon extends her hand, and Greer takes it and smiles. "So nice to meet you. It's Bellissima? No wonder I love it. I have the perfect place for it in my home." She bites her lip. She looks so cute when she does that. "Would you deliver into The City?"

"We have a service that can bring it in and hang it for you."

Greer looks at the painting a few more moments, taking it in, before announcing, "I'll take it." She grins widely.

"The artist will be thrilled." Sharon sounds pleased, and I'm not surprised. When my former intern told me she had Sharon agree to take her painting into the gallery and that she was going to sell it for her in the mid six figures, I was shocked. I appreciate the talent though, and I'm glad I know where the painting will hang.

Turning to me, Sharon says, "I think Lydia will need to do more paintings."

After we get everything wrapped up, we head into a little café filled with wine paraphernalia and overstuffed chairs that invite casual conversation and relaxation. We sit at a bistro table and take in the menus.

"You're on the wine list," Greer notes.

"Yes, Christy was one of the first to order cases of Bellissima. She asked if we were related to my father's vineyard, then committed to buying our wine before we planted our first vine."

"She did? I love that story."

"Yes, she's a true connoisseur of wine. I like her list because she always showcases the up-and-coming bottles. Would you be okay to try one?"

"Absolutely. If I order the chicken salad, what do you suggest to drink with it?"

I chuckle. "None of them go with chicken salad, but I'll order you a nice white chardonnay from one of the new vintners from an area south of my family's vineyard in Italy. Also a glass of the syrah from my neighbor here in St. Helena. We cultivate our grapes the same, but the fermentation process is different, and I like his wine. Something to compare."

I order pasta with pesto and shrimp, and while we wait, we talk.

Resting her hands on her chin, she asks me questions about the business and my aspirations. She listens so intently, probing gently as she asks questions. I feel like I'm a king as she hangs on my every word.

When our simple lunch is placed in front of us along with our glasses of wine, Greer lets out a shuddering breath, then lifts each glass of wine to her nose and inhales deeply. Just looking at her makes me think of sex. Raw, pussy-grinding sex. That little crease between her eyes pops up. I've been learning her expressions. The crease is a clue that she can't decide—in this case which glass to taste first.

Leaving the restaurant after our meal, we walk down the street, window-shopping, when we smell the sweet, velvety aroma of chocolate. Her pace quickens, and I follow her.

"You do like chocolate, don't you?" She looks at me intently, and I know this is a make or break question.

"Without a doubt. Who doesn't like chocolate, particularly paired with wine or coffee?"

We walk in, noting several cases full of chocolates. They're all decadent and smell like heaven.

"There's something in the dark brown sweet I had always found beautiful. The way it glistened when it melted. The way it crumbled when it was hard. It's exotic, made from far grown cocoa beans. Once it's finished, all eaten, my heart aches for more. I love all sorts of chocolate." Her sultry voice makes chocolate sound better than sex. I love her enthusiasm as she studies the cases and carefully chooses a pound of chocolate for a box. She adds three to a bag, and we set off to explore the next store.

She checks her watch, the same conflict on her face that I feel inside me, like a ball of twine knotted and pulled in many directions. She turns to me. "This has been a wonderful weekend. I hope we can do it again soon."

"Why are you so formal? I told you I'm coming down this week, and I want you to come see Bellissima Grande."

"I know I come with some baggage, and I know you may change your mind. I just wanted you to know that I understand, and I had a magnificent time with you this weekend."

I bring her in for a hug and whisper in her hair. "I won't change my mind." I need to tell her about my own baggage, but I can't right now. She could very well run from me once she knows my truth.

GREER

*A*s I cross the Golden Gate, the sun is shining, and it's a perfect Sunday afternoon. I left a part of me in St. Helena. I love the vineyard. I know Andy calls himself a farmer, but I can't help but remember the way his eyes lit up as he talked about his passion for the winemaking process and the business. His voice is smooth as silk, and I love his slight Italian accent. It just makes me all gooey inside. I'm starting to fall hard for him.

Traffic slows, but that's normal. I finally inch my way to my place and ask the doorman to leave my car out because I'll be heading out shortly.

Walking into my apartment, I drop my bags next to the door and breathe in the smell that comes from the roses and lilacs on my patio. I text Andy: **I made it home. Hope to see you soon.**

Andy: **How does Thursday look for me to come into town? I can do a few things around The City on Friday while you work, then have the weekend on your turf?**

My heart warms at the thought of him coming to visit me.

Greer: **Sounds like a perfect weekend.**

I can't wait for Thursday. But for now, I need to concentrate on today's meeting.

California "work appropriate" clothes can range from suit and tie to bathing suits, but I feel a partners meeting, while informal on a Sunday night, deserves better than a lightweight sundress. I change into capri pants and a cute sweater, putting the finishing touches on my makeup before climbing back in my car and heading down to Hillsboro for the meeting.

When I arrive, CeCe pulls me aside. "Hey, chica! You're positively glowing."

"Hey, yourself. What's up?" We link arms and walk in. We've been friends for so long that her parents' house is a second home to me.

"You know that guy we had dinner with at Fashion Week, that the one your cousin set me up with?"

"Todd, right?"

"Well I've been talking to him. He's thinking about coming out to San Francisco."

I step back, not sure I like this guy who's inviting himself for a visit. CeCe can certainly take care of herself when it comes to men and her wealth, but I'm always on guard when she doesn't tell me about a man pursuing her. Her radar must be up. I'll need to call my cousin and get the real scoop about Todd and his motives for the trip. "To visit or to live?"

"Apparently Vanessa's husband wants to open an office here, and he would head it."

Vanessa hasn't said a word. I'll definitely need to hear about the plan from her lips to know if it's true.

"How do you feel about that?"

A big sigh escapes her mouth. "I don't know. He was fun when we were there, and we've exchanged some saucy texts, but I'm not sure I want more than that with him."

"Why not? He's single, and as a senior manager at a hedge fund, he has some money. Most likely he may even have more money than both of us."

"I'm sure he does. I just don't feel that spark with him. Am I crazy to think it should be lightning in a bottle? I'm not even that excited to talk to him when he calls."

That's why she hasn't told me anything. She's not into him. "Just be honest with him."

"I know. Now enough of that. How's your mom doing?"

"She's going to be in the hospital for a while. I got her place cleaned. It was the worst I've ever seen it, and it looks like she'd been off her meds for a while. I had them throw out everything that couldn't be cleaned or saved, and now her condo's essentially empty."

"Oh, honey, I'm so sorry."

"Thanks. I was at Bellissima, and one of her friends confronted me about how crazy my mom is. Andy was my knight in shining armor, kicked her out of the tasting room."

"Really? That's awesome! Did you spend some time with him while you were there?" she asks, trying to be sly.

"You know Eve had her final break at Bellissima and was wandering his fields essentially naked. Andy found her and kept her while I drove up." She gives me a gentle squeeze of encouragement. She's experienced the ugliest of Eve and is still supportive. "I don't want you to get your hopes up. He's coming to town on Thursday, and we'll spend the weekend together."

Her eyes widen and she jumps up and down, squealing, "I knew it! I knew it! I knew it!"

This is exactly why I don't tell her about my love life. She gets more invested than I do.

I throw my head back, laughing. "It's still early, so don't go and start planning a wedding. He's only had a small taste of Eve."

"Honey, he sounds like he handled Eve like a pro. Don't push him away. You deserve to be happy."

"I know," I mutter.

"Greer, I can't tell you how happy I am for you. I mean, I called several of my friends this week, and we all donated to Mark's competitor, and I'm funding a political poll to determine his weaknesses. I'm going for the jugular."

"Remind me to never cross you."

"Honey, that man used you and hurt you, one of my best friends. He's dead to me. There's nothing you could ever do or say that would make me hate you like I hate him."

"I love you."

"I love you, too. Now, what are your plans for the weekend? You can't just hole up in your apartment and have sex. Okay, yes you can, but how about showing him off a bit?"

"I was thinking we would do something with everyone Friday night."

"Emerson, Hadlee, Sara, and I will get it organized. You both just need to show up."

"Don't scare him away. Something easy and simple."

"Okay, okay. I hear you." She gives my arm a reassuring squeeze, then goes off to find the girls and begin planning. She has no real concept of easy and simple, so I'll have to make sure the girls know. They can help tame her a bit.

Mason arrives with his girlfriend, Annabel, who looks like she's been crying.

"Hey, guys." I step in and greet them both with a cordial hug.

Mason turns to me. "Annabel thinks everyone here hates her. Can you tell her that isn't the case?"

We do hate her, and unfortunately he's the only one who can't see it. Still, I try to be reassuring. "Annabel, what makes you think that? I can't believe Mason drags you to these things. When we retire to Charles's office after dinner, it must be so boring."

Sniffling, she tells us, "It is, especially now that Hadlee comes with Cameron. She and Margo laugh and talk, leaving me out of the conversation."

Mason sighs in exacerbation and, just loud enough for the two of us to hear, says, "You're being childish, Annabel."

I'm stunned by his comment. I agree with his assessment, but for him to be that direct is pretty shocking. He always seems to think we're crazy when we're less than complimentary about her. But I know exactly why Margo and Hadlee exclude her. According to Hadlee, she asks what they know about the agenda of the partners meeting and is only interested in Mason or herself. However, I can't be rude, so I choose my words carefully. "Oh, honey, I'm sure they don't mean to. I'll mention it to Hadlee, and we'll make sure you feel included."

Mason gives me a nod of appreciation, then turns to Annabel. "See, you're just imagining this. Have fun tonight. You were the one who wanted to come, remember."

"Well, if I didn't have to worry about Cynthia trying to steal you away from me, I wouldn't have to come and could've stayed home."

I can't hear what he tells her in response, but I think she's off her rocker about Cynthia.

Seeing Cameron and Hadlee in a deep conversation with Dillon, I approach and Hadlee excuses herself. "CeCe told me all about Andy coming down to spend the weekend with you. I'm in for planning."

"Great, just make it simple. I don't want to do any private rooms or anything that might overwhelm him."

"I understand. I think CeCe was planning to meet at a pub and throw darts at Mark's picture. Too much?"

"You're funny. Yes, too much." I laugh. "But I'm game for Wednesday night if you all are up for it."

"That's my girl." She looks over at Annabel. "I see Cruella is here."

"She's convinced Mason that we all hate her."

"We pretty much do. Even Margo can't stand her, and she likes everyone. We caught her last week hanging outside the meeting trying to eavesdrop."

"Why isn't someone saying anything to Mason?"

"Dillon and Charles both have. He just thinks they're making it up."

The housekeeper rings a bell and calls us to the dining room. We all sit at our regular places, and Margo announces, "I was in the mood for some comfort food, so tonight we're having meatloaf, mashed potatoes, green beans, and peach cobbler for dessert."

"That sounds delicious," Dillon declares.

"I want seconds already." Cameron grins.

Cynthia, sitting on the other side of Mason, says, "My diet can start tomorrow. Bring it on."

Annabel glares at Cynthia, who has a perfect figure, and I've never seen her abstain from anything for a diet. Mason sees the dirty look, but it doesn't seem to faze him. Maybe he's starting to see what we all see and will dump Annabel. Even if she isn't our mole, she's not right for him. He's very good-looking, smart, and he's a billionaire—a real catch by anyone's standards—and he needs someone a little more independent and self-confident.

Dinner conversation centers around a motorcycle ride that Hadlee and Cameron took, and a vacation Mason and Annabel are considering.

Andy assures me he's serious about my joining him in when

he goes home to Italy. The idea excites me—not the meeting his family part, but getting away together. However, if I don't get it on the calendar with the partners, someone else may take those same days off, leaving us too shorthanded for me to also be gone. I throw out, "I've been invited to Tuscany next month with a friend. I've checked the dates, and it's around two filings, and I think I can make it work. I know I took a few days to deal with my mom though, so I'd understand if you'd prefer I not go."

Mason pipes up. "Greer, you've hardly taken any time off since you started with us at SHN. Unless anyone disagrees, I say go have fun."

"I agree," Sara says.

Cameron tousles my hair with brotherly affection. "Enjoy your time with your mystery man. I can't wait to meet him this weekend."

Looking at CeCe, I sigh in exasperation. "Good to see nothing is secret around here."

She proudly announces, "Not with us, babe," and he table erupts with laughter.

Our dinner conversation deteriorates into a big rowdy family dinner. At one point, Dillon asks, "Anyone up for seafood?" and he opens his mouth full of food. Emerson elbows him hard in the stomach while we all laugh, and then Cameron and Trey both open their mouths as well. We seem to relish the role of children at Margo and Charles's table, and they love it.

Eventually, the partners and advisors move into Charles's office for our meeting. I try to give Annabel a reassuring smile as she's left behind with Hadlee and Margo, but she just looks pissed off and is scowling at Mason. If her eyes had lasers, she would've cut him in half.

Cynthia leans in and says, "She's not a happy camper."

"No, she really isn't."

We all take our usual places, and for the first time, I realize Cynthia doesn't even sit close to Mason. Her regular spot is between Charles and Sara across the room, while Mason sits between CeCe and Emerson. So odd for Annabel to be jealous of Cynthia of all people. If she was jealous of CeCe, well, that'd be a different story.

Our meeting is uneventful. I end up with some work to pre-pare for a few upcoming deals, and I'll be doing some research on our competitor Benchmark. I know the one of their founders, Jeannine Pierce, and Mason have a strong personal connection—I think they love to hate one another. This could create quite the media blowup, and I want to be prepared.

At the end of the night, I head home. Putting my favorite flannel jammies on, I crawl under the covers and grab my Kindle to read something fun—a naughty but sweet novel.

My cell phone pings, and my curiosity gets the better of me. I'm expecting CeCe with some comment about tonight, and it's actually Andy. **Just thinking of you. My bed misses you.**

I smile, the message making me warm all over. **My body misses you.**

Andy: **I can't wait to taste you all over on Thursday.**

Me: **I have big plans, but CeCe and friends want to see you on Friday. Hope that's okay.**

Andy: **I'd prefer you to myself, but I suppose we should be cordial.**

Andy: **Buona note, cuore mio. Sweet dreams, and know I'm dreaming of all the things I plan on doing to you this weekend.**

I involuntarily shiver in anticipation. If you keep talking like that, I won't be able to wait.

Andy: **Trust me, I feel the same. You taste better than the chocolate you left me.**
Me: **Good night.**

Lying in bed, I'm getting nervous about joining him in Italy. I wish Sophia was coming—at least then I'd know someone. Apparently she hates these meetings. This just seems to be moving so quickly, something I'm not at all used to.

All of his brothers and sisters will be there with their spouses and kids except for Sophia and her husband; his parents thrive on big tables. I grew up with our family dinner table often being either my mom and me and maybe a boyfriend of hers, but mostly eating by myself in front of the television or eating over the sink. Or my dad and the current wife and their kids. At the most at a table, there might have been five of us. Andy tells me there will be close to fifty people there. Just the thought gives me anxiety. I know many of them speak English, but his parents really don't, so I'm not expecting to have many people to talk to.

But despite all this trepidation, there's something about going that just feels right. I want to see Andy with his family around him. How he responds. I wonder if they'll act like Dillon, Trey, and Cameron did tonight at dinner—silly and completely immature.

My mind wanders to Andy. I love the way his brown eyes light up when he talks about his family. He has six older brothers and four older sisters plus two younger brothers and two younger sisters. How did his mother manage that? I can't even imagine.

I wonder how alike they all look—though there's no way they're as handsome as my Andy.

God, I miss him.

EVERY DAY, I FIND MYSELF thinking about Andy while I should be working. We continue to trade a few saucy texts each day.

We're really building our foreplay with all this naughty talk, but we also share more and more about ourselves each day as well.

While not a practicing Catholic, many of his opinions really dive deep into his upbringing, so I know when we're at his parents', we'll be given different rooms. I'm a guest in their home, so that doesn't bother me at all. I worry about being lonely at night, but he assures me that's never an issue. We also talk about our work and our plans for the future. I'm surprised at how comfortable I am when we discuss a future together.

I'm staring out my window, watching a sailboat tack hard across the whitecap waves on the bay, when my phone rings and brings me out of my trance. Looking at the caller ID, I see it's CeCe. Before I can even say hello, she asks, "What time are we meeting at the pub tonight?"

"The pub?"

"Yes, you told Hadlee we could throw darts at Mark's face tonight."

"I was only kidding."

"Well, we aren't. Sounded fun to everyone else."

"You're evil, you know that?"

"Yes, and yet everyone who meets me loves me. What does that say?"

Glancing around my desk, I see piles of papers and plenty to do that will keep me busy for the next millennium. "Okay, how about seven?"

"Perfect. I'll e-mail the girls, and they can alert their men."

A short time later, Emerson walks over and sticks her head in. "Did you drive today?"

I look at the clock to find it's well after six. *Where did my afternoon go?* "I did. Do you want a ride?"

"Why don't you leave your car here and we get a ride share? It's going to be me, Dillon, and Cameron. Mason will swing by and pick up Annabel. Cynthia's with a client and will meet us there."

"What about Sara and Trey?"

"They're going to meet us there, too. More wedding planning."

I believe "wedding planning" is their code for a nooner; they always look so relaxed and a bit flushed each time I see them.

"That works. See you by the elevators at six forty-five?"

"This is going to be so much fun."

I get to a decent stopping point in my work and meet everyone by the elevators. Cameron's been texting Hadlee and has a goofy grin on his face. I would guess they share their own bit of saucy, naughty texts. I've known Cameron long enough to know he's most likely up to no good. Hadlee is a perfect match for him.

We all pile into the Nissan Armada ride share and head to our favorite pub. When we arrive, CeCe has a big sign outside the pub that says "Jennifer Chang for Congress."

I shake my head. She's positively crazy, and I love her.

She's reserved the back room, and it's stuffed full of people—ones I don't know. "Who are all these people?" I mumble.

She puts her arm around my shoulder and sheepishly explains, "Well, I might've called her office and told her what I was doing."

I hear "Bullseye" yelled over a group of people. There's a buffet table piled high with bar food and a beer tap.

Dillon kisses CeCe on the cheek, and in a convincing Irish brogue, he says, "Caroline, you've outdone yourself." He hands her a $100 bill, and Emerson does the same, followed by everyone else.

CeCe walks over to where a young woman is standing next to

a box and puts the money in a slot on the top. "I need five brace-lets, please."

The young girl counts out five of the same red plastic brace-lets and hands them to CeCe. Everyone at our not-so-little fun-draiser seems to be wearing one. CeCe hands everyone the bracelets that signify our admittance to the private party, then ushers us to a table in the corner where we all grab food from a well-stocked buffet.

After filling our plates with typical bar food, we make our way to the table. Cynthia turns to me, "So, Mark Morris is your ex?"

I nod. "He is. We dated for almost five years and were engaged at the end. I got him onto the city council and set up his platform, and then one day he decided I had too much baggage for politics."

"Sounds like a real jerk." Cynthia may be new to our group, but she fits in just perfectly.

"He is. I just hope this doesn't make me seem petty."

"Not at all. You didn't even know CeCe would go all out."

"Well, we've been friends for years. CeCe doesn't do anything halfway."

She laughs hard. "So I've come to realize. I also think this party tells me to never piss her off."

I vigorously nod in agreement.

Hadlee approaches the table with her arms open. "Leave it to her to organize a fundraiser around a joke."

"I know. I'm feeling a bit silly right now."

"Don't you dare," Cameron demands.

Pictures are being taken, and I recognize it as one of CeCe's contacts from the *San Francisco Chronicle*.

This is going to end badly. I just know it.

We all laugh as someone else yells, "Bullseye!"

Usually, we don't need an excuse to get together, but having this impromptu fundraiser really has been fun.

As things begin to wind down, Jennifer, our guest of honor, arrives to thank everyone for coming and laughs when she sees the dartboard. We can't convince her to throw any darts, but I understand why—that would make the national news, and not in a good way for her. We collected over ten thousand dollars, so she's thrilled.

CeCe points to me, and Jennifer nods and walks over.

"You're the one I have to thank for this."

"No, it was all Caroline, really. Hadlee"—I point to her—"had the idea, and Caroline ran with it."

"Well, he's running a tough campaign, so I appreciate the last-minute fundraiser."

I motion for her to sit down and, after an internal debate, tell her, "One good way to turn his constituents against him is to ask him about his platform on the homeless in San Francisco. Chances are he'll crumble, because I came up with it and managed it for him, and he really doesn't understand it or quite frankly care about the homeless problem in The City."

"Thank you. I'll have to do that." She stands and extends a hand. "I'm really sorry for what he did to you, but you have some great friends who look like they're taking good care of you."

"Enjoy your night, and good luck with the campaign. I hope you're victorious."

She leaves, and before long we're all making excuses to head out while the fundraiser rages on.

I grabbed a Lyft home, and just as I begin to lie down, my cell phone pings. It's Mark, which takes me by surprise. I haven't heard hide nor hair from him in almost a year. **You fucking bitch. I heard about your fundraiser. This is exactly why I dumped your ass. You're as fucked up as your mother.**

I forward the text to CeCe. **I guess he heard.**

CeCe: **I could forward this along to the papers because of his slanderous words about mental health, but we're just going to hold on to this for a while. Don't let him get to you.**

Me: **I promise. Looking forward to seeing Andy tomorrow.**

CeCe: **See you Friday night. Promise not to mention Mark.**

CECE'S FUNDRAISER MADE THE FRONT PAGE of the Local section of the *Chronicle*. She and the candidate were interviewed, positioning it as a feel-good for a friend he'd dumped. Mark was asked for a quote, and he responded with a veiled threat of his impending victory. He's apparently forgotten what happens when you scorn CeCe, but that does explain his late-night text.

Shortly after three, my cell phone pings with a message from Andy. **I'm leaving now. Where should I meet you?**

Me: **My place. It may take you over two hours to get here leaving now. I understand if you want to wait until after 7 so it'll take about an hour.**

Andy: **Can't hold me back. I'm looking forward to seeing you and ravishing you all night.**

My insides go all gooey, and I feel as if I'm walking on air. I text him my address and work a short while longer. Yesterday I got a fresh pedicure, and today at lunch I got a bikini wax, so I should be ready for our weekend.

Just before five, I grab my things and head out. Emerson sees me and gives me a broad grin and a wave, mouthing, "Have fun."

I nod. "I'll see you tomorrow morning."

One of the new guys in the bullpen says, "It must be nice to be a partner and get to leave early."

I'm annoyed by the comment, as these guys have no idea how much time the partners work. Then Mason steps out of his office, points to the man and asks, "Can you come in here, please?"

I'd hate to be that guy right now. Mason's not very forgiving when it comes to negative behavior.

MAKING IT HOME IN RECORD TIME, I arrive just as Andy does. A broad grin spreads quickly across his face as I walk up to him. "Perfect timing."

"You live in this building?" he asks.

"I do. Grab your stuff and come upstairs."

We walk into the elevator and he pins me to the wall as we make out like two teenagers. Only when it dings upon our arrival at the penthouse do we break apart.

"I've missed you so much," he breathes. I giggle and grab him by the hand, leading him into my apartment. "This is your place?"

"Yes." Now I'm starting to get nervous. We've never discussed our financial situations. He must know CeCe is one of *those* Arnaults, and I've told him we've been hanging out since childhood. My great-grandfather started a major transportation manufacturer. I inherited a few billion dollars at six years old, and with good financial planning, I've managed to double that. I work because I love my job and because I believe it helps me to keep a clear head and besides, what else would I do? Sit by a pool all day?

"When you said you had an apartment that was from a friend's mother, I didn't expect it to be this grand."

"Does it matter?"

Turning to me and taking me in his arms, he shares, "No. Not at all. I guess we'll have to figure out what to get a girl who has everything."

"I don't have everything. In fact, right now, I'm thinking I'm missing an orgasm or two."

"Then I'm at the right place."

His lips come crashing down on mine in a fiery, passionate kiss.

"I've missed you this week." He grips my shoulders tightly and pulls me to him, kissing me hard once more.

I rip the buttons off his shirt, flinging it open and exposing his sweaty masculine chest. He holds me against the wall, and I wrap my legs around his waist and my arms around his neck as our kisses become aggressive. My panties are soaking wet, and I need more.

Grabbing him by the hand, I lead him to my bedroom, which overlooks Alcatraz and the bay. I push him back against the bed, his cock tenting in his pants as I begin a slow striptease. Swaying my hips from side to side, I lift my shirt over my head, revealing my taut breasts constricted by my tight lace bra. I palm my nipples, which sends electric currents direct to my clit. Turning away, I tuck my thumbs into the waist of my skirt and slowly pull it over my hips. I can feel his eyes riveted to my every move. Facing him again, I step out of my skirt once it pools at my ankles, then reach behind me to unhook my bra, turn my back to him to prolong his excitement. Rocking my ass back and forth, I pull and twist at my nipples and moan.

"I want to see you," he pants.

"Be patient." I cross my legs at my ankles, then slip my thumb in the edges of my panties and slowly begin to pull them down. Turning to look at him, I find his eyes riveted to my magic spot. I rub my fingers along the crease, giving him a good peek at what he's going to enjoy.

I pinch and play with my nipples as I walk slowly toward him. I stand at the edge of the bed above him then lower myself so I'm straddling him, grinding my pussy onto his erect cock as I press my mouth to his and his breathing becomes labored. I can feel his cock grow to full mass quickly, sandwiched between his stomach and my moistening pussy.

Going into great detail, I share how I intend to rip his jeans open before tearing them down and throwing them across the room. Stroking the hair on his stomach just above his waist, I continue telling him how I intend on throating his cock, wrapping my lips around the shaft and swirling my tongue around the head.

He listens as I tell him how I'll lather his cock until it's dripping wet from my tongue, and how I plan on making his cock spew hot white cum into the depths of my hungry mouth. He can do nothing but listen and shudder with eager delight as I plant my lips on his chest, nipples, belly, and beyond.

I snake my way down his body, hooking my fingers into the waistband of his undone jeans as I plant kiss after wet kiss along his abdomen. He shudders and watches, helping by wiggling his hips to aid my eager hands as I work his jeans down off his legs, tossing them to the floor like an animal in heat.

Thrashing my head back in his direction, my hair falls like a curtain in front of my face as I crawl my way back to him, coming to rest between his legs. I tilt my head to the side, exposing my eager mouth as I drizzle long trails of saliva onto his hard cock that's growing harder with each moment, rising up to meet my open mouth.

My seductively poised head lowers, my mouth opening wider as my hand wraps firmly around the base of his cock and guides it slowly to my waiting mouth. I see him close his eyes and he takes a deep breath, filling his lungs before slowly releasing it. Hungry and lusting, my mouth continues to pour saliva onto his cock as my hand guides it round and round, sliding his quivering head over my pursed lips. Stroking up and down the length of his shaft,

I work the lather of saliva into his flesh, his moans of approval harmonizing with mine.

Pulling a pillow under his head to raise it, he watches me. Our eyes remain locked, and he grins in delight as I lower my mouth onto him, engulfing his length. It turns me on knowing how much he's enjoying this. Heat fills my core as his cock disappears into my wanting mouth, intensifying at the moment my lips close around the base of his cock. I suckle gently on his shaft, then harder as my mouth works its way up his cock before releasing the head with an audible pop. I can't help but rub at my throbbing clit, the slickness matching my feral desire. I repeat the process over and over again, brushing my hair aside occasionally to refresh my view.

As the pace quickens, my head bobs faster over his shaft, his throbbing cock fucking my hungry mouth as fast as my lips will let it. He tries to buck his hips up into my mouth, but I press down on his waist to stop his movement, wanting to be the one who pleasures him, who controls his movements. He eventually relaxes and lies back, allowing my assault on his beautiful cock. I let his dripping cock stand at attention, bobbing for more consideration. One hand is still wrapped gently around the shaft, firmly stroking it as my tongue runs deftly along the underside, down toward the base and then lower over his balls.

My mouth opens wider, a perfect O as I suckle his balls between my lips, lavishing them with great attention as I work them one at a time, lifting and caressing them with my tongue as my hand strokes him tighter up and down the length of his cock. A hunger mounts within me, my desire to get him off almost more pleasurable than my own climax.

I lift my head and swallow his cock back down my throat, followed by a loud groan of pleasure from him. I answer it with a moan of my own, sending exciting vibrations through his rigid flesh and pushing his head deep into the pillow as he looks to the heavens, panting.

Up and down my head bobs, my hand planted firmly against the base, kneading the dripping saliva into his taut flesh every time my mouth hovers over his head. I stroke him faster, harder as I look up to him and begin a monologue of naughty teasing that sends his body into overdrive.

"C'mon, baby. Do you like my hand stroking your big cock? Come for me, baby. I want to taste it. I want to feel that cum in my mouth. Please, baby, please," I beg, urging him on as my pace quickens.

His body tenses as my hands caress his sac and my mouth continues its oral ravaging of him. Faster my lips fuck him, up and down, sucking and slurping noises more and more audible now. I tighten my grip every now and again to milk the precum from his head, my tongue massaging him, pressing into him in unison with my hands kneading his balls.

I start to stroke him violently, leaving my mouth open and dangling my tongue over the shaking head, my other hand snaking up and pinching my nipple as I drizzle stream after hot stream of saliva onto his cock for lubrication as I piston away at his shaft. His body goes rigid, hips bucking violently as it happens.

His head rocks back onto the pillow, and a loud groan echoes throughout the room as he spurts hot white ropes of cum into my waiting mouth. As the flow begins, I close my lips around my head and stroke him faster and faster, harder and harder, milking his cock into my mouth, appeasing my carnal hunger only slightly. My head bobs again, lips suckling tightly around him, coaxing out pulse after erotic pulse of his warm salty cum down my throat.

With a loud gasp I release his cock, catching my breath as streams of his juice ooze down my lips and over my chin. I lower my head once more and lick up stray streams of white dripping down his shaft. His body shudders, convulsing with each touch of my tongue against his throbbing cock. His moaning eventually subsides, and he crooks his arm over his eyes as he catches his breath.

I release his softening cock, spent and still throbbing, twitching now and then. He opens his eyes and tries to adjust his vision to the dim room. I kiss him deeply as his hands wander to my wet pussy, opening my legs to allow him entry. His strokes are firm and probing.

"God, baby, you're fucking awesome," he whispers.

"As are you, babe. Your cock is simply exquisite," I reply, resting my head on his still-heaving chest.

I rub circles with my fingers in his chest hair, and I'm sure he's fallen asleep when he kisses the top of my head. "Your turn."

"I thought we weren't counting."

His mouth suckles my nipple, and his fingers explore, teasing me before pumping in and out of my pussy, one finger and then two curling deep inside me. His thumb circling my clit as his mouth continues at my nipple. So much sensation. I don't realize I'm holding my breath until he shatters me and I yell, "Andreas!" so loud that I'm sure they heard me in Reno—almost two hundred miles away.

He licks his fingers, and I can feel his throbbing cock against my belly alive and ready. I reach to the side table and hand him a condom as he presses kisses all over my firm breasts, my nipples sending an electrical pulse to my core. He pushes my tits together and licks at the peaks in tandem as he growls over and over.

He rubs himself against me, and I whimper in response. Lovemaking can come later; I need Andy to take me hard and fast. I've missed him, and I need him again.

As he sits back and rolls the condom onto his steel rod, I can't help but watch in awe. Staring at my wide-open pussy, he smiles as if he's found treasure. "Tell me if you need me to slow down or if I'm hurting you, *cuore mio*." He moves back as I drive against his hard cock pushing against my core.

"Stop talking and start fucking me." I groan as he drives forward, opening me up and working his way into where he belongs, deep inside me.

"You're so damn tight," he grunts.

I mewl and push back, taking more of him. He grips my hips and rocks against me, picking up speed as he grunts softly. Pleasure rolls through me in waves, my shallow breathing increasing as I enjoy the intense pressure of his thickness.

He leans forward and kisses the side of my neck as his fingers slide between the wet folds of my sex. I arch my hips forward and jerk back in rhythm with his deep thrusts as he softly pinches my clit.

"I want to feel you come again," he whispers against the damp skin of my neck, and as if he's already gained mastery over my body, it responds to his desire. I let out a guttural cry and come hard, his words commanding and voice thick with passion as I lose myself in it.

"Oh my God," I groan and rock against him, never wanting the moment to end.

He collapses on me, both of us spent, and we drift off into euphoric sleep.

ANDY

I LOOK OVER AT GREER. She's always so beautiful, like a pinup girl from the twenties with her beautiful straight dark hair and post-sex glow about her. She pulls the sheets up close under my scrutiny. "You up for some coffee, hot tea or scotch? That's pretty much all I have."

"No wine?"

"Nope. I drank it all." Her lips curl, and there's a twinkle in her eyes. I can't be sure if she's giving me a hard time or if she's serious.

"I did bring a bottle from my brother's place in Argentina."

Her eyes grow wide, and I can see the excitement in them. "What does he grow in Argentina?"

"Malbecs mostly."

"Sounds delicious. Does anyone in your family grow whites?"

"Yes, I have a brother in Greece who does pinot grigio, a brother in New Zealand with almost a dozen kids who grows sauvignon blanc mostly, and finally we grow a great chardonnay in South Africa."

"A dozen kids?"

"He's child number two. My first brother went to France. Dominic went to New Zealand and met a wonderful Kiwi, and I think they spent most of their first five years in bed."

"Well, if he has half the talent you have, then I can see why."

I roll on my back and let out a deep belly laugh. I'm actually embarrassed, and Greer must be able to tell since she changes the topic. "Your father really must like wine."

"It's in our blood."

"But it must be hard for your mother to have her children so far away."

"Through our quarterly face-to-face meetings and our weekly phone calls, we work together as a team to make sure the Bellissima name is well represented on all continents. In your world, you'd call it branding. In ours, we want the best of every variety of grape to fall under our name."

"Actually, I have a Bellissima champagne and a few different reds I bought last week when I was at your vineyard."

"Sophia charged you for wine?"

"Of course. Why wouldn't she?"

"That will never happen again. She knows better." Sophia knows I'm serious with Greer and that she shouldn't be charging her for wine. That bugs me. There aren't many perks for dating a guy who works twenty-four hours a day, seven days a week, three hundred and sixty-five days a year. A case of wine now and again won't kill us. Not if I'm missing over forty barrels.

The initial conversations with my dad about this missing wine have been me mostly talking. I've had some salespeople stop by the vineyard, and I have some ideas that I need to fully vet before I go, but hopefully, if I have a plan, they'll move on to other issues instead.

Greer rests her head on my shoulder and holds me tight. I kiss the top of her head, and she asks, "What do you feel like for dinner? We can order in."

"I would love a good seafood pasta. Would that work for you?"

Being Italian is in my blood, and sometimes I crave the carbs I grew up on.

"I know just the place. I have a menu for them here on my phone." She sits up and hands me the phone. It looks like food my mother would make, and I start a mental list of all the things I want.

"This looks perfect. May I call and order?"

"Of course. I've never had anything I didn't like on their menu. We can send a messenger to bring it to us if we don't want to go pick it up. I'm fine either way, and of course, if you want to get dressed and eat there, I'm good with that, too."

The man who answers their phone has the same accent I do, and I fall into Italian as we talk. He and his wife are from the next town over from where I grew up. Conversation is easy as we talk about what we miss and don't miss about the home country. I share that I want to show my girlfriend some good authentic Italian food from the old neighborhood, and he tells me he'll make me the best meal and deliver it himself.

We hang up, and I turn to Greer and say, "That was easy. You're going to like what I ordered. They make their pasta like my mother does."

"They're a favorite of mine, but usually I need to send someone to pick it up."

"Oh, no worries. They agreed to deliver it here. Is that okay?"

"Of course, though I didn't think they delivered. When did they say they'll be here?"

"I didn't ask. Sorry. Do you have one of the Bellissima Grande wines I gave you?"

"Yes."

I hate to ask, but I think he'd really appreciate it, and I can always get Greer more. "If I promise to replace the one bottle with a case, may I give it to him for making the delivery?"

"Of course, but I think you should also give him one of your wines from Napa. He needs to see how mature your wines are. Your dad's will remind him of home, but yours will let him know he can get a piece of home right here in Northern California."

"You're a marketing genius." I kiss the top of her head once more.

I hear her stomach beginning to growl. I'm also getting hungry. "I ordered many things that aren't on the menu. We're in for a treat."

I look up to find she's changed. I would've been fine if she wanted to be naked for the rest of the weekend, but I like the yoga pants that hug her every curve, and she's wearing a long-sleeved Giants baseball T-shirt. We snuggle on the patio watching the lighted sailboats glide across the water as we wait for our dinner to arrive.

The sun begins to set behind the Golden Gate, and it hugs the bay with a vibrant orange glow that creates a warmth all on its own. "You really have the most stunning view."

"Thank you. It was CeCe's godmother who was selling, and she really did give it to me for a song. She wasn't spending much time here any longer. She has a beau in Marin, and after many years of commuting, he finally talked her into moving in with him."

She wants to downplay her wealth, but I don't care about money like that. It's the European in me. I knew people who had buckets full of money and drove old beat-up cars when I was growing up. Money is a curse sometimes, and I think Greer would agree with that. "She didn't want to marry?"

"No, I think because they weren't going to have children, she didn't see the need."

"Just because they weren't going to have children doesn't mean the union isn't important." I have to be careful, my Catholic upbringing is coming out.

"Well, they're both well off financially and didn't want to mix their money."

"Do you think the same way?"

She takes a deep breath before she answers. "I don't know if I want to marry. I don't need to for financial reasons, and I don't think I'll ever have children, so I just don't know."

Her phone rings, alerting us that our dinner has arrived and she's escaped a difficult conversation.

I thought all women wanted to get married, so I'm a little surprised by her comment. I'll come back to it later; she's not off the hook.

THE OWNER ARRIVES and introduces himself as Filippo. He loves the wine and won't accept it, but Greer steps in and stresses, "It's a piece of home for you and your wife to enjoy together. And we hope you will try the Napa Bellissima Valle and order it for your restaurant so you can share a bit of home made here in Northern California, just like your amazing food."

His eyes begin to mist. In a thick Italian accent, he says, "You are wonderful people. You know, he's from a town just over a few hills from where I grew up, and we know people in common."

Greer takes the food and disappears into the kitchen with it as Filippo and I talk. After almost twenty minutes, Filippo's phone rings and his wife is scolding him for spending too much time with us. Greer returns, and he tells us, "The wine will make her happy. Thank you for your generosity. Please send your salesperson to my restaurant. I will buy cases, I promise."

I'm in awe over how easily Greer turned him into probably a big customer for us. "You were amazing."

"Your wine did that, not me." She removes the aluminum takeout containers from a warming rack in her oven. "So what did he bring us?"

With each container I open, my mouth waters and I get more and more excited. "We're going to eat so well tonight." I plate generous portions of various kinds of antipasti, a seafood pasta, salad, and bread on our plates. This is heaven.

I'll need to make sure Sophia knows about this place. She and Luke will want to drive into the city for this. We've been on the hunt for restaurants of this quality since we moved to the States.

"I set the table on the patio so we can watch the night sky and enjoy the evening outside. Our window of great weather is fleeting." I nod, understanding that San Francisco is actually colder in the summer than the winter because of the dense fog created by the hot desert on the other side of the bay.

"Filippo knows my brother in France, and I know his sister, who's married to a friend. What a small world."

"Wow, that's amazing." Popping a shrimp into her mouth, she smiles as if she's been caught with her hand in the cookie jar.

"I don't mean to change the subject, but we've not really talked about our histories. You mentioned before that you don't want kids. Why?"

All the color drains from her face. "It isn't because I don't like kids. I love kids." She takes a big breath and continues, "You've met my mother. She's bipolar, and it can be genetic. I don't show any signs and may never have it, but I could pass it onto my children. My mother and her sister are very tortured by their illness. When my mother is in a depressive cycle, she's often suicidal. Since there's a chance I could pass that on, I can't do that to an unsuspecting child."

"I understand, but you do take exceptional care of your mother."

"I hate to admit this, but not always. It's really hard. She says awful things to me, and when I was younger, before I understood her illness, I often said awful things to her."

"Teenagers often say things to their parents when they're emotional." Picking up her hand, I bring it to my mouth and kiss the inside of her wrist. It's very sensual, and her eyes hood as she looks at me with carnal need, but I won't be deterred. "Have you ever been married?"

"No, though I came close with a guy who CeCe is tormenting right now."

"How is she doing that?"

She goes into all the details, and I think it's really funny that so many people showed up to throw darts at pictures of this guy. However, I'm bothered by his threatening text. Is it really necessary to say such awful things about her mother? The guy is a complete ass.

"That's ridiculous. You have no control over your mother's disorder. It isn't contagious." Before I go on a rant, I take a deep breath. "I'm really sorry he hurt you, but I'm also glad you're here with me. If I ever meet him, I'll shake his hand and thank him for breaking up with the most amazing woman I've ever met."

She leans in and gives me a soft and yearning kiss. "What about you?"

"I've been married, though it didn't last long. We met too young and didn't really want the same things. We met at UC Davis, and both had a love of wine. We were crazy in love, but she wanted to go to fancy restaurants and drink the wine and didn't really have the patience to grow and cultivate the winemaking process. We divorced five years ago. We have a child. My daughter's name is Genevieve, and she's eleven. She lives in Sacramento with my ex-wife, Melanie."

I'm ready to run after her if she gets angry about this new information, but she only smiles broadly at me.

"Is she the young girl in the picture with you and Sophia at your apartment?"

"Yes, that was taken last year. I see her most weekends, but she hasn't wanted to see me recently. She's my world, but Melanie's dating someone seriously, and Genevieve's worried about it and doesn't want to leave her mother. I tried to get her to join us on our trip to Italy, but she wouldn't come." She isn't running away, that's promising. Looking down at my hands, I do the only thing I can—I apologize. "I know I should have told you sooner. I'm sorry."

"Sophia mentioned she and her husband didn't have any kids, so I figured the girl in the pictures was your daughter." She shrugs like it isn't a big deal. "I always hated when my parents were dating people when I was growing up. My mom would bring the flavor of the night home, and I'd have to pretend I didn't hear her moaning like a porn star."

"Oh, that's awful." I laugh.

"I know, isn't it?" Getting serious again, she continues, "But my dad would wait to introduce his girlfriends to me until they were engaged or already married. So that was equally hurtful." She seems to struggle with something, then finally confesses, "My father had guilt over leaving me to care for my mother. My parents never said it to me, but I know I was always an afterthought. 'Oh yeah, I need to introduce you to my daughter.' I don't want Genevieve to feel that way about me. Hopefully we can meet one day, because you're a package deal."

"I'm sorry if you're upset about Genevieve. I should've told you earlier."

She reaches for my hand. "I'm really okay with it."

"I haven't dated very much since my marriage broke up. At

least no one seriously until... you. This may be an adjustment for her."

"We'll figure it out. One day at a time, right?"

I look at her and my heart skips a beat. I'm in love with this woman, I have no doubt. We haven't been with one another long, but every time we're together, I find something else to love about her.

I hope she's right about taking this slow for Genevieve's sake, because I'm not ready to have to choose between them. They both feed my soul in different ways, and I need them like I need air and water.

We enjoy our Saturday morning wandering the farmer's market, running into Cameron and Hadlee there. I met them at Sara's birthday party. While we're catching up, Dillon and Emerson arrive.

Hadlee says, "We're looking forward to hanging out with you tonight."

"I think CeCe has a few things in mind for this evening. If Greer hasn't already warned you, she doesn't do anything understated," Emerson adds.

Dillon laughs, and I share, "Believe it or not, that doesn't surprise me."

"We'll try not to be too hard on you," Cameron confides.

"Don't you dare, Cameron. Andy is a good guy, and you can't scare him away," Greer warns.

Dillon asks, "What's the plan? I just go where my wife tells me."

"Tell me about it," Cameron mutters.

Hadlee pats him on the arm. "And you never complain."

"We're meeting at the Japanese Tea Gardens in Golden Gate, and I think she has a picnic of some sort planned," Emerson says. "And I think we're going on the swan boats in the lake." Turning to look at Dillon and Cameron, she warns, "And the first one to tip or cause someone else to tip will be sleeping at the Fairmont, or if you're lucky, Mason will take you in."

I laugh at the visible blanch from both men. I'll have to ask why later. "I'm up for whatever you guys want to throw at me," I tell them honestly.

We chat for a short while longer before we all go our separate ways.

"See you later this afternoon." Hadlee gives me a hug, then mutters in my ear, "Don't let them scare you."

As we walk hand in hand back to the apartment, Greer gives me the rundown on Mason and Annabel. "We really need to accept her. If he decides he's going to marry her, then she'll be in our social circle for a very long time. Honestly, I think we all really wanted Mason and CeCe to get together."

I just nod as she fills me in on all the company gossip.

"Maybe as an outsider, you'll see it differently and we're just jaded by our hopes for them."

"I can do that."

We spend the remainder of the morning relaxing on the patio. Greer studies her computer carefully, and I read an Italian mystery. Reading in Italian helps keep my vocabulary strong, so I try to read all I can in my first language. I'm not getting very far in my book, though, looking over at Greer too often to focus. She's so beautiful. And she's smart, sexy, funny, and amazing in so many ways, too.

Greer's cell phone is ringing like a doorbell. She looks up at me as she turns it off. "Okay, the torture—I mean picnic is in a little over an hour."

Laughing, I ask, "I'm not worried. Should I be?"

She stands and reaches for my hand to pull me up. "They're my friends and really, outside of my mother and father, they're my family. They'll be protective of me, but I don't think you have anything to worry about."

"You did say we had 'a little over an hour.' Does that mean we have time to relax a little bit?"

She kisses me softly on the lips. "That's exactly what I was thinking."

I pull her gently to me. She smells of vanilla and orange spice, and I love exploring where she hides her perfume. Our lips meet, the silky slow kisses continuing as I reach for the hem of her T-shirt and pull it over her head. Her hair falls over her shoulders, and I take in her vulnerability and need.

My tongue and lips tease her as I nip at her nipples and move to the insides of her thighs, making her shiver in pleasure and sending lightning through my body. I slide my hand between her thighs, my thumb teasing her clit, and she whimpers.

She reaches for my shirt and pulls it over my head before pushing me back on the bed, our bare chests pressed against one another as we kiss passionately. We've become impatient in our lovemaking, but this time we're going slow and enjoying ourselves.

My warm breath teases her skin as I move down her body to the apex of her thighs, her fingers tightening on the bedsheets.

I drag my tongue over the beautiful nub and growl into her, rolling it in small slow circles. I move with slow, achingly teasing movements, my tongue swirling in mind-blowing circles and pushing the tip deep against her. Her entire body starts to shiver and melt as I work her precious clit. She explodes all over, screaming her orgasm into the sheets, clawing at them and twisting them in her fists.

My cock hard and ready, I enter her slowly, wanting to make love to her. I'm tender as I move in and out, our eyes connecting as she plants small kisses on my chest. This all feels right. It takes time, and we enjoy the joining of our two bodies.

My orgasm is the most intense I've ever had.

I would prefer to just remain naked and in bed all weekend, but I suppose we should give my dick a break. I don't think I've ever come this much in twenty-four hours. She has the magic touch.

"I know you told me, but who will be there this afternoon?

"I'm pretty sure you've met everyone—CeCe, Mason, Annabel, Emerson, Dillon, Sara, Trey, Hadlee, and Cameron. You should've met Cynthia before, too, and I think she's bringing a date. And one of Mason's exes just joined the firm, but we all adore Quinn, and I think she's also coming with a date."

We grab a quick shower, her eyes filling with lust as she bites her lower lip and watches me carefully while she soaps my swollen cock.

"Do you think they'd miss us if we didn't show up?" I ask.

She continues to stroke me. "They'll all show up here, and then we'd never be alone the rest of the weekend."

Regretfully we both finish our shower and get ready. I know this is a test, and I'm trying not to be nervous. She's very close with her friends, and if they don't like me, we won't last long.

The Lyft is downstairs waiting to take us into Golden Gate Park when we exit her apartment.

During the drive over, I ask, "How did you meet your friends?"

Greer goes through meeting CeCe and Hadlee in high school, and Emerson was CeCe's college roommate. Emerson owned her own company that was purchased by SHN, which is where most of her friends work, and where she met Dillon. I like everyone, so I'm pretty confident that I'll be okay with this group. After all, I'm crazy about Greer, so why wouldn't they like me?

The Lyft drops us off at the Japanese Tea Gardens. We walk

hand in hand and Greer leads me. I've seen it from the outside but never ventured into the gardens. Just inside the main gate, there's an amazing clipped hedge in the form of Mt. Fuji. I marvel at the hours it must take to maintain the simple yet very ornate gardens.

To the left of the Mt. Fuji Hedge is the Dragon Hedge, decorated with a backdrop of illuminating bamboo. A pathway filled with beautiful Japanese flowering bushes and plant guides you to the Drum Bridge; it's like we've been transported to Japan in the middle of San Francisco.

Just over the bridge is a small walkway that leads us to the gazebo, decorated as if he had transported to Japan with golden lanterns and beautiful white plum blossoms. I was expecting blankets and cold cut sandwiches sitting in one of the park areas, but this is much more elaborate.

Everyone is dressed very casually, and CeCe walks over and gives us both a tight hug and kisses on both cheeks. "Welcome! Our guests of honor are here with a beautiful glow." She winks at Greer, who turns a vibrant shade of crimson.

The evening is surprisingly fun. There's a subtle Japanese guitar known as the shamisen playing over loudspeakers, and we eat a traditional Japanese dinner of various types of sushi, saba shioyaki (grilled mackerel) as a main dish, nikujaga (meat and potato stew) and sunomono (cucumber salad) as side dishes. Miso soup and genmai (brown rice) are also served. As we sit on mats on the floor around a large table, we enjoy hot tea, Japanese beer, and sake.

Everyone is very polite and asks general questions, but nothing too invasive. As we finish our meal, CeCe announces, "Time to take this party over to the swan boats."

I spend time watching Annabel and Mason. She seems unhappy, and he seems indifferent. That's what the last few years of my marriage were like, so if I had to guess, their relationship is beginning to peter out. As we wander over to the boats, we walk along with them, and I ask Annabel, "What keeps you busy since you left SHN?"

She lights up. "I take care of our home, and I'm very active in several charitable organizations."

"You must miss working."

"No. Mason has been very firm that he wants me to be available for certain work activities, and an employer would never understand my need for flexibility, plus my volunteer work is incredibly fulfilling. I've been asked to sit on a committee by the mayor of San Francisco."

CeCe, who's been listening to our conversation, asks, "Wow, I'm impressed, Annabel. What committee?"

She very proudly says, "The Shelter Monitoring committee."

I see a slight smirk appear on CeCe's face. "You would certainly have your hands full."

"I'm very excited."

We end up in eight swan boats, and we paddle around the lake. I want to wander off and find a quiet spot to make out with my girl, but I notice between Cameron, Trey, and Dillon, they're going to make sure that doesn't happen. Finally, to show my humor with their pestering, I'm able to splash them with water. I grew up with eight brothers; I can play their game. The girls are all screaming, and before we know it, we're all soaked and laughing. I'm ready to get a tongue lashing from CeCe, but she's equally wet and laughing just as loudly as the rest of us. I really like this group of friends.

Exiting the water, Dillon pats me on the back. "Well played, man."

Trey says, "My sister was even laughing, and that says something. Greer's like a sister to me. Please be gentle with her. She means the world to all of us."

I nod and shake their hands. "Sounds like a plan."

CeCe asks, "I know you two would like to be alone tonight, but how about we keep this going and head over to one of Trey's favorite bars, Bourbon and Branch? It's only eight o'clock."

Everyone is looking at us, and I see the conflict on Greer's face. I finally say, "We'd love to."

STANDING AT THE BAR with a smooth caramel-colored bourbon over a perfectly round and completely clear ice cube, I'm being interrogated by Trey, Dillon, and Cameron.

"How do you like living in St. Helena?"

"How serious are you and Greer?"

"What are your intentions with her?"

"How will you manage living ninety minutes apart?"

I answer every question honestly, often as simple as "We haven't discussed that yet."

After the guys are done with me, I get a different reception from the women. CeCe is all hugs and proudly telling everyone, "I knew you two would hit it off."

Sara and Emerson talk about their favorite wines, though they're also protective of Greer, asking about Genevieve and Melanie and what my plans were long-term. I was still being tested by the women, only it wasn't as obvious.

Surveying the group at the end of the night, and knowing Greer's situation, I'm really glad she has so many people in her life looking out for her.

ANDY

$\mathcal{S}$OPHIA IS STAYING BEHIND to manage the vineyard while I go home. There's no one I can trust more than my sister. She has a real handle on the business, and she couldn't care less to go back to these meetings. My older brothers and my father are of another generation and don't treat my sisters as the partners they really are and she would rather stay here and work.

I know my mother's talked to them about it, and those of us who have one of our sisters for help plan on splitting our vineyards with them. We're from a patriarchal family, and women are to support the men, though most of us disagree with this attitude. I see Sophia as my equal and treat her as such. She may not be on the deed or any of the loan documents, but no decisions are made without her input, and one day once the vineyard is all mine, I'll give her half.

I leave in a week, but I'm mentally ready to walk out the door today. My inventory is still off, the total growing to almost fifty barrels. Each barrel produces fifty cases, or six hundred bottles, and it's strange to have so much gone missing.

It's time for some fresh eyes. I must be missing a storage location that should be obvious to me but apparently isn't.

"Michael, are you up for a project?" As one of our interns, this is the third year Michael has come to work for us. He grew up in the area and is studying to become a vineyard manager like his father. He's a hard worker, someone I'd like to promote and bring up within Bellissima, though he knows that to be a good manager, he needs to start at the bottom. "I need an accurate counting of each barrel and location."

"Not a problem. Is there something I should be looking for?"

"My inventory and counts aren't matching, and I'm hoping you can help. We've outgrown our space, and it seems we may have been careless in some of our storage. This will take us the better part of a week. If anyone asks what you're doing, you can tell them. If they have any other questions, send them to me. But I expect you to climb in some dusty areas and tag each barrel and mark their location."

"Yes, sir."

I send him in one direction, and I go in the other, each independently hand counting every barrel of wine we have on-site. His stickers are green, and mine are yellow, and I'm impressed that he got to some of our best wines in some of the hardest to reach spots. Unfortunately, we're both coming up with the same number—we're short an even fifty barrels, which leaves me with a pit in my stomach. Someone has stolen barrels of wine from us, though I don't know how. Pretty sure I'd notice if someone pulled a truck up and took one barrel, let alone take fifty.

Sophia and I came up with the same amount of forty-one barrels missing. Now we're at fifty. I'll talk to my brothers about it, and together we'll figure out where we're going wrong.

I'm not ready to face that I have a thief at the winery. It can't be. I trust everyone like they're family. I mentioned it to Sophia, and she doesn't think its possible either. We're both racking our brains trying to figure out what's going on.

I drive into San Francisco, where I'll leave my car at Greer's and take a ride share to the airport. My anxiousness about the trip begins to increase as I approach the city. My mind races, thinking about Greer constantly. I want her to have fun without any pressure. If my family's too difficult, Greer could very well walk away. I take a few breaths to calm myself. I have to believe this time will be different. My mother is getting her wish, and I'm bringing Greer home. I think despite the language differences, they'll get along famously.

My mother is disappointed that my daughter isn't coming on this trip, which will add to the pressure on Greer. During our last call, I explained, "Unfortunately Genevieve can't leave school to come home, but I'm bringing my new girlfriend, Greer, to see where I grew up." I've set the expectation that I really like her, but it's still somewhat new. Hopefully that'll convince my brothers and sisters to keep the talk of marriage down.

Mom was silent on the subject. She's always pretended Melanie died the minute we broke up. My mother is nothing but loyal to her children.

GREER

*A*NDY AND I have been spending almost every weekend together. I've been going up on Thursday nights and seeing my mother on Fridays. Right now the conversation with her doctor is that she needs to stay put for a while. Her episodes are increasing and not being well managed by medication, lasting longer and becoming more pronounced.

"Greer, I know this is difficult to understand. During one of Eve's manic periods, she was talking so fast no one could understand her, and she became highly agitated and threatened someone."

I knew in my heart of hearts when I saw her condo that chances are she'd be hospitalized for a while, and possibly for the rest of her life, but it still bothers me to my core. When I was growing up, some of my best memories come from my mother's manic episodes. She was fun, and we would do things that most parents would never consider. I was studying the great sequoias in school, and she decided I needed to see them. She woke me one night, and we piled into the car and drove all night to Sequoia National Park. It was exciting spending the day exploring the forest with her. She was fun.

The doctor continues, "During a depressive episode, she threatened herself, and she threatened others with physical harm."

My mother has been like this for as long as I can remember, so this isn't really a shock to me.

"Greer, you're over thirty years old. You're at the end of your window to show signs of bipolar disorder. It may run in families, but just because your mother and her sister share this illness doesn't mean you or your cousin will have it. Is Vanessa still not showing any signs?"

"Not that I'm aware of, and we both share the same concern, so we talk about it often."

"I'm worried about Eve living alone right now. Her desire to not take the medication is severe, and when she hits her lows, she's suicidal and threatens to harm others. She isn't safe right now on her own."

"She can stay as long as she needs." It's a private hospital, and they'll keep her as long as she has money, which she has from her parents' inheritance and my parents' divorce, and of course I have no problem contributing should she need it. She isn't that old, and a long-term stay would be significant, but if she runs out of money, I'll always make sure she can stay. My mother's comfort and health are important to me.

I decide I should share about Mark's threats because it could create some security challenges for the hospital. "Dr. Phillips, I thought you should know my ex-fiancé is running for Congress and is in the news. He's been texting me about my mother."

Dr. Phillips sits up straighter and seems slightly alarmed. "How so?"

"He's threatening to out her illness. I know it isn't a secret, but please know if that happens, you'll have a lot of visitors by way of the press. Please make sure no one sees her except my father. And he hasn't made any contact with her since I graduated from college."

"I'll make a note of that. Don't worry, we have you covered.

Your mother's health is important to all of us."

"I'll be heading to Italy with a friend for two weeks. Do you think I should stay?"

"No, not at all. I think you're a wonderful daughter and she knows that. But I also think you need a break from this. We'll take good care of her, and I can always call you if we need to talk to you. And of course, you can call as often as you'd like."

I make my way back to Hillsboro and the Arnaults' for my Sunday partners meeting. When I think about everything going on, I worry that going to Italy is a mistake. Work is ready to crack open at any time, and we all know it'll happen the minute I leave the country. That's just Murphy's Law.

Sitting at our meeting behind closed doors, I share with the group, "Okay, I'm leaving in the morning for Tuscany. We'll be gone for two weeks. I'm reachable by cell phone, and I can get home in a matter of hours. Our public relations firm is on standby, since we know the shoe is going to drop with Benchmark shortly." I look around the room, and everyone is paying close attention. "Maybe I should stay just in case something goes sideways with Benchmark?"

Mason vigorously shakes his head. "Absolutely not. Go. We can manage this."

Dillon and Cameron both agree.

"You need a break, Greer. We've bounced from one crisis to another, and you've handled them all like a pro. Enjoy yourself," Cameron implores.

"Just don't come back married," Emerson adds.

I laugh, her wisecrack making me feel better. "I don't think that'll be happening. I've already been warned that the men sit in meetings and the women cook and clean," I share.

"That's a good idea. Maybe when you get back, you can run a training on that here?" Dillon teases.

Emerson throws her pen at her husband. "In your dreams, buster."

Charles, who rarely contributes to our ribbing of one another, says, "Dillon, I tried that with Margo years ago, and she went out and started a whole new company. We fell in love with these women. It's too late to change them."

"That's right," CeCe exclaims, staring down her brother.

"I don't disagree." Trey holds his hands up in mock surrender.

As our meeting breaks up, I walk up to Mason. "Call me if something breaks with Benchmark. The PR agency can only do so much on their own."

He hugs me. "Go have fun with your boyfriend. Don't worry about us. I've learned there's always something."

Charles puts his hand on Mason's shoulder and says, "He's right, Greer. SHN is high-profile. You're in people's sights, and we can only be proactive part of the time and reactive the rest. You deserve a break. Go enjoy some wine and the valleys of Tuscany."

CeCe came out earlier this weekend to spend time with her parents related to her work at Metro Composition, and I agreed to give her a ride home. As we drive into San Francisco, we talk about my mom. The girls and my cousin Vanessa are the only ones who know all I've dealt with. "Would you like me to go visit Eve?" she asks.

"I think she'd like that, but I've warned the doctor about the press, so her visitors are limited to my dad and me."

"If you change your mind, just let me know. I'd be happy to go, as would Hadlee."

"Thank you. I'll e-mail him, and if he thinks it would be a

good idea, I'll let you know. But don't feel any pressure to go."

"What? Go wine tasting *and* visit your mom? Sounds like a brilliant Saturday afternoon if you ask me."

"I'm going to miss you."

"I'll be here if you need anything, but I really want you to have a good time with Andy and his family. And if he has an eligible brother who needs me in some exotic location, I'm willing to travel."

"You're funny. Like you'd ever leave San Francisco." CeCe snickers, and I attempt to change the subject. "How are things going with Todd? Is he still talking about moving out here?"

"He is. He's looking at coming out in a few weeks to look for a place to live. He's hinted at living with me, but I made him a reservation at the Fairmont, so he's cluing in. He's a great guy, but he's not the one for me. I actually have my eye on him for someone else."

"You and your brother both say all the time that 'we all meet our soul mates at different times in our lives.' Yours is out there."

"I believe that, too." We pull up outside her building and she gives me a big hug. "Have fun, and send pictures."

"Be strong, and I promise many pictures coming your way."

GREER

$\mathcal{W}$E ARRIVE IN MONTALCINO, the actual town in Tuscany where Andy's parents' vineyard is located, and the pictures don't do it any justice. The hills are a patchwork of green, made even more varied by the shadows of passing clouds. They're every hue from new spring grass to deep forest pools, covered in rows of grape vines alternating with olive trees—rows of vegetation as far as the eye can see. Steep paths that take you to one side of a rolling hill and then down to the next valley below. Occasionally we see dwellings and compounds for the collection of various crops, the birds overhead and in the trees singing their songs. It's so peaceful.

We flew from San Francisco with a short layover in Paris and then into Florence. Exhausted when we arrived and not able to make the two-hour drive into Montalcino, we spend the night in a beautiful hotel in Florence. Enjoying one last night alone before the chaos that fourteen children along with their spouses and children create as they descend upon Bellissima Grande. Andy warned me that we might be segregated at times, as the women will work in the kitchens, cleaning and constantly preparing for the next meal while the men deal with the business side of things.

That idea seemed okay when he told me, but now that we're here and together, and I don't really speak any Italian, I'm a little nervous.

Stopping in town before we drive out to the vineyard, we pick up a few things his mother requested. As we wander the cobblestone streets, Andy reaches for my hand and points out places where he and his brothers would play hide-and-seek or put coins in the fountain. I'm awestruck by the town perched high atop a hill with its rustic streets and buildings, many of which were built in medieval times and still stand tall today. We walk only a few steps before people are yelling for Andreas, who's clearly well known here. He's always polite and introduces me, but I can't keep up with the rapid-fire Italian that sounds to me like Bedouin leaders chanting in the desert.

Andy buys cheese from one of the storefronts his mother requested and eventually picks up a few odds and ends from a produce market. I see his energy expand and his chest puff a bit bigger. When I mention it to him, he tells me, "Nothing feels as good as being home. I love St. Helena, but Montalcino will always be my true home."

I squeeze his hand tight, knowing I would say the same about San Francisco.

We finally get in the car for the last leg of the journey. It's only a ten-minute drive to the family homestead, but in that time, my palms sweat and my anxiety rises greatly. Andy reaches for me as if he knows and it immediately calms me. Together, we can do this.

As we arrive, I can see why it isn't a big deal that so many people are converging on Bellissima Grande. The home is a former medieval castle and is large by everyone's standards. It's been in Andy's family since it was built, which they believe was in 500 AD.

We drive into the courtyard, and kids and dogs all come running. Many are disappointed that Genevieve isn't with us, but I'm introduced to hordes of people, all of whom look similar to Sophia and Andy. As the introductions continue, I realize there are small towns with fewer people than the Giordano family. I'm an only child with six half-siblings, and the only time we'll probably all be together is at my father's funeral.

As we make our way through the crowd of people, I see who I assume are his parents standing at the door, waiting for us to come to them. Finally, after introducing me to almost all of the brothers and sisters, spouses, and kids, Andy leads me by the hand and greets both his parents. I'm able to follow some of the conversation despite the Italian before he stands aside and gestures to me. *"Mama, papà, questa e la mia raggazza Greer Ford."*

I'm given a stern look and a nod. I greet them in basic Italian I learned just for this introduction. *"Buon pomeriggio, signore e signora Giordano. Grazie per avermi invitato a rimanere nella vostra bellissima casa."* From my bag, I remove a beautiful small Dale Chihuly glass sculpture and curtsy.

Andy's dad gathers me in his arms and welcomes me with kisses on each cheek. His mother nods and gestures for us to follow her into the house.

Andy whispers to me, "That was terrific. My parents love you."

I'm still nervous and a tiny bit apprehensive as we wander the many dark halls, each looking the same. *I may never find my way around here.* "I don't know about that."

"I forgot to tell you that initial meetings with my parents don't always go as planned. With most of the wives, they stand at the door uncomfortably for hours before my mother relents to let them in. You got in immediately. Are you kidding? My parents love you. My family will be talking about this for days." He holds my hand and squeezes it tight. "Your Italian was perfect. Who taught you that, Sophia?"

"Actually, it was Google Translate. I do hope your family doesn't expect me to speak Italian, because that just exhausted all my abilities."

Andy releases a deep belly laugh. "You'll be fine. I think my mother speaks more English than she lets on, so don't let her play too dumb."

Bringing us to a wing of bedrooms, his father says in broken English, "Here your bedroom."

I place my bag in the room, and in rapid Italian, Andy and his father speak before Andy brings his things in. Looking at me, he says, "Well, looks like we are staying together. This is a first. My father says they're using my bedroom for storage, so I'm to stay with you. Are you comfortable with that?"

The weight of being alone immediately evaporates, and I'm thankful for the sudden change in plans. "Of course. I'm relieved, actually."

We make our way downstairs, and the family is all sitting outside at a giant table where lunch is ready for everyone to enjoy. I'm told where to sit, Andy taking the seat on my left with one of his sisters on my right.

"Hello. I'm Maria. Sophia really likes you."

"I really like her. I'm sorry she didn't come."

"She hates these gatherings. She's probably the only one who can get away with not coming. She's very headstrong and butts heads with my father and several of our older brothers. She knows a lot about the business, and our brothers discount her opinions despite her helping to run the second largest vineyard in the family."

"Bellissima Valle is a success because she and Andy work so closely together."

"Yes, that's so true. But our brothers and father are stuck in the old world."

"Where do you live?"

"I live in Greece. My brother Antonio is a pig, but he's learned over the years that I know what I'm doing. Now that he has a young Greek wife and small children, I've been able to prove to him how valuable I am."

The dinner conversation is in Italian. I meet several of the wives, and many of them speak English, so I don't feel too isolated. The children run around the table, and I can see the pride in Signora Giordano as she watches the next generation of her family that's full of many accents, yet they all get along. I realize all I've missed with my crazy family, and I fall in love with this chaos immediately.

When the sun sets, we remain at the table. His father and brother take up guitars, and several slow dance to the music. As we get up to join them, we're stopped by a man who could be Andy's twin. The two men do a bit of back-slapping, and then I'm in Andy's arms. Unlike Mark, who kept his body a polite distance from mine as we danced, Andy takes one of my hands in his, slips the other down my back and uses it to pull my body flush with his. Damn, this feels good. We rock back and forth, moving slowly around the dance floor. The music fills the warm air, and the song is beautiful. I don't think I've been this happy and content in a long time.

As the night wears on, I talk to several of the wives and sisters. It's a beautiful night, and I'm struggling to remain upright. We've been going for almost thirty-six hours without a good rest. Andy leans over and asks, "This party will go on for hours. You look exhausted. Would you like to go to bed?"

"I'm good if you are."

He smirks. "I was hoping you'd say you wanted to go to bed so I could go with you."

"Then let's tell them we're jet-lagged and ready for bed."

Andy holds my hand as he stands and announces we've been awake for hours and need to rest. He confirms the time of the meeting in the morning, and we say our good nights to everyone. Andy's mother rises and kisses me on both cheeks, saying something to me in Italian. I smile and nod, and the people who heard what she said all laugh and cheer.

I turn to Andy with a questioning look. He shakes his head. "You don't want to know."

Honestly, I'm too tired to care. Andy leads me to our room, and I'm so turned around that I'm glad he's coming with me. My exhaustion is overwhelming, and I can hardly think straight. I'd be completely lost without him.

We're barely able to get undressed before we collapse into bed. Our heads don't seem to have hit the pillows before we're out.

ANDY

"WHAT DO YOU MEAN, you lost fifty barrels of wine?" my oldest brother berates me in Italian.

"I live on-site. I would've noticed if some truck pulled up and took off with fifty barrels." I pass out the inventory sheets to everyone. "As you can see, we've taken a careful inventory. I even had another set of eyes take a look besides Sophia and me to make sure I wasn't missing anything. We've had good years, and the grapes have been plentiful, so we ran out of space to store them. I need to invest in a storage system. Plus, it'll make any theft more obvious."

"I can't believe you lost fifty barrels. What's that going to do to our profits?"

"Look, they don't come from one year or one grape. Overall, it'll be a small bump, but it shouldn't affect one year any more than others."

My father has been sitting and watching my brothers cross-examine me. Finally, he puts his hand up to stop the assault. "We had this happen to us here when I was a child. People can be thieves. I want you to order the Australian storage system. It'll cut into all of our profits, but you have the largest vineyard outside of Bellissima Grande. I understand there's a French tracking system we can install that's unidentifiable to the naked eye, and we can catch the person stealing from us."

My brother who runs a small vineyard in Hungary is quick to add, "I think it may be too much for Andreas to manage. Maybe Napa needs to be moved to someone with more experience and knowledge."

I bang my hand on the table, and the squabbling stops. "No one knows the American market better than I do. Plus, I'm the only one who's legal to live there, so there's no option beyond Sophia and me to do this."

"Sophia is to blame for this," my brother Marco insists in rapid-fire Italian. "She should be sleeping on a cot in the warehouse."

"She's not to blame. Neither of us would allow her to sleep in the warehouse." Looking around the table, I can see the differences between my oldest siblings and my younger ones. The oldest group is more like my father, the younger is the most liberal, and the middle group is a combination of both.

My youngest brother has been watching the exchanges. He mutters something, and my father asks him to repeat what he's said. "Andy knows Sophia deserves half of Bellissima Valle. If you don't make that clear, she'll leave Andy."

My shoulders sag. I know what he says is true, but this isn't the time for an equality fight.

The table erupts in yelling and fighting, and I turn to my father, "May I go into the office and order the shelves, forklift, and the trackers so they arrive before I return?"

He nods and I walk away, completely understanding why Sophia hates these meetings. Many of my brothers are pure Neanderthals, and they don't understand why the wine business in America is so different than on other continents.

I head into the office and find Greer studying her computer.

"What are you doing?"

"I'm using the Wi-Fi to check my e-mail. What about you?"

"Escaping World War III in our meeting. One of my older brothers wants to take control of my vineyard because he's sure the missing barrels are my fault, while another think it falls on Sophia."

"I'm sorry. I'm not very good with family politics."

"You're doing wonderfully. What have you been up to this morning?"

"Besides fending off five different breakfasts? Your mother has indicated I'm too thin, and she wants to fatten me up."

I pull her flush to me so she can feel my partially hard cock against her belly. "I'll love you no matter what size you are." Her eyes widen, and I realize what I just said. *Crap.* I've known for some time that I love her, but I didn't want to tell her like this. "I should've chosen a better place to tell you the first time, but I do love you. Every tiny thing I get to know of you makes me love you more."

"I love you, too," she whispers.

There's yelling down the hallway as my brothers approach. They enter my father's office, obviously ready to continue their assault, until they see Greer. Thankfully they won't emasculate me in front of my girlfriend.

I sit at my father's computer and order the trackers and storage units. The trackers are just a small GPS dot that's placed beneath the metal ring, so if the barrels disappear, we can locate them with a few simple clicks on a computer.

I call the manufacturer's rep, in the California central valley and tell me they can drop the trackers off that afternoon. "Ask for Michael when you deliver them. He'll be expecting them, but please make them nondescript." I feel I can trust Michael, and I want only him and Sophia to know what I'm doing.

I put in a call to the distributor of the barrel stacking system and leave him a message that I'm in Italy but to call me on my cell phone when he can get to me. This system will more than double our space, and because of how they're stacked, it'll be difficult for someone to remove a barrel without anyone noticing.

I dial Michael, who answers after a couple rings. "Andreas?"

"Hi, Michael. There will be some trackers for the wine barrels delivered this afternoon. Would you be able to attach them to each barrel for me this week?"

"Of course. I mentioned to my father about it. I'm sorry if that was out of turn, but I wanted his perspective and thoughts on how they may be disappearing. He suggested the trackers."

"I'm glad he's on the same page, but Michael, let's be careful what we share with our competitors."

"I understand. It'll never happen again. He did say it's a problem across the valley right now, but no one wants to admit they've been hit."

"No surprise that they don't talk about it, but it's good to know it isn't just us. Ultimately the various vintners are still a community that competes with one another. Call me if you have any problems. You can have Jose help you, but tell no one else what you're doing."

"Yes, sir."

I end the call and lean back in my father's desk chair, staring at the ceiling. I can't imagine not living in Northern California. I spent my life learning the rules around the environment, the process requirements, and of course, how to market to Americans.

My youngest brother will be going to Davis in the fall, and he's destined to open a winery for pinot noir grapes down in Southern California. Sophia has been watching the land prices, and we know we need to start buying.

So many things to do.

GREER

$\mathcal{S}$AYING OUR GOODBYES to the family is very bittersweet. I really had a nice time. I spent a lot of time with Chiara, Andy's oldest sister and the one their parents turn to for direction. She's married to a lawyer in town, and her children are grown and working for the vineyard, with the exception of her one son who's a priest. She's a lot like Sophia, very direct and down to earth, but regularly decked out in top-of-the-line, high-end Italian designers.

Chiara is at the end of the line as we're heading out. "Remember what I told you. If Andreas gets out of line, you must put him right back. Don't let him walk all over you. He's a Giordano and is a bit headstrong, but don't let that fool you. When it comes down to it, he's a pussycat."

"I promise I'll put him in his place if I need to."

"Good girl. And please tell my sister that these meetings aren't near enough fun when she's not here. In three months I expect to see her."

Andy steps in. "Chiara, we love you and we'll miss you, but if we don't leave now, we'll miss our plane out of Florence."

Water wells at the corner of her eyes and she says something to Andy in Italian that I can't understand. He nods and promises in English, "I'll take good care of her."

As we navigate the long and winding roads out of the Tuscan valley, I'm sad to be leaving, but I also know I'll be back. We really had fun the past two weeks. I loved all the kids, and every member of the family was loving and supportive of Andy. They may fight and argue, but it's a shared passion for wine and the artistry of winemaking that pushes them. It really is inspirational. They think we're a little more serious as a couple than we might be, but that's okay. I can live with that. I wouldn't mind being more serious anyway.

I'll admit that I'm looking forward to being alone for a bit. Or at least alone with just Andy for a while. "When we get back to San Francisco, I want to hide for a whole weekend, just the two of us in my apartment. No people."

"You've been great these past two weeks. I know my family can be overwhelming at times."

I giggle. "At times? I think when you aren't used to having so many people around you who hug and kiss you hello and good-bye, it can be a little overwhelming. But please don't get me wrong, I loved every minute of being here with you."

"My mother tells me you came to her in a dream. That's why she put so much pressure on me to include you."

"I did? When did she tell you that?"

"The first night we were there. She feels we're good for each other."

"I like your mom."

"My whole family likes you. Are you ready for the trip home?"

"Yes. I can tell things are going to be crazy for a few weeks when I get there, so I'm glad I got the rest these past two weeks."

WE'RE NOT IN THE DOOR even two minutes when my phone rings with a call from CeCe.

"Hello, my long-lost friend," I answer

"Welcome home! You were very quiet during your trip. I hardly heard from you. Did you have fun? Please tell me you and Andy didn't get married. I'd be crushed if I wasn't there. When can we get together?"

"Come over any time."

She hangs up, and in less than twenty minutes she's at my door. It's so nice to see her. "Did you lose weight while I was gone?"

"From your lips to my hips, I wish!"

We hug and she again asks me a slew of questions that I can't even follow. When she finally takes a breath, I'm able to talk. "It was a wonderfully quiet two weeks. We didn't do many touristy things. We'd get up in the morning and take walks around the villa. There were close to fifty people there, all related to Andy. It's so different than how we grew up. They're close, much like your family but on steroids. Kids everywhere running around and laughing. It was a controlled chaos."

"Did you spend all your time with Andy, or were you on your own?"

"Andy would join mostly his brothers—a few of his sisters would be there including his oldest sister, Chiara. Who I absolutely loved and so would you. Always decked out in high-end Italian designers and looking incredibly chic."

"I can't wait to meet her."

"I told her all about you, and she hopes to meet you soon, too."

"What did you do to keep busy?"

"While Andy had meetings, I would offer to help clean or prepare the lunch, but I think Andy told them I wasn't much of a cook, so they pretty much just shooed me out of the kitchen while they worked."

"You're a good cook. Why would he tell them that?"

"Because I can't boil water. I'm good at ordering food, not making it."

"I've had food I watched you make. I think you're not giving yourself enough credit."

"Stir-fry of precut vegetables and adding a precooked chicken isn't cooking CeCe. Anyway, I used the time he was in his meetings to check my e-mails, and one of the sisters-in-law is a yogi, so she'd lead a yoga class for all the girls. Even Andy's mom joined us one day. I was impressed."

"That *is* impressive."

"They'd serve a late lunch that was as big as our dinners each day. It was always three-plus courses—pasta or risotto, then a beautifully cooked fish or meat with a lot of vegetables followed by a salad made from vegetables in their garden. I don't think I've eaten so well in years. I swear I gained at least ten pounds."

"Somehow I doubt that, but it sounds amazing. I think I'd be comatose all afternoon if that was me. Did you find any neat trinkets?"

"Of course, and I may have brought one or two for my friends." I smile and pull a beautiful hand-carved box with a stained-glass top from my bag.

She accepts it gracefully and gives me a warm embrace. "Thank you. It certainly wasn't necessary."

"I saw it and thought of you. And I brought something back for my admin and the receptionist. It isn't much, but I thought of you often."

We sit in my living room, and she kicks her shoes off and tucks her feet under her on the couch. "Tell me more about his family."

I describe the various family members and how much they reminded me of Sophia and Andy. I learned stories of Andy's childhood and how he and his siblings terrorized the nuns at the local schools. It was a really nice and much-needed vacation.

"It sounds like you really had a good time. Do you still like Andy?"

"We said the L-word."

Her eyes light up, and she smiles broadly. "Oh, Greer! I'm so happy for you."

"You're a good matchmaker, CeCe. I just wish I could find a good guy for you. I met all of Andy's brothers, but they live too far away. I couldn't have my best friend live so far away."

"Don't worry about me. I'm not giving up yet."

We make plans to meet later in the week, and I head out to the bedroom and find Andy sleeping as a soccer game plays on the TV. He'll drive home tomorrow, and our lives will go back to the way they were before. I'll miss seeing him every day, and I've never slept as well as I do when I'm curled up with him. He hasn't even left yet and already my heart aches that he's gone.

Laying down on the bed, I cuddle in close. His arm wraps around me and he kisses my head as he mutters, *"Ti amo."*

ANDY

*A*T ELEVEN YEARS OLD, Genevieve is young enough that she still has the exuberance of youth, but by all standards of beauty, she's stunning. I know every father thinks that of their daughters, but she has that movie star look, not overly tall but still willowy. She walks with the confidence of someone a decade older and radiates an intelligent beauty.

We sit together watching the soccer match on the television. I know Genevieve would rather watch some silly teen angst show, but instead she's here at my side and doing what I enjoy. *"Papa?"*

"Yes, baby." I wrap my arm around her shoulders, wishing I could freeze her at this age right now. I know she's hard sometimes, but she still hangs on my every word, she hugs me, and she tells me things about her life and her friends. "I've missed you so much."

"I've missed you, too." She stares at the game, absently asking, "How was the trip home?"

"It went well. You were missed by many of your cousins."

"Mom needed me."

"Are you sure about that?" I know that isn't the case, but she's doing the only thing she knows, and that's to be around her mother and mark her territory like a cat.

"Yes. She's been seeing a dillweed named Tomas. He's trying to get serious, and she isn't seeing him for what he is."

This should be interesting. An assessment of an adult by a preteen. "What is he?"

"Well, he's a dillweed to start with, and he isn't right for her." She says it so matter-of-factly, like she believes that alone should be reason enough that her mother should move away from Tomas.

I know from conversations that Tomas and Melanie are very serious, but I can't help but wonder if she doesn't hope her mother and I will rekindle our relationship. "Baby, you know your mom and I won't be getting back together, right?"

"Yes. You weren't meant to be together. Mom says that all the time. But he isn't right either."

"I think you should give Tomas some time. Speaking of which, I've met someone. I took her to Montalcino with me."

She sits up and screams, "You did what?"

"Genevieve, I think you'll like Greer. She works for a company in San Francisco, and she's smart and beautiful, just like you."

"No." She shakes her head vehemently.

It was probably a mistake to mention Greer, but I want the two of them to meet. I know Greer has agreed with Melanie's approach to waiting an appropriate amount of time to make sure we'll be together before I introduce them, but I want them to become friends. "Well, let's not worry about that today. I'd like you to meet her eventually."

"Never."

I need to change the subject or this will go nowhere fast. "What are we going to do today?"

She visibly calms down. There's so much change going on, and now I know I need to tiptoe into my relationship. "I want ice cream from the creamery."

"Today is a perfect day for ice cream."

I shut the television off, and we get in my car and drive into town. Genevieve chats aimlessly about her friends, and I try hard to keep up without drifting into my own world.

I LIE IN BED THINKING about my last conversation with Michael. When Mark applied trackers to the barrels, two more were missing. I think this is going to drive me over the edge. I wanted to talk to Sophie, but she left for vacation as soon as I returned. She deserves the break, but I never even got the chance to tell her about the meeting. She'll want to know the family's decision about the trackers and stacking system and my brother petitioning for us to lose our stake in Bellissima Valle. I don't know how much more stress I can take, but I also don't want to burden her with all the vineyard's problems, as she takes everything so personally.

Genevieve is becoming difficult for both her mother and me. I know in parenting circles they warn you about your sweet little girl turning into a bitch as she begins puberty, but isn't eleven too young for that? She's struggling with her mother getting serious with Tomas, but I know from our conversations that Melanie dated Tomas for over a year before she introduced him to Genevieve, and they're planning on getting married. We've always made it clear to Genevieve that while she wasn't a mistake, her mom and I just weren't meant to be anything more than good friends, but we love her dearly. Melanie wants Tomas in her life, and I want Genevieve to like Greer. And it's important that she see a loving relationship. I need the women in my life to get along.

GREER

I FINALLY FEEL like a normal person again. It's only taken a week to completely recover from my jet lag and get fully in the groove of things at the office.

I look through the final issue of the business journal I missed while I was out and see a few things that are concerning. It's time to make a preemptive attack. I came up with an idea while I was in Italy, and now I'm rested and ready to implement.

I call a friend at the *Silicon Valley Business Journal.* "Hey, Wiley, it's Greer Ford."

"Hey, Greer. How are things at SHN?"

"They're amazing, actually. We were thinking of doing a roundtable with several of our reclusive CEOs. Any interest in covering it for *The* SVBJ?"

"You've caught my interest. Tell me more."

I take the time to go through my vision. It's a total puff piece, but a few of the names I drop will be very interesting for Wiley to cover, as they've been in the news dealing with issues of sexual harassment, tax avoidance, device addition, working with the government under less than ideal circumstances, and the challenges of working in a highly changing environment and how they're adapting. I haven't run it by the partners but will do so after I put this into motion. It's going to bring our mole out in full force, and Benchmark is going to go crazy.

If this goes sideways though, I could very well lose my job. I've resigned myself that if it comes to that, I'll move to my mom's condo for a while to relax and date Andy.

I pick up the phone and make lunch plans with Jim, our private investigator, then decide to include Dillon last minute so I have some senior partner buy-in.

Dillon pops into my office. "I noticed you didn't include Mason on the lunch."

"Yes, normally I'd invite Mason, but while on vacation I came up with something that I've launched with the media to flush out our mole. Plus, he's understandably raw about Jeannine."

Jeannine Pierce was, I believe, Mason's first serious girlfriend, and he's still a bit protective of her. And she's the CEO and founder of Benchmark Capital, a rival venture capital fund. "I understand. Let's see what Jim says. If he has a problem, can we roll back what you've promised?"

"Yes, but it'll be ugly. I don't think Mason's going to like it, and he'd probably veto it out of the gate."

I work the afternoon on my personal laptop that isn't attached to our network in any way, watching my e-mail and newsfeeds from my work computer. By eight I have my entire plan written down, and tonight I'll make copies of it from home, so no one who might have access or can hack our work network has anything to steal.

The group all gathers for drinks after work to casually catch up. We discuss the new partner joining us in emerging markets and get hints on the final plans for Sara's wedding that's coming up. Given Trey's a paparazzi darling and has been since he was twelve, there's a lot of misdirection going on. We don't discuss any details for fear of being overheard, but I can't wait. Sara won't have any bridesmaids, but her two sisters will join her as flower girls, and her foster father will walk her down the aisle. Beyond that, we don't know a when or where, so we're all on high alert.

Emerson's drinking club soda, which makes me think she might be pregnant, but when I hint at her beverage choice, she tells me she has more work to get done tonight and needs to be fully aware since its budget planning for her teams. I'm not sure I believe her excuse, thinking if she isn't currently pregnant, then they're probably trying. The idea of little babies running around SHN is actually exciting. I'm a very good aunt.

Cameron and Hadlee are also busy planning a wedding, something small for the ceremony and a big party with all sorts of people invited.

Annabel turns green with envy. I'm not sure, but I have to wonder if Mason doesn't hear a little bit of what our concerns are and is slow to commit. They live together, but she wants to be his universe, and I don't get the impression that she is. Selfishly, I can't help but enjoy her jealousy, and I feed it a little bit by digging into wedding plans that are being made, but I'm not a total bitch about it.

Cameron stands up and straightens his shirt in a fit of nervousness as Hadlee glides in. Her eyes light up, and the chemistry between the two is obvious and smoldering. After a quick but deep kiss with her man, she walks over and hugs the two of us. "Hey, ladies. Funny meeting you here."

Emerson sardonically shares, "This stool has my butt prints on it, we come here so often."

Hadlee looks up and sees Annabel watching us. "Hi, Annabel, I didn't see you there. Sorry."

"That's all right, I hear the wedding planning is coming along."

"Slowly. I'm okay with a long engagement, but this big ol' lug here is in a hurry."

Hadlee had no idea that her innocent comment would only make Annabel more envious. Her lips purse and her smile becomes plastic, and I think the pained look on her face is because she must have a hemorrhoid with how restrained she's acting right now. Hadlee has no idea how she was before, so she doesn't know that she just threw gasoline on the fire. Annabel excuses herself, and I see her take a big breath.

I feel a little bad for her. She loves Mason—I think—and it isn't reciprocated. I consider going after her, but Mason gets a text message and walks off for a minute. When he returns to the table, he sits down heavily. "Annabel apologizes, but she isn't feeling well and is heading home."

"I'm sorry to hear that." I cringe, feeling a bit guilty about how much I had to do with her early departure.

"I think all the wedding talk is hard for her," Emerson sympathizes.

"I don't know why," Mason says matter-of-factly. "I've told her it isn't in the cards until we've lived together for at least two years."

"Two years?" slips out of my mouth before I realize it. "I mean, that's a long time. Don't you think you'll know before that?"

"No, I don't," he replies curtly.

Hadlee soothes him. "Well, I hope it works like you want. We'll support you regardless."

We talk for another hour or so before I excuse myself and head home. I need to print this proposal for Jim and Dillon, and I want to talk to Andy before it gets too late.

THE NEXT MORNING GOES IN A FLASH, and before I know it, Dillon and I climb into a rideshare for our lunch across town in

Ghirardelli Square. While we ride, we make polite conversation.

"Are you and Andy getting serious?"

I'm crazy about him, but I'm not ready to share that with the world. Instead, I make an excuse. "It's hard to get serious when we live so far apart."

"Well, it isn't like your father's company doesn't make helicopters, and you could use the pad on the top of the building and chopper in every day."

"I didn't know there's a helipad on the roof."

"There is. It would probably be a twenty-minute trip door to door. And no traffic."

"You're funny. Right now I don't know what I'm going to do. We need to date a while and live through my meeting his daughter—"

"He has a daughter?"

"Yes, when we all met, the girls were talking about Genevieve and Melinda. Who did you think they were talking about?"

"I don't know. Maybe sisters or ex-girlfriends. I wasn't really paying attention." Looking sheepish, he mumbles, "Sorry."

I giggle. "Don't worry about it. He's very special to me, and while he's been exposed to an episode of the many dramas of Eve, if Mark is any indicator of the male behavior, he won't stick around anyway."

"You do realize that Mark is a fucking idiot. And honestly, it wouldn't surprise me if he wasn't really a man."

I chuckle. "I know he's an idiot, but I also think when most men realize how difficult it can be and the prospect that I could also become that batshit crazy, they run for the hills."

"Not if they love you they don't."

I'm grateful when we arrive at the restaurant, though I'm relieved to hear what he said. Maybe he's right.

We jump out of the car and walk in, searching for Jim. He's already arrived and found us a table in a corner far away from any possible eavesdroppers.

We quickly order, and once the waiter leaves, I bring out the proposal and walk them through my thought process, including how I think it'll play out with the media and with Benchmark.

Dillon is silent as he processes what I've laid out. Jim leans back in his chair and scrutinizes me carefully. "You did this on your personal computer and didn't get on any network, right?"

"That's correct," I assure him.

"This is pretty risky, but I would imagine it's going to send your mole into overdrive."

"The first roundtable is Saturday, and we expect the Sunday *Chronicle* to have a small piece. The *Silicon Valley Business Journal* will have a complete spread with over fifteen interviews. Each one will have a take on the things they're struggling with and how we've helped to manage it."

"Don't get me wrong, Greer. I think it's brilliant, but I think the chance of this blowing up is about 40 percent," Dillon confides.

"I'm prepared for that. If it goes sideways, I'll resign from SHN and move to my mother's place in Napa."

"I don't think that's necessary. We'll figure it out if it comes to that." Looking down at the proposal as our food is delivered, Dillon continues, "I think this is positively brilliant and it's a good risk. I know Mason will struggle with it because of the risk to you personally, but if you're willing, then I support you regardless of the repercussions."

We eat and talk quietly about different aspects to make sure I've covered all my bases, and I have. When they clear our plates, I say, "It sounds like I have buy-in from both of you." They nod, and Dillon says, "I'll call a partners meeting at my place tonight. Jim, can you make it?"

"I can."

"Why don't we make it my place?" I offer. "That way we don't put Emerson out, and I can take care of dinner and other details."

"That works." I watch Dillon type out an invite stressing it's for partners' eyes only. He also includes Charles, Trey, and CeCe. His phone pings successively, and it looks like everyone will be converging on my place at seven.

As I leave the restaurant, I call the Italian restaurant and order dinner for ten people, then the liquor store to order a case of Bellissima wine for dinner, and finally prepare a table outside with a screen and projector. People can't steal the screen like they can a discarded proposal.

My cell phone pings.

Mason: **Is everything okay?**

Me: **Yes. I met with Jim today and included Dillon last minute. I'll walk through my proposal tonight.**

It takes him a few minutes to respond. I know not including him most likely hurt his feelings, and I'll have to work hard to make it up to him.

Mason: **See you shortly. Can I bring anything?**

Me: **I adore you, Mason. You're incredibly kind for offering, but I think I have it covered.**

The wine arrives first, and I put it aside. Then dinner is delivered by the wife's owner this time, who's also from a town close to Andy's. She sets up a buffet-style spread with a heat source so none of the food gets cold. I promise to bring Andy by soon, and she thanks me profusely for the Bellissima Grande wine. It was a special memory from their past, but she assures me that Bellissima Valle gets front and center stage at their restaurant.

She leaves as my friends and partners arrive. I show them

outside to the patio where dinner is set up along with drinks. It isn't even 7:05 p.m. and everyone is already here.

"Wow, I don't think we've all been on time to anything before. I'm impressed."

"Well it isn't often you call a meeting," Sara says.

"True. Why don't we all grab some food? It's amazing Italian food that's here in my neighborhood, we recently learned the owners are from the next town over from where Andy grew up. There's Bellissima Valle wine to enjoy with it, so you get a real Italian experience."

Fifteen minutes later, everyone is seated and it's just dark enough that I can fire up my presentation. People eat quietly and slowly as I walk through the plan. No one asks any questions while I'm talking, and that makes me nervous. I can't have explained it so well that they understand everything.

Mason is first to talk. "You do realize with this plan that Jeannine is going to come gunning hard for you."

I nod. "Yes, but Jim, Dillon, and I agree that if I'm willing to take the risk, we just might cripple our mole, if not completely take them out."

Cameron turns to Dillon. "You've digested this a bit longer than I have. How do our investments look after this?"

"I do think we'll take a hit, but I think it'll be temporary. These guys are exposing themselves. We may open the market on Monday morning down, but by the end of the day, our companies should all be up from where they closed Friday night."

"Holy fuck, this is risky," Cynthia breathes.

Trey and Sara nod in agreement.

Charles asks, "What do we do if this goes sideways?"

"I take the blame in the media. My ex will get on the bandwagon that my mother is bipolar and chances are I am, too. You'll all have deniability, and I leave the company and move out to Napa to my mother's condo for a while."

Emerson is quick to jump to my defense. "Wait a minute, that seems rather drastic."

Sara adds, "I think we determine tonight if this is what we want, and then we all go down with the decision."

"Wait, that's not part of my plan. While I do think this will work and work well for us, I think it's only appropriate for me to fall on my sword."

Cameron, who has been quietly reading through everything, sits back in his chair. He's often reserved, so when he has something to say, everyone stops and pays attention. "Sara's right. We're all behind this and will go down with the sinking ship, but I don't think it'll turn out that way. I think this is going to upset our mole and frost Jeannine. Mason, you'd better change your phone number. She's going to be pissed."

"It's going to be fantastic." Mason beams.

Charles slaps his hands on his knees. "That settles it. Sounds like we're all on board." Turning to me, he adds, "This took some serious balls to pull off. I think the company is going to catapult after this, and we'll have you to thank."

I take a deep breath. I want to cry and run to him for a hug as I did when my dad left my mom when I was young. Instead, I murmur, "Thank you."

We break for dessert, and the mood lifts exponentially. Hanging out and drinking wine, I look around the group. I'm excited they're allowing me to run with my idea. I do think if it goes bad, I'll need to leave, and the thought alone makes me want to cry, but knowing some of the Bay Area's smartest minds think it's a good idea makes me feel a little better.

My phone rings, and it's Andy calling on FaceTime. I greet

him and tell him what's going on, then show him the group all enjoying the food and wine.

"I wish I was there," he pouts.

Emerson says, "We wish you were, too."

I turn the phone back to me. "Can I call you later?"

"I'm heading to bed. Can we talk tomorrow?"

"Call whenever you can. I'll try to get away, or you can always wake me up."

"Okay, good night."

I miss him.

ANDY

T TAKES ME A MOMENT to realize the noise is the alarm at the farthest warehouse from the villa going off. I grab a pair of jeans and pull on a T-shirt as I stumble in the dark with only my cell phone to cross the grounds. It doesn't take long before the alarm company calls asking if they should send the police. "Someone has kicked in the door to one of our warehouses. Please send the police."

"Sir, they're three minutes out. We don't suggest you enter the property," the operator informs me.

"Thank you." I disconnect the call and stand for all of probably five seconds before I walk in ready to confront the person who broke into the warehouse.

I don't see anything immediately. Flipping the light switch on and off gets me nothing. I'd bet they cut the electricity to the warehouse, which is what set the alarm off.

I walk farther in and smell it—fermenting wine.

This isn't good.

Using the flashlight function on my cell phone, I see wine spilled on the floor. Then I see stars.

I WAKE COVERED IN WINE, and my head is killing me. A police officer is leaning over me. "Sir, are you okay?"

I reach for the back of my head and notice a ringing in my ears. "What happened?"

"Seems like someone hit you from behind. You have a nasty gash, and you're bleeding."

I'm soaked in various stages of wine fermentation. "What did they do to my wine?"

"Stay still, sir. The ambulance is on its way."

I hear Sophia before I see her. "Let me in. This is my family winery, and that's my brother." They must have let her pass, because she shrieks and then I feel her at my side. "Andreas! Are you okay?"

"I think so." I struggle to sit up, the pain so strong it's like I'm being hit from behind over and over. I look at my fingers and they're red, though not from wine.

"Ma'am, the ambulance is on its way. Your brother was knocked out by the intruder. He needs to be looked at by the EMTs."

Sophia jumps up and covers her mouth in horror. "Oh my God!"

I follow her line of sight and see what has her upset. Four barrels of wine have been destroyed. Four of our oldest wines.

I lean back and close my eyes. That was probably close to a million dollars in sales, given the vintage. This is going to send my older brother here for sure. "Shit."

The ambulance arrives, and they insist on taking me to the hospital. Sophia remains to deal with the police.

It's shortly after 5:00 a.m. They've X-rayed my head, gave me twenty-seven stitches, and determined I have a skull fracture. Doping me up pretty heavily, the nurse warns me, "You're going to have a headache for quite some time."

I dial Greer, who answers out of breath. "Hey, baby. Good

morning."

I moan into the phone. "Good morning. You're breathing hard."

"I'm just finishing my morning run. You're early."

"Someone broke into the warehouse last night. When I went to investigate, I was hit from behind. I'm at the hospital."

"Oh my God, are you okay? I'll shower and be right there."

"No, I'm fine. Really. I only wanted to hear your voice. I'm going to have one monster of a headache for a few days."

"Oh, sweetheart, I can work from the hospital today."

"No, really. I'm okay. Plus, Sophia's here and bossing everyone around."

She chuckles. "I'm sure she is. What happened?"

"The alarm went off, and I went to find out why." I tell her what happened, leaving out that they told me to wait outside for the police.

"I'm going to get a few things done and head up there. I have a big weekend with work, so I'd love to see you for moral support."

"Really, you don't need to do that."

"I'm sure I can find a way to make you feel better," she whispers seductively, and my dick becomes hard as a board.

Laughing only makes my head hurt more. "I'm sure if anyone can make me feel better, it's you."

We talk for a few more moments and end the call. I'm being moved to a room for a few days of observation. With my sister fussing, I see Melanie and Genevieve arrive.

"Genny heard about what happened, and she wanted to come see you."

I pat the bed next to me. "Come here, *cucciola*." She sits beside me and looks like she's been crying. "I'm okay. Don't worry about your *papa*." I knock softly on my forehead. "This thing is hard as a rock."

She lunges at me with a big hug. "I was so worried about you."

I wince from the movement, but hold on tight and tousle her hair. "I'm okay. I promise."

Melanie looks at Sophia. "May I leave her here for a few hours? I need to get some work done, and there's no way I can get her to go to school today."

"Of course."

Doctors come and go, and I'm taken for blood tests and CT scans. Genevieve is a trooper, and she's taken over the television and is texting her friends. She's quick to take care of me, but in a way an eleven-year-old does.

After a while, Sophia asks her, "How about we go find some lunch down at the cafeteria?"

Genevieve jumps at the chance to move around a bit.

I lie in my bed and keep thinking about what happened and why someone would break in to vandalize barrels. There's no value in destroying them, and up until now, they've only been stealing, which is money.

When I look up, I see Greer. I can't tell if it's a mirage or if it's really her.

"Hey, handsome." She puts her bag down and glides over to me. With a look of concern, she asks, "How are you feeling?"

"I'm doing pretty well. They're going to keep me for a few days."

She sits next to me and rests her head on my chest. "You can't worry us like this. Why didn't you wait for the police to arri—"

"Who the hell are you?" Genevieve fumes.

Greer bolts to a sitting position and turns to look at my daughter.

I explain, "Genevieve, it's okay. This is my friend Greer. I told you about her."

Greer starts to speak. "Ni—"

"I don't care who she is. She doesn't belong here."

"Genevieve! We don't speak like that," Sophia admonishes her.

"She needs to leave. This is family business, and she's. Not. Family." Genevieve's fists are balled at her sides, her face flushed.

Greer looks at me with regret in her eyes. "I'll leave."

I grab her hand. "Let me talk to her."

"I've been in her shoes. I understand. I'm going to head back to The City. If you can talk tonight, give me a call." Turning to Genevieve, she says, "I'm sorry we had to meet under these circumstances. Take good care of your father. He needs you."

"You can leave now."

Greer nods and walks out. Sophia is quick to follow her, leaving me with Genevieve.

"That was completely uncalled for. You need to apologize to her this instant."

"No I don't. She's not part of our family, and she doesn't belong here."

"Genevieve, I know you're struggling with the changes with your mom and Tomas, but you need to realize that your mom and I both still love you."

She begins to cry. "I thought when Sophia called, she was going to tell me you were dead."

Sophia returns and shakes her head.

What a mess.

GREER

J GET INTO MY CAR and start to cry. I don't cry often, but I've been where Genevieve is, and I can't do to her what was done to me. My heart is being ripped from my chest as the tears roll in steady streams down my face.

I want my mommy. I don't know if she's going to be lucid today, but I want to see her.

I drive over to the hospital and walk in. My mother's doctor meets me in the lobby.

"What a pleasant surprise. Eve is sitting in the garden and will be excited to see you."

"Thanks. I've had a bad morning, and I'm hoping my mom can make it better."

He looks at me thoughtfully. "I hope so, too. Come with me and let's go find her." We walk along the paths until we find a bench facing a pond, ducks surrounding my mom. "Someone's been hoarding bread to feed the ducks." My mom tucks her hand in her pocket and pretends she didn't hear him. "Eve, it isn't healthy for the ducks to be fed bread."

"Can she feed them a duck food pellet?"

"I suppose." He eyes me carefully.

I sit next to my mom and give her a big hug, and she hugs me back. I fight back the tears and pull my phone out. "Let's order some duck pellets to be delivered tomorrow for you. Would you like that?"

She nods.

"All right, I'll leave you two troublemakers here," the doctor says. "Greer, feel free to see me on your way out if you need anything."

"Thanks, Doctor."

My mom is in a good place today. I tell her all about Andy and what's happened, though she doesn't register that my Andy and her Andy are the same person. "Oh, sweetie. That's too bad. There'll be another."

That isn't what I want to hear, but my mother was never one to be affectionate and loving. I should've known better to hope for more. "Thank you for being my mom today."

I can tell all the stimulation is getting to her because she's becoming agitated. Deciding that's my cue, I tell her, "I love you, Mom. I'll see you again soon."

"You're leaving?"

"Yes, I need to get back into The City and get some work done today. I have a big project due on Saturday."

"Oh, okay," she says softly as she watches the ducks.

I walk inside to the doctor's office to let him know how the visit went.

"Did you get what you needed from her?"

"I don't think I ever got that from Eve. I love her with all my might, but she's missing the compassion gene."

"I know you've talked to someone about it."

"Yes. I know what she's capable of. I'll be fine. Thanks for allowing me to order the duck food pellets. I ordered a twenty-pound bag that should arrive tomorrow. Maybe those who are interested can feed the ducks?"

"I think we're going to have a lot interested, but the gardener is going to send you a bill for picking up their waste."

I laugh. "Send it over. If it makes Eve happy, I'll cover it." I leave his office and head back to my car, feeling slightly better than I did when I arrived.

As I drive back into town, I call CeCe and tell her what happened.

"Are you okay?" she asks once I've finished.

"I will be. I just can't do to Genevieve what my father did to me. It's about her happiness, not his or mine."

"I think you're being too hard on yourself."

"They're a package deal. She has to like me at least a little bit."

"She's almost a teenager. Is that even possible?"

"I won't force it. Sophia told me she's taking out her anger with her mother preparing to remarry."

She pauses a moment. "So, how are things going for the forum this weekend?"

I'm happy for the subject change. "Amazingly well, actually. We got everyone lined up and scheduled for who's talking to who and when. I have all the local papers, *the Wall Street Journal, the Washington Post, the New York Times,* the *LA Times,* and a few others. I'm getting nervous."

"It's all going to go without a hitch. Do you want to meet for dinner tonight?"

"I shouldn't. I've taken the morning off, and now I have a lot to do to prepare for Saturday."

"Well if you change your mind, please call. I'll leave my evening open, or I can call in the girls or everyone if you need it?"

"I'm good, really."

I somehow managed to turn off the ringer on my phone, and I miss several calls throughout the day. None of the work calls were pressing, but I also missed CeCe and Andy.

I listen to CeCe's voice mail first. "I'm still hoping I can tear you away for dinner. Let me know if you've found the time. Sending big hugs and kisses."

I then listen to Andy's message. He sounds loopy and definitely drugged, and my heart breaks for him and all he has to deal with. "Hello, *cuore mio.* I really am sorry about Genevieve. She and I talked about it. Once I break free from here, we'll organize something for just the three of us. I miss you and wish you were here. I'm really sorry."

I really want this to work out with him. The distance makes it hard, but I keep thinking about what Dillon said about my dad owning a company that manufactures helicopters. I've never been too extravagant, but this may be a way I can make it work with Andy.

There's a rainbow at the end of this ordeal after all.

I pull out a bath bomb from my favorite spa, The Meadowood in Napa, and crawl into a warm bath that smells of lavender and vanilla. I'm almost ready for Saturday, so it's time to relax for a bit.

Staying until the water is tepid, I finally make my way to my room and crawl between the sheets before I crash.

I NEVER SET MY ALARM, so I sleep in a bit for me. Waking on my own usually means I can remember my dreams, but I can't remember last night's—though I know it had something to do with Genevieve and my mom sitting in a press room. That would be a mess.

I shake it off, determined to make today a good day. I dress for my run and head out, my mind wandering as I push myself hard. I used to find sweating so gross, but now I can't go three days without running until I'm sweatier than all of those I see. When my hair is saturated and the salty drops run into my mouth, it's a kiss of life, the reassurance that I can still run, still enjoy the body God gave me for years to come.

After returning from my run and showering, I dress in all white to counter my dark mood and head to the office. My day is quiet as I continue to work outside of the office network to prepare for Saturday.

My head is buried in my work when my office phone buzzes, and I almost jump out of my skin at the sound.

"Yes, Monica?"

"Hi, Greer. You have a delivery. I can bring it to you when I have relief in about an hour, or you can send someone up if you'd like it before then. Sorry, but I've been instructed to never leave the front desk without coverage." Mason's insisting that we have the front desk fully manned to make sure only those allowed are in the office.

"You're very mysterious."

She giggles. "I have to entertain myself somehow."

She hangs up and I smile. I like Monica. She's always cheerful and never lets the pressure of working for one of the Bay Area's most successful venture capital funds get to her.

I've been sitting all morning, so stretching my legs sounds like a good idea—plus I'm curious what was sent. Locking my computer screen and closing down my personal computer, I walk out front. Last year, Sara had someone go through her computer after turning it off and leaving for the evening, and now we're incredibly careful about them.

I pick up a Diet Coke and a snack for Monica; she always has a Diet Coke on her desk, and I know she'd appreciate it. Walking into the lobby, I hand her my small token of appreciation and see my delivery—a beautiful bouquet of white and lavender dancing-lady orchids and a note: 'Flowers for *cuore mio*. Miss you. A.'

"They're so pretty. Who are they from?" Monica asks.

I smile. Not really wanting to give her all the details, I quickly determine a light version is how I should answer. "I had a tough weekend, and a friend sent them to cheer me up."

"I hope it worked."

"It did. Thanks."

Finding the perfect place in my office where I can see them as I work at my computer or talk on the phone, I text him. **Thank you for the beautiful orchids. They're perfect.**

Andy: **Sorry I can't be with you this weekend, but I know it's going to go well.**

My heart beats a tiny bit faster. He's so thoughtful. He has so much going on, and yet he remembers that my life is crazy and sends these.

I'm so lucky.

SATURDAY STARTS EARLY. We have a forum for our clients who are making rounds with the press. They've been encouraged to speak frankly about some of their recent issues and taught how to avoid questions that would derail the interviews. With each press person, there's someone from our PR agency to prevent any catastrophes.

We bring everyone together for lunch, and Mason gives a wonderful speech before we send everyone along late afternoon. Each news outlet spoke with over ten companies, and it was a buzz of technology announcements.

Despite the long day, I'm exhausted, but the PR team and the partners all decided to go out for drinks, not only to celebrate clearing the first hurdle but also to share our anxiety of what the coming week will bring.

Our account manager announces to the group, "Greer, that went incredibly well."

"Don't congratulate me until we see the press clippings this week."

I really am nervous and excited about how it's going to all turnout. The feedback from the press and my PR people inside the room is all positive, but they've known for two days this was coming, so it's the dirt they dig up that will affect how this all plays out. I raise my glass. "To my having a job at the end of the week."

We all clink glasses, and there's a collective optimism with the group. We talk about some of the funny things that happened throughout the day, and we bask in our glory for at least the evening. I'll watch the wires tonight to see how the first stories drop. I have to wait, and patience isn't my virtue. I can't concentrate on the conversation and figure it's time to head home. My nerves are peaked and I need to be by myself in yoga pants and a sweatshirt while I wait anxiously.

WALKING OUTSIDE, I watch the fog blanket the bay for a few moments before returning to the living room and turning the TV on. You'd think with over five hundred stations that something would pique my interests, but none do. I fluff pillows and re-arrange chairs, even try reading my book, but my brain is worrying about the storm I've just created. All I'm left to do is pace until the stories start to hit.

They begin to post shortly after 2:00 a.m. for the East Coast papers. I sift through the various articles and e-mail them to the team as they come in. They're incredibly complimentary, which eases my mind for a moment. Over the next few hours, I watch the Midwest papers and then the West Coast.

Round one goes to SHN.

Since I was up half the night, I sleep late into the morning, knowing Benchmark will strike as soon as they see what's going on. Checking the wires after grabbing my first jolt of caffeine, I note several papers that weren't invited but are rewording the stories for their local audiences. I go for a late-afternoon run, quickly finding that, while there's something to be said for what the push of endorphins does for my mornings, it's not as strong for the afternoon.

Our clients have been instructed to contact us if they receive any calls about commenting on less than positive coverage, but I haven't heard anything. Crickets. The silence is making me very nervous. *Living in Napa for a while wouldn't be too bad. At least I'd be close to Andy and my mom.*

Staying up for the second night, I watch the newswires. My nerves are worse than they were last night. All I can do is pace. The stories start at 2:00 a.m. and push across the wires in the early hours. The more in-depth coverage continues to be relatively positive. We hit some bumps with our clients who have government contracts, pushback from their internal employees about hiring issues, and those accused of skirting tax avoidance and harassment. I pull the newswires on Benchmark, Argent Capital, and Carson Mills—our major competitors. There's some bad-mouthing us from Carson Mills, but the reporter responds by calling them out on it.

Then I see what I've been waiting for. Benchmark does a piece on the inaccuracies of our forum and where we're wrong. Things that were planted for the mole.

I e-mail the team and Jim. **Okay, here we go.**

Jim is the first to respond. **I'm tracking their information.**

Mason adds, **When do you respond to the news source?**

I tell them, **I'm on it. I'm using the New York Times this first round. Stay tuned.**

After a few clicks and a brief phone call, I see our counter to the Benchmark article that proves our information correct. I then watch the other papers pick it up.

Round two, SHN.

I begin receiving notices from our PR agency that clients are receiving calls validating possible misinformation. This is where it gets tricky. The agency is well-versed in spin, but we need our spin to be factual and how we're going to back it up. This is where it could become interesting. I'm getting regular updates, and I start feeding compressed updates to the team via a secure server outside of SHN's network.

We watch our first piece of coverage go sideways. The article discusses the falling apart of SillySally, which we heavily invested in. Their CEO was having multiple affairs, his wife was suing him for divorce, and some less than positive actions got him booted from the company by his board, which we orchestrated. The company has struggled to find their footing with their new CEO. We knew this would be coming.

We then see some articles about old clients where we didn't manage things correctly. This was also expected.

This round goes to the mole.

It's Wednesday when the hit pieces start. The hardest isn't with our investments, but the team personally. With me, they concentrate on my mother's mental illness. They have quotes about Cameron being into S&M, which actually makes me laugh to think he likes spanking Hadlee. Whatever floats their boat. They call Dillon an alcoholic and talk about how Mason makes constant mistakes and the team covers for him. Sara is a primadonna, and Emerson is a tyrant, both of which couldn't be further than the truth. There's a big hit piece on the Arnaults and their association with SHN, asking the question of whether Charles is really the person behind SHN and our success. None of our news sources are asking why these hit pieces on us about our personal lives matter, and I'm getting nervous.

I put a call in to my cousin. "Vannie?"

"GiGi, I'm watching this from New York. This is getting ugly."

"It is, and I'm vulnerable right now. The press is going for page reads and not content. What does your brilliant mind think?"

She launches into her opinion on page reads and pushes for a solution, just as I hoped she would; I'm too close to be objective since they're attacking my friends and me. She comes up with an idea, and I like it. "Are you sure you're comfortable doing this?"

"Absolutely. This is when our jobs get fun."

"Thank you." I feel Zen and know this is the right avenue to take.

"I'll call you after I have some luck."

"I'll be by my phone."

I'm stunned when she calls back twenty minutes later. "That was quicker than I'd expected, but then again, I started planting stories this morning," she explains.

"What did you do?"

"Oh, I might have gone after the CEOs of your main competitors, figuring they were going to go low."

I see the wires pick up stories about our three major competitors' failures, with comments about the leadership in all three instances. This is either going to get people to back off, or the news sources are going to drive this to page reads and a war among venture capital companies in the Bay Area where no one comes out on top.

This is a no-win for any of us.

I pull out my grand finale, which will either work or it won't. I call my contact at *The Wall Street Journal* and arrange for the typically reclusive Charles Arnault to do a one-on-one interview later this afternoon at the Fairmont Hotel.

Tanya from the *Journal* arrives, and she's ready for this no-holds-barred Q&A session. I'm in the back chewing on my thumbnail. Dammit. I hate when I do this. I've had too much coffee and not enough food this week.

I listen to her question Charles, starting soft and then attempting to go for the jugular. He answers each of her questions with confidence and acknowledges problems when necessary. I notice after a while that she isn't reading from her prepared questions, but I don't want to break up the conversation. She's running late, and I'm getting nervous that she's going to miss her deadline and this won't run, which will send us into the weekend with the lousy coverage.

Finally, I hear her say, "Okay, I have what I need, and I have a deadline. Can you excuse me"—she looks down at her phone—"for the next twenty minutes?"

Everyone stands back, and Charles and I step into the hallway outside of the room. He pulls me in for an embrace. "Greer, this has gone better than we expected. Regardless, we're ahead."

When Tanya emerges, she hands each of us a copy of the article she posted. I thank her but don't want to be too eager, waiting until she leaves to read it.

In 1984, Charles Arnault cofounded Sandy Systems with his wife, Margret "Margo" Lerner Arnault, to market the technology they codeveloped for connecting computer networks. The Arnaults designed and built routers in their house and experimented using Stanford's network. Initially, the Arnaults went to Stanford with a proposition to start building and selling the routers, but the school refused. It was then that they founded their own company and named it "Sandy Systems," taken from the name of the city to the north.

Sandy Systems' product was developed in their garage and began selling in 1986 by word of mouth. In their first month alone, Sandy Systems was able to land contracts worth more than $200,000. The company produced revolutionary technology, giving them domination over the marketplace. Sandy Systems went public in 1990, Charles Arnault retired from the business five years ago, and their son currently sits at the helm. His experience with venture capital money was not positive.

"After funding the company for three years by mortgaging everything we owned and putting everything on credit cards, we made an absolute bozo no-no. We decided to take money from a VC. He got 30-odd percent of the company for $2.6 million. Margo and I were very naïve. We used his lawyer and agreed to a four-year vesting agreement. We would get 90 percent of the founder's stock after four years, but we didn't put enough in writing and learned the hard way."

Charles Arnault is the grandson of Winston Arnault, the famed shipping and railroad magnate. When he chose not to join the family business, he and Margo were on their own. "Margo's family had a small business. I always thought if someone invested in your business, that meant he or she believed in it. I assumed our investor supported us because his money was tied up in our success. I didn't realize he had decoupled the success of the company from that of the founders."

It wasn't until a friend of their daughter, Caroline, came to him and asked for his advice that he ever wanted to work with a venture capital fund again. "I don't believe all VCs are adversarial, but the first thing I tell everyone is 'You need to look out for yourself.' I'm an advisor to Sullivan Healy Newhouse. I was introduced when a friend *of my daughter's was being approached by them to buy her business. I was incredibly impressed by how they presented themselves. We had set the expectation that the business would be worth a certain amount, and SHN came in with a better than competitive offer. They were honest and very forthcoming. Their ethics drew me to advise them when they asked. I have nothing but respect for the team at SHN."*

When asked about his advisory role, Arnault is quick to downplay his input. "These guys don't really need my advice. Doesn't mean I don't offer it, but I'm more of a sounding board as they grow and face multiple situations that they've never faced before, having reached personal success at such young ages."

As SHN grows, so does the Arnault input. Charles and Margo have contributed personal income into SHN's funds as payment for his time. "Having my children involved adds another layer to the advice. Both Trey and Caroline run large successful companies in their own rights, and they bring a younger perspective that I've never dealt with."

I do a cursory glance through the remaining article, stunned at how hard she went after him and yet essentially wrote a nice puff piece. "This may just end it all with us landing okay."

"Greer, I've never been prouder of you." He brings me in for another tight embrace.

An enormous weight lifts from my shoulders. I bite back the tears, realizing with everything going on with Andy, work and my life, this is exactly what I needed.

Sending the article out to the team, I include a note: **Jim, it's up to you and your team. It looks like the hit pieces on us have some real inside information.**

Just as I press Send, my phone begins to light up as it hits the wires. Taking a deep breath, I attempt to calm my nerves. What the stock market does next is what will determine if I fucked up.

Dillon reports, **Our investments are going like crazy. Some are up over 200 percent and others 50.**

I got something accomplished this week. For a change, I was out in front of the news rather than reacting to it. I may not have to move to Napa after all.

I can't help but be a tiny bit disappointed about that fact. It would've been the perfect excuse to be close to Andy.

Now I want to see my boyfriend.

Me: **Are you home this weekend? May I come for a visit?**

Andy replies almost immediately. **I've been told they're releasing me tomorrow. I need a nurse. Will you be my nurse?**

Me: **Only if I can wear a short white uniform with no panties and lots of cleavage.**

Andy: **I'm hard already.**

Me: **I'm leaving The City now. I'll come by the hospital tonight and be there when you check out. I can stay at my mom's.**

Andy: **You can stay at my place.**

Me: **My mom's is good until Genevieve is comfortable. Even if that takes a year or two, I'm good with it.**

Andy: **You're too good for us.**

Me: **I love you, and you're a package deal.**

Me: **See you soon.**

Andy: **I love you, too. I can't wait to see you. (Nurse uniform not required.)**

Me: **Okay, I'll leave it at home.**

Andy: **What? Bring it if you have it.**

THE TRAFFIC LEAVING THE CITY is terrible. I was hoping for a quick trip up to St. Helena, but unfortunately the traffic is thick both ways, and it's after five when I finally arrive at the hospital. I walk up to his room and peek in before I enter, finding Sophia talking to him in rapid Italian.

She sees me and breaks into a wide grin, then offers me a hug. "So wonderful to see you."

"It's been very busy at work."

Andy breaks into a giant grin and holds his arms up for a hug. "We've been watching the newspapers. Your work has been very exciting this week."

"I think it's going to calm down for a minute."

Throwing her arms up in frustration, Sophia says, "I'm glad you're here. The doctor isn't telling me much because of some silly privacy laws. Maybe you can get him to tell us what he's not supposed to do so I make sure he follows doctor's orders."

"I'll try. No promises though." I chortle as if I have any influence in getting the doctor to talk to me.

She leans down and kisses Andy on the forehead, then leaves in a flourish.

He hasn't let go of my hand since he hugged me, running his fingers over my knuckles. "Hey, where's your nurse uniform?"

"You're not home yet," I tease.

"No sneak peeks?"

I'm shy all of a sudden. Our last visit was not what we expected, and nurses are running in and out of the room, so I'm not interested in giving him any shows. Instead, I ask, "How are you feeling?"

Andy lets out a sigh of boredom or frustration—it's hard to tell for sure. "Ready to go home and sleep all night in my own bed without interruptions."

"Well, I might've brought something to lift your spirits." I remove some cartons of Italian food from his favorite place. "Don't tell anyone. It's not as hot as it should be. The traffic was terrible." I look around, making sure there aren't any spies hiding in his room. "Do you want me to find a microwave?"

Andy spots the takeout dishes and his eyes twinkle. "No. I knew there were many reasons to love you. Any woman who'll bring contraband into the hospital is an angel sent from heaven."

"You may be disappointed, because I think I'm half angel, half devil," I flirt.

He scoops a big piece of ravioli into his mouth, and I'm not sure if his moans are for my comments or his dinner, though I'm assuming the latter. He eats as if he hasn't had food in a month, taking little time to breathe or even say anything.

As he finishes his last bite, a nurse walks in and spies the empty food containers. "Where did that come from?" she asks, eyeing me carefully.

Uh-oh. I'm in trouble now. I mean really, what can they do to me? Kick me out?

I scramble and finally say, "I'm sorry. It was my dinner, and he was just finishing off the leftovers."

"Just a small taste," Andy says as he stifles a laugh.

"Uh-huh, sure." Turning to me, she adds, "Next time bring some for the staff, too."

I nod. "Yes, ma'am."

"You breakin' him out tomorrow?"

My heart beats faster, and my smile is so wide my cheeks hurt. "That's the plan."

"Well, make sure he doesn't go crazy. He's going to get one hell of a headache if he works too hard. They'll send you home with instructions. Make sure he follows them." She abruptly turns and leaves.

Andy waves toward the door. "See what I put up with?" He lowers his voice and teases, "I need a naughty nurse to take care of me."

"We'll see. When's Genevieve due?"

"I don't think she's coming."

I'm completely floored by his response. I'm not nearly as close with my father and I would still go out of my way to be at the hospital when he was being released.

"Are you sure? I would think if her father is getting out of the hospital after a five-day stay when he originally told us it was only going to be three, she'd be here to push your wheelchair to the door."

"I'd be surprised if she knew." He tries to sound nonchalant, but I can see it bothers him.

I know he doesn't mean to be callous toward his daughter and her feelings, but I'm not interested in being the reason they fight. I sit on the bed next to him and rest my head on his chest. "I don't want what happened at my last visit to happen again. Can you call Melanie and find out?"

"Right now?"

I sit up and look him in the eyes so there's no question of my sincerity. "Yes, before it gets too late."

He grabs his phone and makes the call. "Hey, Melanie. Greer's here to take me home tomorrow. Is Genevieve coming by?" He listens a few minutes, then replies, "She is?"

My heart sinks. I've had a long week, and I want time with him, but not to exclude her. Melanie is doing most of the talking, Andy giving the occasional "Uh-huh." Then he says, "No, have her come. Greer and I will make other plans. Is she planning on spending the night?" He listens for a few moments. "Okay. See you tomorrow."

His face falls in disappointment, and I know what he's going to tell me before he does. "It seems like you're right." He tosses his phone on the table in frustration. "I want a naughty nurse."

He's so cute when he pouts. I love that he looks like a petulant little boy, but I need to reassure him. "We have plenty of time for the naughty nurse. Figure out when you're coming down to San Francisco. My mom had a furniture delivery this week, and my plan is to stay tonight at her place, sleep until I can't stand it, and then drive home tomorrow morning after I can function again."

He's still pouting, but we both understand this is our reality when it comes to us dating. "This is the second time you've been accommodating."

"As long as you're keeping track. We need to ease her into a relationship with me. I've been in her shoes, and when I was forced, I never got there."

"She doesn't know how lucky she is to have you."

I kiss the top of his head. "Soon."

My visit with my mom wasn't much different than the last one. We fed the ducks and talked about how she was feeling. I tried to tell her how great my week was, but she isn't interested.

I head back into town and call CeCe on my drive.

She answers with a smile in her voice. "How did it go with your knight in shining armor?"

"You mean the hour I spent with him last night in the hospital?"

"What?"

"Princess Genevieve was coming to break him out of jail today, so I visited Eve, and now I'm headed home."

"I'm sorry. He's lucky he has someone who understands as well as you do."

"He knows that."

"Have you seen today's *Chronicle*?"

My stomach drops and I hold the steering wheel tight. I was hoping the issue with the press was behind us. "No, why? Did someone do an ugly piece on SHN?"

"Nope. Our good friend Mark made a giant gaffe with his biggest donor, and it was recorded and is playing on TubeIt with almost a million downloads as of about an hour ago."

Now I'll need to look out for the backlash coming at my mom and me. "What did you do, CeCe?"

"Me? What would make you think I did anything?" She plays innocent, but I can hear she's being facetious.

"Because I know you."

I pull over and evaluate what my next steps should be as she goes on. "It's a recording of Mark spewing a lot of hate speech about the blacks who live in low-income housing. I might've had someone recording everything he says and does, waiting for a gaffe I could upload to TubeIt, but I didn't bait him into saying anything. I just knew he'd say something on his own. His political career is over. His campaign manager quit this morning, and he's lost most of his endorsements."

Jeff Jenson, his biggest donor, may be an old Southern boy, but his son is gay and has a black partner, and together they've several adopted interracial children. San Francisco is a very progressive city, and they don't tolerate bigotry. "You're part evil, you know."

"Only when someone goes after my posse."

"How about brunch tomorrow and some shopping? I could use some retail therapy after this week."

"Great. I'm in. Have a good night, sweetie."

"You, too."

ANDY

I WAKE TO THE PHONE RINGING. My head's still killing me, particularly when I'm tired—which comes regularly and easily. Genevieve is here as often as she can and is trying to nurse me. I talk to Greer almost every night. It shouldn't be this hard to have a relationship with someone who only lives an hour and a half away, but we're determined to make it work.

Glancing at the caller ID, I answer the phone knowing it's Melanie. *"Buongiorno."* My voice cracks from just having woken up.

"Andreas, I'm sorry I woke you."

Yawning, I say, "It's okay. I think Genevieve is still sleeping."

"I called to talk to you." I sit up in bed, not sure I'm ready to hear what she has to tell me. "Tomas and I are getting married next month in a small ceremony at the capitol. The governor has time in his schedule and is going to do it for us."

This has so many implications for us, and not all good. I haven't paid spousal support in years, and I happily pay my child support, so it doesn't affect me financially, but Genevieve is going to be very upset. She doesn't like Tomas. I'm confident it's because he takes time away from her mother's attention. I've met Tomas on many occasions; he dotes on both the girls and is good to them. "Congratulations. I'm very happy for you."

"You know Genny is going to have a tough time with this news."

"She'll be happy for you."

"Maybe one day. She's so worried about having younger brothers and sisters and being lost."

I'm a little thrown by the comment. Melanie was never sure she wanted to have kids, and I know when she got pregnant she struggled with the idea of being a mom. Sure, we were young, but she never was excited about kids. "She likes Tomas."

"She likes him personally but doesn't like what he represents."

"What do you mean?"

"That you and I are no longer—"

"We've always told her that we wouldn't be getting back together."

"I know." Quietly she adds, "I just wish she could be as happy for this as I am."

"She is. She just doesn't know it."

"What do we do if she decides she wants to come live with you?"

"I'm certainly fine with that, but I can't see her wanting to be away from you for very long." My life may turn upside down with this news if Genevieve decides to move in with me, but my goal is to help use it for Greer. "When are you going to tell her?"

"Soon. She tells me you have a girlfriend?"

I'm not surprised she knows, but I'm not fully prepared to discuss Greer with Melanie. "She lives in The City, and Genevieve's struggling with the idea of sharing me, so I understand where you're coming from."

"So much is changing for her."

"Melanie, in life, things are always changing. She'll adjust. We'll be there for her, and the change gives her examples of what loving relationships are supposed to be."

"I know you're right, but she's so hormonal already. I'm not ready for the teen years."

"I can hear her in the kitchen. Do you want to talk to her?" I ask.

"No, we'll probably tell her this afternoon."

"See you then. I won't say anything."

I get up from the bed and wander into the kitchen. *"Buongiorno."* I look around the kitchen and notice she's started the latte machine. "A little young for coffee."

She hands me a steaming cup of frothy latte and a saucer. "I made it for you."

It smells divine, and with a perfect mix of warm and frothy milk. I take a lengthy sip. "Ahh, your mother has taught you well."

She comes in and gives me a big hug. I miss the days of unconditional love. These days I sometimes get it, but the rest of the time it's judgmental love. "What do you want to do today? Your mom should be here in a few hours."

"How about we go downtown for lunch and walk around?"

"Sounds like a great idea."

We get our things together and head downtown, though I'm distracted by my thoughts of Greer and my problems at the vineyard. The police are involved and investigating. This has been happening with several other vineyards in the area, so they're asking a lot of questions that I don't have answers for. I'm still puzzled why they broke in and destroyed the barrels. I need to ask Michael if he was successful in putting the trackers on each one. We'd scheduled a time to talk the day of the break-in, but it didn't happen.

I watch the people wandering the shops like they don't have any place to be. The weather is like a kiss of sunshine without the fiery heat of summer in August. The grass is a soft green with a hint of indigo, and in the sky is a perfect shade of blue accentuated by just enough pristine white clouds. The concrete of the sidewalk must be warm under Genevieve's bare feet; she removed her sandals and is enjoying walking downtown.

I close my eyes so I can focus on the sounds around me. I hear a blackbird song and wonder how anyone could not say that was music. Opening my eyes, I let the light flood back in, bringing the late February day right back into focus.

We pick up a few sandwiches from the deli and sit cross-legged on the well-manicured lawn, enjoying the last few minutes of our time alone. I know Genevieve is going to be upset when her mother tells her about the wedding, and I want to cushion the blow, but it really isn't my news to tell news. It breaks my heart that my daughter's struggling with the changes in her life. I only wish I could tell her that things are going to be all right and have her believe me.

Melanie and Tomas approach, joining us on the grass, and we stare into the final days of perfect weather before the unforgiving heat descends upon us.

Genevieve eyes her mother and Tomas carefully. "Why did you bring him?"

Tomas squeezes Melanie's hand, and she explains, "Sweet-heart, Tomas and I are really excited. Next month, the governor is going to marry us."

"What? No!" Genevieve screams. She stands and runs away.

Melanie follows her, and I watch them exchange terse words. Tomas is as uncomfortable as I've ever seen him. "I'm very happy for you both," I tell him, trying to break some of the tension.

"Thanks. We're really excited, and we've known this wasn't going to go over well with Genny."

"She'll adjust. She had words with my girlfriend, who means a lot to me. I'm hoping she can realize that her mom and I are better apart than together."

We watch them approach. Genevieve's eyes are swollen red from crying. I stand and give her a hug. "*Cucciola*, it only means you have more people who love you." Turning to Melanie and Tomas, I ask, "May I talk to her for a moment?"

Melanie nods with tears pooling in her eyes as Tomas leads her a little farther away.

I pull Genevieve in for a hug and stroke her hair. Just out of earshot, I tell her, "Tomas loves your mom more than anything. If you wanted him to leave, he would, but you know they would both be heartbroken. Please don't make your mother choose between you and Tomas. I promise you'll win, but at what cost?"

"I just want us to be a family again."

"I know, *mia piccola cucciola,* but that isn't going to happen. We don't love each other anymore. Your mom and I love you more than anything, but we're only friends. That's all we can be."

I pull her into a tight hug, and she cries, "What if they have babies?"

"Then you'll have even more people to love you."

I let her get her tears out, and then her mother approaches.

"Are you ready to go home?"

Genevieve nods, and I kiss the top of the head. "Congratulate Tomas and your mom when you can. They're very excited."

I watch them leave. My heart aches for Genevieve, but she'll learn this is a good thing.

My mind wanders to Greer.

I need her. Of course, I love her—that's a given—but it's more than that. I respect her and want her and lean on her. I didn't realize how much I'd missed having someone to talk about my day, and to spoon at night. I miss all the little quiet moments that slip by almost unnoticed but are just as much magical as the big, dramatic ones with her.

My life has felt three-dimensional since I met Greer, and the funny part is I hadn't even noticed it was flat before. And it's clear to me that I always want her in my life. Sure, there could be other women, but it's Greer I love and really want to be with. Anyone else would be second-best.

After that realization, I go into planning mode. I can't wait to show her how important she is to me. I know I can make her as happy as she has me. How to convince her of that may be my problem. I know she worries about her mother, but Eve is who she is. She met my crazy family and still seems to like me. Not to mention my daughter's been a total bitch to her, and she's taken it in stride and still come back.

I run through a list of everything from hiring the high school marching band to getting an aerial banner, but I know the grand gestures alone aren't going to change Greer's mind. She was hurt by her ex because her mother is imperfect, and she needs to know I accept her and anyone in her life—same as she's done for me. I'll show her how much she means to me.

I start making a plan to become that guy, and just in case it would help my cause, I'll work on a grand gesture to let her know.

GREER

OUR MONDAY MORNING partners meeting has grown, having added a new partner in emerging markets. Christopher seems like a great guy. I give him props for sticking with us, as he came on the week all hell broke loose. Gotta love perseverance in the eye of a storm.

I watch him flirt and flatter his way through most of the women. He's good with them and has them eating out of his hand in no time. He's not my idea of handsome, but it's clear what women might see in him. He's definitely a ladies' man.

"Dillon, how are our investments looking?" Mason asks.

"With a few exceptions, most are doing extremely well. We have an offer to buy Prophecy Software. They don't want the team, but they'll take the technology."

"Speaking of Prophecy, they have one of the strongest technology teams in our portfolio. Mason, would you be willing to sit down with the them and work on a business plan for a new company? If the buyer is going to throw them away, I believe we should finance their next adventure. I'd be shocked if they didn't have something they're working on outside of the company, particularly if they see the writing on the wall," Cameron says.

"I'll call as soon as we're done." Turning to me, Mason asks, "And how are the news wires holding up?"

"They're good. It seems the technology and business press has moved on to the next shiny object."

"Jim, you're next on the agenda."

Jim passes around a package of paper. "In your packets, you'll see what my team observed. We identified a mole at Perkins Klein. Her name was Heather Martindale. She was in their accounting department, and she was feeding our information and PK's information to Benchmark."

"Fuuuck," Cameron exclaims.

"They had a mole, too? This is serious shit," Dillon agrees.

"We believe our mole sent the insider information on Netronix and SillySally we planted, and a separate person who may or may not be a mole fed the press the information on all of you."

Mason him looks over carefully. "So you know who it is?"

"We believe so, yes."

"And?"

"With Sara's help, we identified her legal secretary, Elizabeth Monroe."

Every eye in the room turns to Sara, and it doesn't seem that I'm the only one who's shocked. I fully expected it to be Annabel.

"There was a small piece of information that got out that I was pretty sure only Mason and I knew until I realized Elizabeth would know as well," Sara explains. "She sees all the contract details and enters the Ts and Cs in our system. So I mentioned it to Jim, and we set a trap for her."

"She never was very friendly," Cynthia volunteers.

Emerson interjects, "But she's fairly new. The espionage started before she joined the company."

"That's true. We found the handheld device and phone she was using to pass the information along, and we were able to grab the information she was sharing. Elizabeth was arrested this morning. Her initial statements seem to be that she doesn't exactly know who's behind everything, but she was paid well in a Cayman Island account. This information is what's going to help us find who's behind all this espionage. Currently, all signs point to various people who are feeding the information to our competitors and sources, but right now we can't figure out who's behind it all."

Annabel is still on my list.

Multiple conversations erupt at once. I'm stunned that Elizabeth was behind at least the release about me. Just above a whisper, I say, "But how did she know about my mother? And all the things about the three of you."

Mason nods vigorously. We all concur there's more to this, and Jim assures us that he understands, stressing, "There's most likely one person behind this, and they're using multiple people at all of our companies."

Mason ends the meeting, saying, "Jim, thank you and your team for pursuing this. And I want to really thank Greer for putting herself on the line and personally getting singed."

We talk for a short time and then break. I go back to my office. We have three companies going public with highly technical concepts, and I need to translate it to Wall Street so they have successful initial public offerings.

Every time I read the technology briefs from Cameron, I start to think about Andreas. He's been extra attentive as of late. We talked at length about his ex-wife remarrying, and I know Genevieve is struggling.

I remember when my father remarried. It was soon after he left my mother, and I wasn't invited. He went on a business trip to Paris with his assistant and came home married. They presented me with an emerald tennis bracelet and told me. Immediately she was competing with me for my father's attention, and I always felt like I was in the way. I remember overhearing them talk about sending me to boarding school, and I was devastated. Not only could I not leave my mother, who couldn't get out of bed because her depression was so bad, but they were ready to just hide me away. They were married for three years, and then my father married his next assistant.

I want to help Genevieve with this adjustment, and I hope this weekend will be a fun way to get her out of her shell. There's a music festival we plan to take her to, and Andy assures me that she knows I'm coming. I'm ready to have some fun and enjoy some time with them both.

WHEN I ARRIVE AT THE VINEYARD, I watch Sophia arguing with someone in Italian on the phone. She doesn't hear me walk in, so I quietly take my place in a corner and play with my phone. I have no idea what she's saying other than the word "vino," so I'm sure she's talking about vineyard business.

She waves when she sees me and stops her conversation abruptly, whispering something unidentifiable into the phone before hanging up and turning to me. "Greer, I didn't hear you come in."

"I'm sorry. I didn't want to interrupt."

"No, you're fine. I've been arguing with my family again. They're upset with Andreas and me, and want us to leave and have one of our older brothers run the vineyard."

"Oh no, that's awful. Can they do that?"

"It would be incredibly hard. The vineyard is in Andy's name, as are all the loan papers, but it rolls up underneath Bellissima Holdings. Plus, they'd have to figure out how to get the immigration status to come and work here."

"I hope it works out for you. I'd hate to see you both leave."

She gives me a strange smile, then picks up a walkie-talkie and alerts Andy of my arrival. Excusing herself, she leaves me to wait.

A young couple arrives and asks me, "Are you open?"

I'm not really sure what to do, so I gesture to a nearby table. "Please have a seat. Someone just walked to the back and should return momentarily."

They sit, and we all wait. Andy comes flying in and greets me with a hug and kisses on each cheek. "Where is Sophia?"

"I'm not sure. She called you and stepped out back."

He looks annoyed and walks over to the couple. *"Benvenuti a Bellissima Valle."*

I watch as he introduces them to his wines, and then several others come in. I put on an apron and help him. After what seems like forever, Sophia eventually returns. Now we're going to be late to meet Genevieve.

I see Andy give her a dirty look, and together we leave. When we're out of earshot, I can tell he's upset. "Please don't be angry with Sophia. When I arrived, she was arguing with someone, I think from your family." He looks shocked by my comment. "She told me they want one of your brothers to take over the vineyard."

"She told you that?"

"Yes. I know it bothers her."

"I'll talk to her about it later. Genevieve is waiting for us. She's going to be upset that we're running behind."

"How about I drive? I can drop you so she isn't waiting as long, and I can find parking and catch up with you."

"Don't be absurd. She can wait for us."

"Really, Andy. I've been where she is. No matter what you tell her, she'll blame me. Please go to her."

"It isn't very gentlemanly."

"I'm okay. Really. She needs you, and we need today to go well."

We climb in my car, and I drive us to where the festival is being held. I drop Andy at the gate, and it doesn't take me long to catch up with them. Genevieve doesn't look at me, and Andy keeps trying to bring her into our conversation, but all I get is a cold shoulder.

This is going to take some work, but I can be patient. I just hope Andy can be patient with her.

I did get a smile from her at one point, but once she realized she'd smiled at me, I received an equally daunting look of disdain.

After hours in the sun, lots of junk food, some great music, and about six words said to me by Genevieve, I return them both to the vineyard and head back into The City. I think about the fun music, all the crazy people, but mostly I think about how Genevieve is so vulnerable right now. I know she wouldn't believe me, but I want her to adjust and be happy.

ANDY AND I ARE HOPING to develop a nice routine—alternate weekends of coming into San Francisco and staying with Genevieve in Napa. Until then, we escape our work when we can. The office has been crazy, and I'm barely able to keep up.

My cell phone rings and I pick it up without even looking at the caller ID. "Greer Ford."

"Hello, Greer. This is Melanie Giordano, Genevieve's mother."

Please don't chastise me for dating your ex-husband. I swear I don't want to be Genevieve's mother. "Oh, hello. Umm, how are you?"

"I'm good. Genny tells me you all had a great time at the music festival."

"We did." I'm sitting up straight in my seat, waiting for the shoe to drop. "We tried to avoid the pot smell and drunks and enjoy ourselves."

"That's what she shared."

There's an awkward pause, and I'm still not sure why she's calling. "Congratulations on your impending marriage. The governor of California is going to marry you? That's pretty impressive."

"My fiancé grew up with him in Central California."

"He seems like a nice guy."

"He is. Look, the reason I'm calling... this is so awkward, but I really am supportive of you and Andy. I only know what Genny's told me. I know she's really difficult right now, but I promise she's a wonderful girl. She admitted to Andy that she really wants us—Andy and me—to get back together, even though we've assured her a thousand times that it isn't going to happen. And she's worried about younger brothers and sisters—"

"I've been where she is. My father left my mother in less than ideal circumstances. He remarried several more times, and this last one seems to have stuck. I never knew he was dating anyone until he came home with a new wife who never liked me. I understand how it all feels to hope your parents get back together and they don't. I assure you, I'm not pushing. I've told Andy that I don't think I want children of my own, so I'm in no hurry to marry, and babies are not in my future. We've agreed to take it super slow, and I do see Andy and Genevieve as a package deal—it's all or nothing."

"I think Genevieve is very lucky to have someone so in tune with her situation. Is that why you didn't spend the night?"

"Partially. I know Genevieve is still sensitive to me, but I've also been in her shoes with my own parents following their divorce."

"Driving up from San Francisco is a long trip for only a few hours."

"My mom has a condo in St. Helena, so I sometimes stay there."

"She doesn't mind?" Melanie asks.

"She's not using it right now."

"I'll be in San Francisco in a few weeks. Would you be willing to join me for lunch?"

"I think that would be lovely."

"I'll let you know when I have the date figured out."

"Thank you for your call. Genevieve is a very passionate young girl."

She chuckles. "That's one way to put it. But thank you for understanding. I'm not sure why you don't want children, but I think you'd make a wonderful mother. Goodbye, Greer."

"Goodbye."

I sit back in my seat and can't help but think I may have passed the test. That was surprising. I'm still not 100 percent sure why she called, other than to check to make sure I'm on the up-and-up, but I'll tell Andy about it when I talk to him.

TWENTY-SEVEN

ANDY

ICHAEL ARRIVES a few minutes early. He's dressed for field work—jeans, T-shirt, sun hat, and work boots—but he's clean and seems prepared to meet with me. "Andy, how are you feeling?"

It's been a few weeks since I got out of the hospital, and I'm finally getting into my regular routine. Genevieve stayed and nursed me back to life for a few days before I sent her back to her mother's to go to school. I thought I'd be able to go right back to the same rigorous schedule I had prior to the break-in, but if I push too hard, the headaches become paralyzing. Right now I try to work about three-quarters of a day before I can't take it anymore.

"I'm feeling better. I'm sorry I missed our last meeting."

"Well, I'm guessing you would've preferred to meet with me than be in the hospital." His confidence is shining through. He's just returned from a four-day training with the stacking system. I'd like to have joined him, but we sent Jose; I'll go after I'm feeling better. Walking me through the training and how it'll apply to Bellissima, I learn he really has stepped up and has done an outstanding job while I was in Italy and the hospital.

"When will we be ready to use the new stacking system?"

"Jose and I learned a lot in Fresno. We're both certified to run the new forklift, and we understand how to do the stacking. This system will stack up to eight rows high in our warehouse. This is going to make a huge difference in our storage space and make it more difficult for theft."

I really hope so. This thievery is really beginning to put a pinch on our bottom line. If this doesn't stop it, I can go the old-fashioned way and put in a ton of cameras and guard dogs. That's far from foolproof, but if we can make it hard for the thief, they'll move on to someone else.

"That's what we're hoping. How have things been going from your perspective?"

"Not bad. We're on track for the crush, though we had a problem with irrigation out in fields twelve through twenty-eight."

We walk through how he and his team fixed it, and I'm impressed. In my absence, he really stepped up. No one asked, he just saw a missing link and filled it. This has never been Sophia's area of interest, so I'm glad it's working so well.

"I never asked, how did it go with the trackers?"

"Surprisingly well. I did ask Jose to help because I wanted to get them attached as quickly as possible since you were gone, and I didn't want to risk losing any additional barrels."

"Sounds like you have an idea of who's taking them."

"I do, and I'm working on confirming my suspicions. I'll come to you before doing anything."

"You don't want to tell me now?"

"Not yet. I have a few people in mind, and I'd hate to falsely accuse someone."

I suppose that's fair. I can't think straight with these headaches, and I wish I could figure out who could be the thief. Empty, the barrels weigh close to one hundred and ten pounds, and full they're over six hundred pounds. It isn't as if you can tuck one under each arm and walk out with them.

"When do the new forklift and stacking system arrive?"

"The stacking system is here already, and the guys have set up the base for the first two dozen rows. Once the forklift arrives, we'll get it all stacked. It should take roughly a week of three guys working ten-hour days to get it done. You're going to be impressed."

"Michael, I'm already impressed." Sophia and I have been running this winery for over a decade by ourselves. We've hired interns as we've prepared for the crush, pickers to augment our interns for the harvest, a small staff to help out in the tasting room, and I have two full-time laborers who help with the irrigation and other issues around the vineyard. We may have grown to the point that I'll need a real vineyard manager to oversee several parts of the organization. After we make it through this year's harvest and crush, then I can really think about it and position it for my family to approve.

Michael leaves, and I look out the window and watch him go. I wonder who he thinks could be behind the theft and why won't he at least tell me his suspicions.

I hear the beeping of a truck backing up before I see them. The new forklift has arrived.

I'm in my own world, going through invoices and thinking about my conversation with Michael, when my phone rings. I see it's Melanie calling. She usually only calls in the middle of the day if there's an issue or Genevieve is sick, so I'm a little nervous to answer. *"Pronto."*

"Andy, it's me."

"Is everything okay with Genevieve?" I hold my breath, waiting for her to tell me how to feel.

"Yes, Genny's in school and she's fine. I got her report card, and she did really well. She got perfect grades in math. Can you believe it?"

I breathe a sigh of relief. *Perfect grades? She's just like my mother. She's so smart.* "That's great. I'll take her out to celebrate."

Melanie begins to stammer and does some hemming and hawing. There's clearly something else she wants to tell me. "I, uh... I, um, also wanted you to know that I, um, called Greer."

"Why?" Why would she want to talk to Greer? Great. Now I'm going to be fighting Genevieve *and* Melanie about my relationship with Greer. If there's a problem, she needs to discuss it with me first, not go directly to Greer. My blood pressure is rising, and I'm getting upset.

She rushes out, "I know you really like her, and I know Genny is being difficult. I wanted to assure her that Tomas and I support the two of you." My blood pressure drops significantly. *Wow, Melanie is supportive of Greer and me.*

Holding the bridge of my nose, I push the throbbing in my head away and take a few deep breaths. "What did she say?"

"She shared her history with her parents' divorce and how she's being incredibly patient. I think she's great for Genny. And believe it or not, I think Genny likes her—she won't admit it, but she's said some good things about her. I didn't want to undermine anything you have going on with her. My plan was to begin to include her so Genny knows she has the four of us."

Leave it to Melanie to think of that. "Thank you, Melanie. Greer is very special, and Genevieve would be lucky if she wants to stay in our lives."

"I know you're supposed to have Genny this weekend, but with her helping to nurse you back to health, she hasn't been around much. I'm behind on my wedding planning and could use some help. Would you like a weekend with Greer?"

"If she wants to help, I'm good with that. We don't have anything planned."

"She's been helping me with the wedding prep, and I think I can keep her busy with some dress shopping."

It would be wonderful to spend some time with Greer this weekend. She's been so patient with Genevieve and my schedule. I'd like to treat her for a change. "Let me check with her. Maybe I can spend one day with each of them."

"Whatever you need."

We end our call, and I know why I married Melanie. We may have grown apart, but deep down we still care about one another, and together we put our daughter first.

I spend my afternoon paying bills and working through various marketing and sales plans for the next wines. Sophia and I both agree that we're ready to release the first half of the 2015 barrels for bottling. Now the fun with that will begin.

Bellissima Grande has always used real corks. When we started Bellissima Valle, I planted four dozen cork trees along the driveway our first year, but they aren't mature enough, and there's always the spoilage factor with cork. Bellissima Falco Baia in New Zealand has gone to twist top bottles, and they've reduced their spoilage to almost nothing. More of my brothers are considering the twist tops, and I think it's a good idea. I need to make a recommendation to my family; I fear that the loss of barrels and the possibility of spoilage demands we go with twist tops.

My head is beginning to hurt. I want to lie down, but before I do, I place a quick call to Greer. *"Ciao, bella."*

"Hello yourself. How was your day?"

"It went well. The forklift arrived, and the guys will start the new stacking and storage system soon."

"Are you excited?"

"Actually, I am. Melanie called to tell me she reached out to you today."

"I think she was checking to make sure I'm on the up-and-up."

"Actually she wasn't. She knows Genevieve is beginning to warm up, and she wanted to make sure you were good with being patient with her."

She laughs a soft melodious sound, and it makes my cock stir. "Genevieve is warming up to me? That's news."

"It was news to me, too. It's good news, actually. I think what we're doing is working."

"My evil plan to win her over is working. Bwahahaha."

I laugh. "I miss you."

"I miss you, too. Hopefully we can have some alone time soon."

"It may be sooner than you think. Melanie offered to take Genevieve this weekend."

"I love that idea, but maybe not all weekend, so you can still see her?"

How did I get so lucky to have another woman in my life who's so understanding? "You read my mind. I was thinking I'd come to you this weekend on Friday and leave early Sunday morning to drive up to Sacramento and spend the afternoon with her there."

"I love that idea. Anything special you want to do while you're here?"

"Lots of naked time. I'm worried my favorite friend is going to shrivel up and fall off, it's been so long."

"'Your favorite friend?' Your arm?" She stifles a giggle.

Oh, she wants to play that game. "Well, it's the size of a child's arm, anyway."

"In your dreams." She laughs out loud.

"You're right. In my dreams."

She becomes serious and, in a low and very seductive voice, says, "I think it's perfect. And I can't wait to worship it this weekend."

"It's you I worship. I can't wait to see you in less than seventy hours."

"I can't wait. Sweet dreams, Andreas."

"Good night, *cuore mio.*"

GREER

$\mathcal{W}$E BARELY LAST until the doors of the elevator shut, turning to each other at the same time. He drops his bag on the floor and tangles his hands in my hair, our kiss urgent, intense, profound, my body responding instinctively to his. It's clear that he's missed me as much as I've missed him. His hands move up my skirt and pull at the elastic of my panties.

The elevator opens and I break the kiss, disoriented as I fumble for my keys and open the door to my apartment while he picks up his bag.

He drops it once we're inside and shuts the door, pulling me flush to him. Our kisses become more urgent as our tongues aggressively explore one another. His hands tease my breasts before working their way to my center, his fingers rubbing at my core. He pulls at my soaked panties and thrusts his thick fingers deep, my slit wet and welcoming.

I moan softly into his ear, only breaking our embrace to undo his belt and pants, quickly releasing his hard cock. I hold him and stroke it before lowering to my knees, but he stops me. "I'll come too fast if you suck me off."

He pulls a condom from his pocket and quickly rolls it on. Bending me over the side of the sofa, he enters me from behind in one quick move. *God, I've missed him.* He starts slow so I can adjust to his size, reaching around me to find my sensitive nub, applying pressure to my clit with his fingertip. I tense, my breathing already labored. He works viciously, rubbing my hard and swollen nub until I can't take it any longer. I reach for his arm and dig my fingernails in, my legs straight and stiff as my world spins.

"Oh... God... Andreas," I moan.

My orgasm signals that it's time for his pleasure, and he aggressively pounds me hard, slowing his pace before I hear him grit out, "Greeeeer." He pushes hard and deep into me, and together we come almost simultaneously.

Spent and breathing heavy just barely inside my home, I finally tell him, "I've missed you."

He picks up our discarded clothes and playfully smacks my ass. "I'm so happy to see you."

"Would you like a drink?"

"Do you have sparkling water?"

"Actually, I do."

He pulls his jeans on and sits on the couch, leaving me a little self-conscious that I'm naked and wandering around. I hand him his sparkling water. "What would you like to do? I have a reservation at the Italian restaurant in a little over an hour, or we can postpone until tomorrow. But we'll have to go at some point, or they may come hunt me down."

"Oh, that sounds good. Really, I just want to be here with you. I don't care what we do." I raise my eyebrows, not exactly believing him. "Okay, I want a few repeats of what we just did."

I snuggle in close, and he puts his arm around me. "I don't care what we do either as long as we do it together."

We sit and talk about our weeks, our conversation relaxed and easy. I glance at the time. "I guess I should start getting ready. Do you mind if I hop in the shower?"

"Only if I can help." He smiles.

"I think that can be arranged, but I have no idea how you could be ready to go again after what we just did."

In a very husky voice, Andy says, "With you, I always seem to be ready, but this time I think it's just appropriate to wash you down. No sex, I promise."

The shower is large and easily fits us both comfortably. I hand him a bar of soap, and he lathers up a washcloth, then washes my back in slow circles. I run my fingers over his pecs and the glorious curls on his chest. He turns my insides to mush.

"Are you going to be okay?" he asks, genuine concern in his voice as he trails his fingers over my breasts, the skin red from his whiskers.

I kiss him deeply, creating a soft and gentle dance between our tongues. "It'll be the reminder of a wonderful visit." He seems visibly bothered by the marks, but I assure him, "It'll fade in a few days."

He carefully cleans my sex. Like my breasts, it's a bit swollen and tender from all the activity. I look with longing at his erection as it stands at complete attention while he continues to clean my lower half. He wets my hair and adds shampoo, massaging it into the strands, his fingers moving in small circles and relaxing me to no end. After he rinses the soap away, making sure nothing gets in my eyes, I point him to the conditioner, and again he gives me an amazing head massage.

When he's finished, I take the washcloth from him and start with his back. Humming no tune in particular, I stand behind him, slowly moving down to his legs and feet, purposefully avoiding his balls and cock while paying close attention to his inner thighs.

He stands and turns, allowing me to slowly and methodically

wash his arms. His cock bobs at my stomach, begging for more attention, but I ignore it. As I wash his chest, I stop and kiss each of his pecs and lick the nipples. Again his cock bobs, knocking me in the stomach, begging for the consideration it so rightly wants and deserves, yet I continue with his nipples and kissing his chest.

Sitting on the bench in the shower in front of him, I pull him forward by the hips, then lean in and take his full length into my mouth.

He watches me intently as I adjust and flatten my tongue so I can take more of him. As I move up, I flick my tongue across the tip and taste his precum. His hands move to the sides of my face as he helps set the pace of how fast I work his cock. I break the rhythm as I hear his breathing increase, rubbing the underside with my thumb at the base as I carefully suck on each of his testicles. He's panting, and I know if I wait too much longer I won't get to enjoy his climax, so I put his cock deep in my mouth again. It seems as if it's even bigger than it was a few seconds ago. Sucking hard up and down while I palm his balls, I feel them constrict as they shoot their warm, salty cum straight down the back of my throat.

He stands me up, pushes me against the wall and gives me a deep kiss that makes my toes curl.

I turn the water off, and he reaches for a soft fuzzy towel and carefully dries every drop of moisture from my body. My nipples are so responsive that I have a small orgasm when he rubs the material across my breasts.

Taking me by the hand, he leads me to my bed and lays me down. "Spread your legs open for me."

I immediately comply, and his cock is hard again. He easily slips two fingers between my drenched lips. Oh hell, I'm climbing out of my skin, hot with need.

"You really do get off sucking my cock." As he glides his tongue over mine, he takes some of the wetness and spreads it over my clit with his fingertips, rubbing in firm, slow circles.

His lips break away from mine, my husky whisper barely audible. "Oh... oh God, that feels so good." My breath hitches and my hips buck against his fingers as he strokes my G-spot. "Oh my God, please... don't stop." I'm so drunk on desire.

Stepping back, he admires my bare pussy as it glistens from my excitement. Opening the lips wide, he bends down and licks up some of my moisture. "God, you taste so good." With the pad of his thumb, he places a bit of pressure on my hard nub. "Tell me how much you like drinking from my cock."

"I've wanted it for so long. It's so big and tastes so good," I say breathlessly as he works my pussy into a frenzy.

"Tell me what you want."

I whimper as I writhe beneath his touch. "I want you to make me come."

He leans in and gives me a chaste kiss, then settles between my legs. With his tongue, he circles my clit and begins to strum it with direct pressure while inserting his finger into my pussy, rubbing my G-spot once more.

I'm so close. Don't stop.

I grab his head and push him deep into my core as I buck my hips to his rhythm. Moaning loudly, I fill his mouth with my desire, covering my eyes. I don't want this feeling to stop.

Andy stands up and kisses me. "I shouldn't have dessert first or I may not eat my dinner."

Laughing, I remind him, "They'd be very disappointed if you didn't eat."

AFTER OUR WONDERFUL weekend together, it was hard to say goodbye to him this morning. We left my apartment only for dinner on Friday night, ordering in and relaxing the rest of the time until he left this morning to pick up Genevieve.

I'm really beginning to fall for him. He's hinted at how marriage is important to him, so I find myself trying to wrap my head around something I wasn't sure I'd ever contemplate again. I'm in a euphoric glow just thinking of him. I not only enjoy every aspect of his cock, but I really like him. I keep falling more and more in love with him. He's everything I've ever wanted, and considering the future with him doesn't freak me out or make me nervous.

This is right.

ANDY

$\mathcal{L}$OOKING OUT across the warehouse, I'm stunned. This stacking system allows for us to stack two barrels across and eight barrels high. We're able to put six shelves in place side by side, so each row holds ninety-six barrels now, rather than the old system that would hold close to forty-five. Plus, this system makes rotating easier and allows us to keep the spoilage down due to air circulating around the barrels.

"Michael, this looks outstanding."

"Thank you, sir. All of the random barrels in the villa and tasting room are here. We also installed cameras because of the extra room." He hands me a stack of paper containing a bunch of barcodes.

"What's this?"

"This is your new inventory through the software on the trackers. Everything we've tagged is tracked."

"Great. How are our numbers?"

Michael fidgets with his fingers and rocks back and forth. "The last page includes twelve barrels that are no longer on-site."

"Twelve? Twelve in the past month while I was in the hospital and recovering? Can we track where they are?"

"Sir—" He struggles to find his words. "As you can see by the longitude and latitude, they're located here on Pine Street in Calistoga."

I recognize the address. "But why would they be there?" And then I understand. "Michael, if you can keep this between us for a moment, I need to consult my family."

"Of course, sir."

"You've done an outstanding job. Thank you."

Dread hits me like a rock. My trust is completely gone. I'm at a loss as to why this happened.

Picking up the phone, I call my parents. It's just after 6:00 p.m. in Montalcino, so they're most likely just sitting down for dinner.

My father answers the phone. *"Pronto."*

"Papa, it's me. Your son Andreas," I announce in Italian.

"Is everything okay with Genevieve?"

"Yes, *Papa.* I called to tell you that I've figured out who's been stealing our barrels of wine."

I walk him through the evidence, including the new stacking system and how we track the barrels. "Are you sure?"

"I'm afraid so."

"Have you confronted the thief?"

"No, *Papa.* I wanted your advice first."

"I will come to you. Don't say anything to anyone."

"Yes, *Papa.*"

I hang up, dread crawling through my bones.

How could Sophia have done this to our family? To me?

Walking into my apartment, I see my bag from the weekend only partially unpacked. I can't stay here right now. I'm angry, and I'm hurt.

I want to see Greer.

I pick up my phone and call her.

"Hey there. How did your meeting go with Michael?"

"Not great. May I come down and stay with you for a few days?"

"Of course. You don't even have to ask. Is everything okay? Are you losing the vineyard?"

"I'll tell you about it tonight, if that's okay."

Her voice lowers an octave fills with compassion. "Of course. I love you. We'll figure this out."

"I love you, too."

Packing my bag, I put it in the back of my car, then walk into the tasting room. Sophia's there, but I can't even talk to her because I know I can't be civil. She looks up and me and smiles, then continues talking to the clients in the tasting room.

I find Michael. "Hey. Keep what we learned to ourselves. I'm waiting for my family to decide what to do."

"No problem. I haven't said anything—not to my dad, Jose, or anyone."

I clasp his shoulder. "Thank you. I'm headed to San Francisco for a few days. Can you manage this and keep us moving forward toward the crush?"

"Absolutely." He nods vigorously.

I wave goodbye and climb into my car. My sister calls a few minutes into my drive, but I send it to voice mail.

As I near the Golden Gate, my phone rings, the caller ID telling me it's my older brother, Matteo, who runs the vineyard in the Bordeaux region. "*Papa* has given me some of the details. Tell me what you know."

I carefully exit the highway so I can park and concentrate on walking him through what I know in Italian. I struggle with trying to do too much at one time. "I don't know why she'd be doing it."

"Could she be trying to help with storage?"

"No. We've had long conversations about the thief. She knew

all along we were looking for the missing barrels. Are you coming with *Papa?*"

"Yes, and I believe Giovanni is joining us."

My heart drops. "I'm not giving up Bellissima Valle."

"Andreas, no one has said anything. Everyone knows how well you worked with Sophia. I think we're all impressed that you found out the thief was our own sister and shared that with us. We'll confront her together. *Papa* is meeting me in Paris, and if Giovanni is there, we'll all fly in on the same flight direct to you."

"Do you know when you'll arrive?"

"Chiara sent the itinerary to your e-mail. What are you going to do until we arrive?"

"I've left the winery and will stay with Greer in San Francisco. I'm so angry. I believe if I talk to her, she'll run. I want my wine back, I want to know why she put me in the hospital, and I want to know why she did this."

"I think we all do, brother."

"I'll be at the airport to pick you up. But be clear, Bellissima Valle is my vineyard, and I won't be giving it up."

"I hear you, and I agree. See you soon."

We hang up, and I listen to my voice mail from Sophia. "Andreas, darling, when are you returning to the vineyard? I have some invoices to discuss with you."

I'm questioning everything now. She's been taking care of our accounts receivable. What if some of the invoices are false?

Shit. Maybe I *should* let Giovanni take over and just find a regular job in San Francisco, or maybe become a wine distributor.

I decide to text Sophia so she doesn't get suspicious. **I'm heading into The City. Greer has a problem, and I'll be back in a few days. Text me if you need me.**

Sophia: **Okay, but I think we may need to return some of the wine stacking system.**

Me: **Why?**

Sophia: **We've overspent, and I can't make our payment for loans.**

Sophia: **And there's a $15K expense for a company called Tracer. What's that?**

That's the trackers. I realize I never told her about them when we decided to put them on. I can't let her know they're on the barrels or she'll run, or even worse, get rid of the barrels altogether.

Me: **That's for part of the stacking system. This all came out of the quarterly meeting. I'll get some cash from the general fund.**

Sophia: **This stacking system seems to be a big black hole. We'll have to discuss this expense when you get back. We agreed to not spend money without the other's approval. I hope everything is okay with Greer.**

Me: **It will be. Call me if you need me. Michael has the intern crew doing their thing, so we should be good.**

I look through my e-mail. Chiara sent over the itinerary; it appears she's joining them, and they'll arrive tomorrow morning. Wow. In less than twenty-four hours, I'll have four people descending on us.

I arrive at Greer's apartment and head up. She isn't home yet, so I let myself in and catch a glimpse of myself in the foyer mirror. What a mess I am. I look tired.

I hop into the shower, hoping it'll revitalize me, then crawl into bed. I'm just going to rest until Greer gets home.

I HEAR VOICES AND ROLL OVER to look at the time. It's after nine. *Shit.*

I get up and walk into the living room, finding Greer with her hair in a ponytail, dressed in an old T-shirt and yoga pants. She has a pen in her mouth as she sits cross-legged on the couch, studying her computer.

"Hey, I'm sorry. I was only going to rest my eyes for a minute."

Putting her computer aside, she gets up and gives me a hug. "Is everything okay?"

"No. I found the thief."

"That's great news."

"Unfortunately it isn't. The barrels were traced to Sophia's home."

"Her home? What are they doing there? Could she be storing them?"

"No. I forgot to tell her about having Michael put the trackers on. She took four more barrels before the tracking was attached and another twelve while I was in the hospital." I pace and run my hands through my hair. "I can't believe this. We've worked so hard to make Bellissima Valle a success together. And she always knew once my dad passed away, I would gift her half. That was our agreement. Why would she steal from herself?" I walk over to the bar in the corner of the room and pour myself a glass of bourbon. "What would make her so angry that she would hit me over the head and almost kill me, then destroy over a million dollars' worth of wine? I'm angry, but really I'm disappointed."

"I can't even imagine the betrayal you're experiencing. What are you going to do?"

"My father, Giovanni, Matteo, and Chiara all fly in tomorrow morning."

"That's fast."

"I'm not giving up my vineyard."

She reaches for me and gives me a reassuring squeeze. "They can't expect you to."

"We'll meet and figure out what to do."

"Are you hungry? I ordered some Italian food."

"Thank you for your support."

She makes me a plate of pasta, and together we eat. We talk about our work and how Eve's doing.

Looking at the clock, I see it's after eleven. She stands and reaches for me, and together we go back to bed, Greer in my arms. She quiets my brain, and I quickly fall back to sleep.

I HEAR THE ALARM and look over—it's only five. Greer's slender arm reaches from beneath the covers and turns it off. With a small moan, she sits up and stretches.

"You're going to work already?" I ask.

"No, I go for a run most mornings. I didn't realize that when you're here, I don't do that. You're welcome to join me."

I run at home all the time, and I actually brought my running clothes with me, thinking I could get some time in while she's at work. I'm sure I can keep up with her. I put on a pair of shorts I'd normally wear to work out and follow her lead, stretching beside her before we start down the hill toward the bay.

Holy crap, she's fast. I have a longer stride and thought I'd be able to keep up with her no problem. Boy, was I mistaken. I think she does an eight-minute mile.

Heading down to Pier 39, we see the tourists lining up at Boudin Bakery. She slows as the early rush of people walk across her path. She's drenched in sweat with her hands on her head, and looks amazing. We're both breathing so hard, we can hardly talk.

Finally Greer catches her breath. "Are you up for a cup of coffee? They have a Euro breakfast here if you'd like, too."

"You don't eat breakfast."

"I don't, but you do, and I'd love a cup of coffee." I'm embarrassed. I don't have my wallet, and we left so quickly that I forgot my Apple Watch back at her place.

She must see me struggle, as she states, "I have money." She reaches into her shirt and pulls out a credit card and a folded-up bill.

"You must've been a Boy Scout once. Always prepared," I tease.

I order coffee for both of us and pick up a few kinds of cheese, some meats and a nice piece of bread before grabbing a piece of pier far away from the crowds to enjoy our breakfast. I'm up this early every day, but I'm surprised at how active things are in The City. I'm used to the quiet of the vineyard, slowly filling with the sound of the crews arriving and the equipment. Here there's the noise of the markets receiving goods, the grinding of the coffee beans, all the people wandering and the hum of the people talking and starting their day. It piques my senses but calms me at the same time.

My beautiful Greer points to a little girl who's trying to feed the seagulls. We both smile at how cute she is.

Greer looks at me over the brim of her coffee cup. "What time do you pick up your family?"

"They arrive just before noon. They'll need to clear customs, so it could be any time after one."

"Are you nervous?"

I stop and think about the possibility of being nervous. "I probably should be, but I'm not. I want answers to my questions."

"What's the plan?"

"I'm not sure. I know they're all converging in Paris and flying together, so chances are they'll have one when they arrive."

"If you need a place here, you know you're welcome. I have the two guest rooms and my office, and we can also set someone up on the couch."

"You're very generous. I know they'll want the element of surprise."

GREER LEAVES FOR WORK, and I watch the clock. Following the plane's arrival time according to the airport's website, I begin making my way to pick them up.

Sophia's sent me a few more text messages about the company books; I don't ever remember her being so on top of our numbers before. Giovanni's the corporation's accountant, and he'll spend days going through our books to see if everything is on the up-and-up. I have a pit the size of the Grand Canyon in my gut, asking myself how I could've been so blind.

Parking at International Arrivals, I take a seat and watch the people pushing their luggage carts overstuffed with bags and boxes from different parts of the world. I love the airport and watching all the various cultures collide. The colors seem more vivid in the international terminal.

It isn't long before I see Chiara, looking as if she just walked off the runways of Paris or Milan with two large bags trailing behind her. My brothers and father are following her, each carrying a small bag. They silently scream Italian—big gold necklaces, expensive silk dress shirts with the first four buttons undone, high-quality loafers and cigarettes ready to be lit as soon as they're outside. They may run vineyards all over the world, but they're true to their Italian roots.

"Andreas!" My sister and I kiss on both cheeks. Then I greet my brothers and finally my father. There's a lot of cheek kissing and back slapping.

"Welcome to America." I'm happy to see my family, but there's an undercurrent of disappointment among us. "Do we have a plan?"

"Because we bought the tickets last-minute we had middle seats in different rows," my sister informs me.

I scoff. "Let me guess, except for you. You had a first-class seat."

"How did you know?" She smiles, and my brothers and father all light up Italian cigarettes as soon as they're outside. The smell turns my stomach. Chiara and I stand aside, careful to speak in low tones. Just because we're in America doesn't mean someone won't understand Italian.

"Greer has been kind enough to offer us her home for the evening. We can meet up with Sophia tomorrow morning, or we can go up and confront her tonight. It'll take us about four hours this time of day, so it'll be close to five by the time we arrive if we leave right now."

We're all quiet while we wait for my father, because ultimately he makes the decision.

"We go now."

I remember that look from my childhood. I was only on the receiving end once, and that was when I threatened one of my brothers with a vine pruning knife for harassing me. I never threatened anyone again, learning to be more discreet in my retaliation. He's not happy, and I'm grateful his anger isn't at me. I'd feel sorry for Sophia, except she stole from me, and because of her, I landed in the hospital.

I quickly text Greer and let her know we're on our way to meet my sister.

Greer: **Good luck. I know this will be fine for you. I'm here for you if you want to talk.**

During the two-hour drive, we argue the merits of twenty different approaches, but by the time we make our way through

San Francisco and to the villa in St. Helena, we have a plan ready to be executed.

Leaving the luggage in the car, Chiara heads to the tasting room while I walk my father and brothers to the warehouse. Michael's there scrubbing out one of the barrels. He sees us and sends the interns out to pick up the trash from the earlier delivery.

"Michael, this is my father, Luigi, my brothers Matteo and Giovanni."

He pulls his gloves off and extends his hands to each, and they shake.

"Michael started here three years ago as an intern. This year he's been my lead intern. His father runs a neighboring vineyard, and he's finished school to be a vineyard manager. He's the one who installed the trackers, and he oversaw the installation of the stacking system," I tell my family in Italian and then translate it into English for Michael. "It looks amazing. Because of their work, we've doubled our storage area. But also Michael found that while I was in the hospital, twelve additional barrels went missing."

My father asks him a few questions in broken English, then asks me to translate, "Did you suspect Sophia of being the thief?"

"I prefer not to say, sir," he replies sheepishly.

My father turns to us. "So, that is a yes."

I'm angry. I'm ready to find out why she did this. "Let's go get Sophia and drive her to her home. Michael, do you have a truck?"

"I do, sir."

"Good, can you join us?"

"I have an idea, sir. We have a trailer we can load the forklift in. That will help with loading the barrels in the truck bed. It's going to take a few trips."

My brothers and Michael leave with the forklift, and my father and I walk into the villa. Sophia is so excited to be visiting with

Chiara that she doesn't see us at first. As soon as she sees my father, her face falls, and she attempts to run away, but Chiara reaches for her arm and holds her, saying something to her we can't hear.

My father walks up to the women, standing next to Sophia. "Matteo and Giovanni have gone to your home to retrieve the barrels you've stolen from this vineyard."

Panic runs through her eyes in a matter of seconds, and then they're black with anger. "I only took what I deserved."

I couldn't hold back. "What you deserve? I treated you as my partner, and I promised I would sign over half the vineyard once it was mine to share."

"You were never going to do that. Our family would never have allowed that."

Chiara cocks her hand back and slaps Sophia hard across the face. "You fool. Upon *Papa's* death, Bellissima Grande becomes mine. You would've received what you'd earned, but instead you were a spoiled brat. Now you get nothing. I'll make sure of that."

Holding her cheek while her eyes pool, she turns to our father. "*Papa,* are you going to let her treat me like this?"

I'm floored by her audacity. How did she treat me?

Chiara's hands are on her hips, and my father is calm and clear when he tells her, "Sophia, you have two choices. You can come back to Montalcino, or you can remain here, but if you do, you'll no longer be a part of this family."

"I'm not going back."

I hold my hand out. "Fine, give me your keys. All passwords will be changed, and I will be reporting to the police that we found the wine barrels at your home. They can investigate if you're involved in the other thefts around the area."

"You wouldn't dare." Terror rips through her eyes, and she looks like a caged animal searching frantically for an out.

"Actually, I already have." I want to punch her in the face, I'm so angry. Instead, I turn and walk upstairs to my apartment, calling Greer as soon as I'm inside.

She answers on the first ring. "How did it go?"

"Not good. She did it because she felt she deserved it. The good news is that my parents have always planned for Chiara to take over Bellissima Grande."

"I guess since everyone deferred to her at your parents', I always thought that was what was supposed to happen when they passed."

I laugh. Of course, it takes an outsider to see what was in front of all our faces for so long.

"How long is your family in town?"

"I figure they'll stick around for a few days and then head back. Chiara will stay and we'll figure out how we move forward."

"Without any help, how is your life going to change? What will happen to Bellissima Valle?"

"I will run it by my father, but they met one of my employees who was instrumental in catching Sophia. I believe I can promote him without any issues, and I'll work with our staff to cover the tasting room full-time."

"Great. I knew you had a lot going on, and I waited to ask, but Sara and Trey are getting married next week in Hawaii. It's very under the radar because of Trey's celebrity status, so don't say anything, but would you like to come with me? We're chartering a flight, so there's plenty of room. We can bring Genevieve, too."

"If we can talk her mother into it, I think she'd love it, and I'd love to get away with you. I've never been to Hawaii, so it sounds like fun."

THIRTY

GREER

*A*NDY'S BEEN BUSY with his family, trying to figure out the depth of deception of Sophia and her husband, Luke. When they arrived at their home, they found more than just Bellissima barrels, so they called the police, who arrested the couple. They'd been stealing from multiple vineyards over the years, delivering the wines to a bottler in the Central Valley before selling them under their brand to a middleman, who would then sell them to various restaurants and liquor stores. With Andy's help, the police moved the wine into a temperature-controlled evidence lockup, and Andy and his family donated a stacking system until they're able to return the over two hundred barrels they confiscated from Sophia and Luke's property.

I can hear how tired Andy is over the phone. I have no doubt he's pushing himself, and the monster headaches are probably overwhelming. "I'd like to come visit my mom this afternoon before I go out of town. I know it's last minute, and you still have your family visiting, but I'd love to see you. May I stop by?"

"Of course. Chiara would love that. And of course, I would love that, too. Come and stay the night."

Before I dash out the door, I call the Italian restaurant, explaining that Andy's family is in town and asking them to make up some dinner for about eight of us that I can reheat easily in a few hours. They're wonderfully accommodating. I think if I'd asked them to deliver in St. Helena, they would, but they agree to have it ready for me before I leave.

The smell of dinner permeates my car and overwhelms my senses: the sauces loaded with spices and herbs made of the finest plum tomatoes, onion, and basil; the butter and lemon smothering the shrimp in the scampi; the earthy smell of the mushrooms in their natural broth-covered risotto; the freshly made warm bread. It takes all my willpower to not dip into the food. The bad angel on my shoulder keeps whispering in my ear, "Just a small bite. They'll never know." But I also know if I start, I may not stop, and I want to see my mom and check in on her.

She no longer has a cell phone, and she won't answer the phone in her room. I make a quick stop for a bouquet of yellow tulips and head over to the hospital to visit with her.

"Hey, Mom."

"Hi, sweetheart."

"How are you feeling today?" I extend the bouquet to her.

"Thank you for the flowers." She reaches for them, but I hold them back.

"I'll ask again, how are you feeling today?"

"If you must know, I'm angry. They're making me take these medications, and I know it isn't right. I don't feel happy when I'm on them."

This is why she stops taking them every time. If we didn't have the resources, she would be like so many others with bipolar disorder, homeless and not on medication, eating out of trash cans. Or her depression might claim her and she'd be dead. I know she hates it, and I understand wanting to be happy. I want that for her, but she needs the medications because the lows are pretty low. "Mom, the lithium levels you. It means you don't get as many of the manic episodes or the depression episodes. That's important right now."

"I hate the medicine, and I don't want to take it."

"I love you, Mom." It isn't worth arguing with her because she'll never fully understand the importance of the drugs.

We sit and watch the ducks, and she sneaks pellets out of the pocket of her dress. "Are you going to make me stay here?"

I want to put my arm around her and pull her into a hug to comfort her, but she's never really liked personal contact when she's like this. Instead, I reach for her hand and turn to look her in the eyes. "We can't make you stay, but Mom, you do like it here. We can work with Dr. Phillips to regulate your meds better, and you can continue your art classes and stay here for a while. What do you want to do?"

I hold my breath, knowing if she leaves now, she'll go off her meds and will probably become homeless. Not because she doesn't have a place to stay, but her lack of medication will cloud her mind and she won't want to be confined by her condo.

She murmurs, "I don't want to live alone in my condo."

"I know, Mom." I pull her into a big hug. She's hesitant at first, then holds onto me as if she's going to fall if she lets go.

"I'm scared," she whispers.

"I'm here for you, Mom. Always and forever."

She releases me and sits on her bench. "Come visit me again soon."

I've been dismissed. I know she isn't happy about remaining here, and I understand it's hard for her. When the time comes that she checks herself out, it'll be a death sentence. Her depression has become too great without meds.

I hug her and whisper in her ear, "Trey's getting married in

Hawaii, and I'm going to be out of town for a few days. Can you stay here until I return?"

She nods, and I blow her a kiss. Before leaving, I fight back the tears and head to Dr. Phillips's office. I tell him about the conversation, then beg him to make her happy and able to stay at least until I return.

"Greer, your mom already knows she's staying. She's working on coming to peace with remaining here. Enjoy your trip. She really is in a good place mentally right now."

A weight I didn't realize was on my shoulders is lifted, and I tear up. "Thank you."

WHEN I ARRIVE AT THE VILLA, it's a blur of activity. The grapes have bloomed, and everyone is in the fields trimming so they can control the production.

I grab the untouched dinner from the back of my car and walk into the tasting room. Chiara is busy helping people and charming the pants off them. When she sees me, she waves and rushes over. "My love, Greer. You've come to help me balance the male energy for a few days?"

"I've brought a good dinner from a restaurant close to my house in San Francisco."

"At least I don't have to cook tonight."

"I'll start getting this warmed up, and then I'll come down. I'm happy to help you here in the tasting room."

"I'm good. You take your time." She reaches for both of my hands and squeezes them. "Andreas is very excited about your visit."

"I'm excited, too." I've missed him since our visit a few days ago, which now feels like weeks.

"There she is." Andy comes in and gives me a deep kiss before possessively wrapping his arm around me. The tasting room is nearly empty, only a few couples remaining. Once they all leave, and Andy's father and brother return from the fields, we'll eat.

"I have dinner ready to be heated. Where shall I set the table?"

"How about in the private tasting room in the back? When will it be ready?"

"Whenever everyone's prepared to eat. Don't worry about me. I can visit with Chiara, or I can work."

Three hours later, we're all sitting around the table. Andy's father has not left my side. As we enjoy the dinner Filippo made for us, the feeling is somber. The conversation is in English for my benefit.

Giovanni says, "I've gone through the receipts and the books. It looks like Sophia was taking close to $20,000 a month."

"How could I have missed this? $20,000 is pretty significant."

"It was the revenues from the tasting room."

My heart breaks for Andy. Not only did she steel the barrels, but she was skimming off the receipts as well. I hear them vaguely talk about two hundred barrels of wine. How did no one notice? "I don't mean to sound dense, but how were they able to remove these barrels of wine without anyone knowing?"

"They were taking one here and one there. They had a contraption that was used in the old days to move the barrels around. We believe Luke would case the vineyard and figure out how to break in under cover of darkness. Because it was so little each time, no one could point to when exactly the barrels went missing."

Matteo adds, "Some vineyards didn't even know they'd been robbed until the police showed up and told them they had some of their barrels."

How is that even possible?

Giovanni shares, "Most of the barrels were Bellissima because of Sophia's access. She took them from right under Andy's nose."

Andy's father speaks in rapid-fire Italian, I don't understand a word. Everyone is nodding their head and Chiara looks at me and translates what he said. "They weren't prepared for Andreas to put trackers on the barrels. She was hoping he wouldn't notice the missing wine." He shakes his head in disgust. "We've known thieves in our business before, but never from our own family." He looks away from the table and dabs his eyes.

Chiara reaches for her father's hand. "When it was becoming obvious, she and Luke escalated their thievery and hoped to run away after they bottled the wines in a few months."

"Where were they storing the barrels?"

Andy's quick to answer. "Her husband had built a barn that he had temperature controlled on the back of their property."

"Wait, how did no one notice a big barn on her land?"

"Their property is a few acres, but it's long and narrow, so it was built behind the house and wasn't noticeable from the road. Plus, people put up barns for all sorts of reasons." Andy shrugs as if it's hard to explain.

I'm still confused how they moved wine barrels full of wine around without being noticed. No one has answered the obvious either. "Do you know why she hit you?"

"It was actually Luke who hit me with a shovel. I'm lucky that's all he did. I surprised them when I came in. They thought they'd disarmed the alarm when they cut the power."

"Why didn't she use her code?"

Matteo bitterly explains, "She knew if she did, the system would log the time of her entrance."

"I'm really sorry."

Matteo sits back in his chair and looks around the table at all of us. "We trusted our sister. If we can't trust family, who can we trust?" Looking at Andy, he continues, "Don't blame yourself. She'll go to jail, and she can think about what she did wrong."

The table erupts into Italian, and I'm immediately lost.

Andy whispers in my ear, "They'll be angry with Sophia for a very long time."

Andy was at the police station all day being interviewed and briefed. "The police have met with everyone involved here at Bellissima and other vineyards she and Luke stole from. She worked with an attorney and took a plea deal. She'll spend three years in jail and then be deported when she's released. "I've told her she can go home to Bellissima Grande. Luke laid the blame squarely at her feet, and has also served her with divorce papers."

I'm stunned that they feel she's getting what she deserves. We all know Luke had a heavy hand in what happened. Loyalty obviously means everything to them, but she chose him over family, so the family will pretend she doesn't exist until she comes groveling and apologizes—which may likely never happen, and that's clearly okay with them.

Her father nods. "She cannot work in any part of the business at any location."

Matteo shares, "I love her, but I'll never forgive her."

Everyone nods.

"Does Luke get off without any repercussions?" I ask.

"No, he'll serve three years for the assault against me."

"Thank goodness for that silver lining."

"I still love my sister. I know she was influenced by an evil man. I knew he wasn't good enough for her, but she was happy and now look. She's a woman with no country, no family, and her husband is doing nothing to keep her."

I feel really bad for Sophia. She was always very nice to me. I know what she did was wrong, but if losing your family, your country, your business, and your husband all at one time isn't hitting rock bottom, I don't know what is.

ANDY

$\mathcal{L}$EAVING CHIARA AND MICHAEL in charge at Bellissima Valle was hard, but Giovanni is continuing the audit of our books while Chiara works on training Michael, who I promoted to a new position—operations manager. He was thrilled, and we believe there's no one better qualified for the job.

This is my first trip to Hawaii. This is a very small wedding with close friends and family in Poipu on the island of Kauai. We've all been given the lecture on how to spot the paparazzi, and they chartered a plane for everyone. It's beyond extravagant, and Genevieve is constantly saying, "Hey, *Papa,* look at this!" Greer's friends are media darlings for the paparazzi, and all the family and friends are on the plane—but not the bride and groom. They went in a smaller private and jetted up to Anchorage to throw any possible press off their tracks. They'll change planes and be here a few hours after we arrive.

I'm in awe of the beauty around us. When we land in Poipu, we're met at the airport by a friendly couple, each carrying purple orchid leis. They welcome us one at a time and singsong, "Welcome to Hawaii!" while they place a lei over our heads. Once we're all ready, they take us by a small coach with privacy windows to the estate of a friend of Trey's family.

The Andersons have lived on the island for generations. They were sugar plantation owners and bought most of the island from King Kamehameha in the mid-1800s. Over time, they've become the largest landowner on the island, and while they no longer produce sugar, they dabble in several businesses and are in the environmental forefront. Their estate overlooks a stunning emerald green patchwork quilt of a valley and the golden sands of the beach. Luxurious doesn't even begin to describe the house, and its location. I know it's Hawaii, but this can't be normal.

We're greeted by Patrick Anderson, the great-grandson of the founder of the estate and close friend of Trey's. "Aloha. Welcome to the Anderson Sugar Plantation."

We all exit the coach and watch as Patrick's staff unloads our luggage.

"Each of you has a room here on the estate. We have several jeeps for those of you who want to go exploring, and I've made arrangements for helicopter tours of the island. But first, let's get you to your rooms. We can all meet up here in say"—he looks at his watch—"an hour? We'll have a toast to the happy couple, who will hopefully be here by then."

A beautiful petite Hawaiian woman dressed in a floral print dress with a fragrant plumeria flower tucking her chocolate brown hair behind her ear steps forward and begins reading from a clipboard. She calls us each by name, and a houseman picks up our luggage and takes us to our room.

Genevieve and I are in a room next to Greer. "*Papa*, you know I don't need you to stay with me. You can stay with Greer. I know you two have done 'it.'"

I'm not going to talk about my sex life with my daughter. At eleven years old, she doesn't understand relationships and sex, and Melanie and I decided we weren't going to throw that in her face. "We aren't married, so we stay separately. I expect the same from you one day."

She rolls her eyes in a way only a teenage girl can do.

"I thought I'd take Greer for a walk along the beach. Would you be okay if we did that?"

She shrugs. "Sure."

"We'll meet you in an hour downstairs." I knock on the door to Greer's room as I enter. *"Cuore mio?"*

Greer walks out of the bathroom, already changed from the jeans and sweater she wore on the airplane into a beautiful red flowered dress and sandals. She walks over to me with open arms. "Hey, handsome." Placing her hands around my neck, she kisses me aggressively. My cock stirs, and I want so much to take her here, but I have a plan, and part of that's a conversation I want to have with her.

"You up for a walk along the beach?"

"Sounds perfect. Where's Genevieve?"

"She wants to play on her phone and call her mother."

"The ocean is so beautiful here. Let's go check it out."

Holding hands, we follow the sounds of crashing waves. I feel like a young schoolboy excited to be with a girl. We slip our shoes off as the grass becomes sand, stopping to take in the warm breeze and crashing waves. Greer pulls me toward the water. "I love the ocean here." We dip our toes in, and I'm shocked at how warm it is. "I'm really glad you and Genevieve were able to come with me for Trey and Sara's wedding."

"This is beautiful. Thank you for including us. I'm embarrassed to admit, I didn't realize it was such a big deal. Genevieve has pointed out that this is the event of the decade."

She laughs the most beautiful song. "Trey and CeCe are a big deal to some people. But to me, they're my extended family."

"I'd say if they're hiding on an island far away from prying eyes, it's more than some people, but I'm just happy to be here with you."

We stop and enjoy the waves cascading around our feet, allowing the sand to swallow them up. Breathing in the salty air relaxes me. "When I visited you at your home for the first time, you mentioned that the woman you bought it from didn't want to get married because she didn't need to. Is that how you feel about marriage?"

She takes a big breath. "I don't know. I wanted to marry Mark, so I've never ruled it out. But to be fair, I don't want to have any children. I love them, but my mother's illness is hereditary, and I've seen the depth of depression she goes to and how she struggles to take so many pills every day. I just don't want to pass that on to my child."

"So you're fine with committing in front of family and friends to be with another person for the rest of your life?"

In a Southern drawl, Greer says, "Why, *Signore* Giordano, are you asking a particular question?"

I have a plan, and this isn't part of it. "No. I'm just curious where you stand with things."

My heart soars at the idea though. I know I want to spend the rest of my life with Greer. Now I just need to put my plan in place.

We slowly walk back to the house hand in hand.

"There're beautiful drives to parts of the island. If the weather is clear, there are other parts that aren't accessible by car, only by boat or by helicopter. I've scheduled a helicopter ride around the island for tomorrow, if you're up for it."

"I can't wait."

"There they are," a voice booms from the house. I see everyone on the lanai with drinks in hand. Now that Sara and Trey have arrived, the next forty-eight hours are going to be all wedding all the time. I'm taking notes.

Our evening is full of celebration. The hibachi grills are out, and dinner is Mongolian grilled food. My drink of choice was a mac nut martini. The bartender swore to me it was a real drink, containing local macadamia nut liquor and vanilla-flavored vodka and topped with a Donkey Ball—which thankfully is just a chocolate-covered macadamia nut.

Greer alternated between a mai tai and carbonated water, and I loved that Genevieve was glued to her side and drinking alcohol-free mai-tais and the carbonated water. Greer introduced Genevieve to all the guests, and I watch my little girl blossom into a beautiful young woman. She stands tall and composed, and she answers questions like she's at least ten years older. My heart breaks a bit to see her so grown up. I'm not ready for that.

I make my rounds and meet several of Sara's biological siblings. They definitely all look alike with sandy blond hair, blue eyes, and the girls could all be twins. I'm stunned by the story of Sara's upbringing within the foster system.

CeCe's been great introducing me to all the parents and a few others who are part of this group. I meet Emerson's brother, Michael, and his wife, Alicia, learning that Michael and Trey were college roommates at Berkley while CeCe and Emerson were college roommates at Stanford.

This is the entire guest list, not even forty people.

Trey and Sara come over to talk to me. "It's so kind of you to join us for our wedding."

I'm taken aback by Sara's statement. "According to my daughter, this is the event of the decade."

Trey laughs. "It might be the event of the moment, but not even the year, and certainly not the decade."

I really like how down-to-earth Trey and his sister, CeCe, are. I had no idea they were so popular with the press, but I'm truly in awe of Greer and all of her friends. They're all private, but together they can laugh at themselves and enjoy their time together. Genevieve and I are very lucky to be here.

After talking to almost all the people here, I finally get some time alone with Greer in a quiet corner of the lanai. "Genevieve's having a lot of fun."

"She's a delight. Are you having fun?"

"But of course. You have a wonderful set of friends. I realize I've been so focused on my winery over the last fifteen years that not only did I not have any serious girlfriends, but I don't have any friends outside of my competitors, and honestly, we aren't really friends."

"I'm happy to share mine. That's how this group evolved. But to be honest, I want you all to myself."

"I'm regretting sharing a room with my eleven-year-old daughter, too."

I reach for her hands and look her in the eyes. "I'd love very much to have children with you one day, but I understand why you don't want kids. I want you to know that being with you is more important than having any more children."

Her eyes brim with tears. "I love you, Andreas, to the moon and back."

We kiss, and Dillon comes up and pats me hard on the back. "Okay, you two, we boys are heading to the pool house with Patrick for Trey's bachelor party—very tame, I assure you. And the girls are staying here for Sara's bachelorette party."

Greer squeezes my hand and whispers, "Don't forget we have a helicopter tour at ten tomorrow morning. From experience, I can assure you that a hangover isn't really what you want when you're in a helicopter. We can always cancel if you guys get too crazy."

"See you for breakfast tomorrow morning at eight. Have fun, and send Genevieve to bed before too long."

"I'll do no such thing. She's one of the ladies, and our plan is to spoil Sara tonight."

I shake my head as I follow Dillon and the guys out to the pool house. When I arrive, Cameron sidles up to me. "Dude."

I nod.

"Greer is like my little sister. I'll only say this once. She's had her heart broken by a real jackass. If you don't want this"—he holds his arms out at the house and people—"then get out now. Because I guarantee if you hurt her, I know people and we'll hurt you."

I reach for his hand and shake it. "I love her," I tell him honestly, then share my plan. I end with "This weekend is about Sara and Trey, and I know we don't want to overshadow their celebration, but if anyone is going to be broken, it'll be me if she tells me something other than what I want to hear."

"You're a good man. Hadlee and I will help any way we can."

Everyone is listening and nodding their agreement when Michael speaks up. "If you can overshadow this guy"—he knocks Trey in the shoulder—"by all means do it. He's the center of attention wherever he goes."

The night is pretty tame, but even so, I want to go on the tour tomorrow morning, so I stick mostly to water.

As the party breaks up and we all head back into the main house, Trey walks back with me. "Good luck, man. Are you nervous?"

"Hell yes."

"Good. Then you know how awesome Greer is."

"I think she's pretty damn special."

The girls are watching some chick flick on the big screen with popcorn and candy. I peek in and see Genevieve asleep with her head on Greer's lap. Together we wake her and walk back to our rooms. Our kiss lingers as we say good night.

Greer groans, "See you in the morning."

"Good night, *dolcezza mia*."

I dream of Greer and her raven hair.

GREER

T HE WEDDING WAS AT SUNSET, the pink and gold in the
sky making the evening perfect. The only light coming from
tiki torches added to the ambiance. Hibiscus flowers of every
color surrounded the tent.

Dancing to John Legend's "All of Me" in Andy's arms under
the Hawaiian stars, I feel complete. What a beautiful wedding. I
know it sounds so cliché, but Sara was stunning in a Vera Wang
dress and Trey in his tuxedo. It was a simple wedding, just long
enough to know they were married but short enough that it
touched us all with the romanticism.

Trey and Sara's kiss wasn't quick, mouth closed and done. It
was one of those deep, lots of tongue, toe-curling kisses. They
would never have gotten away with it had we not been under a
canopy that kept the long-range lenses of any intruding paparazzi
far away.

Dinner entertainment is hula dancers with bright red lei
po'o—a lei around the head, bracelets of flowers, yellow plumeria
leis, and banana leaf skirts—while a local band performs with
drums and ukulele. Patrick's personal chef roasted a pig in the
ground in the traditional Hawaiian way and served a traditional

luau, which includes chicken long rice—chicken over white noodles—squid luau, lomi lomi salmon, tuna poke, and poi.

The wedding cake was a stunning display consisting of four cakes in total. The ombré rosette had layers of red velvet sponge sprinkled with pink sugar dust. The second was an absolutely dreamy and sophisticated coconut cake, iced with coconut frosting, generously covered with a handful or two of fresh coconut shavings and finally bedecked with a champagne-colored satin bow at the base. Next up was a cinnamon spiced apple cake drizzled with luscious caramel sauce as bourbon-laced brown sugar buttercream oozed in between. And last but not ever least, the topmost was a double-tier vanilla and almond cake with the bottom tier enclosed in edible silver leaf and adorned with a single sugar magnolia to honor the union.

Patrick's staff worked the party, and it was small enough that they were able to do it all themselves. Patrick was even the bartender most of the night. It was casual and extremely fun to have all of us together with Trey's and Sara's families. Very intimate, and perfect in my book.

The reception kicks in and transitions from traditional Hawaiian to more modern music piped from Trey's iPhone to speakers around the area. Smiles abound, and everyone seems to be letting their hair down and enjoying themselves.

Reminiscing at the dinner table with Emerson about Sara's dress and the wedding, I catch a glimpse of some of the bodyguards. "Boy, they're two intimidating Hawaiians. I think they have muscles on their muscles."

"Dillon tells me Patrick has guards at the gates to keep everyone out, as well as patrols on the beach and in boats."

"CeCe did tell me that Sara and Trey will release a few pictures through a publicist. We hope that'll keep the gossip rags away."

Emerson throws her blonde locks back and laughs heartily. "As if that's likely to happen. This is the Arnaults—American royalty."

CeCe sits down and joins us, saying proudly, "My big brother did okay today." We both nod. "I always wanted a sister, and I couldn't have asked for better one."

Genevieve was beautiful in her light blue floral dress. She danced with one of Sara's brothers and spent time with her brothers and sisters. We all learned to hula and just had fun into the early hours of the morning.

Looking around the room, I realize that while my parents may have struggled with the idea, these people here are truly my family. I love them all and know that no matter what, every person in the room would be there for me if I needed them. I'm incredibly fortunate.

As Andy and I walk a half-asleep Genevieve back to her room, she gives me a hug. "Even if I couldn't text my friends that I was here, I had a really good time today. Thank you for inviting me."

Andy tucks her into bed and joins me in my room. "It was a beautiful night, don't you think?"

Holding on to him tightly, I don't ever want to let him go. "I think Genevieve had a good time."

"I know she did. Did you?"

"Yes, but I'd have fun with you no matter where we were."

He kisses the top of my head, and I drift off to sleep still in my dress. Lying in his arms feels so right.

CAMERON

"ARE YOU READY FOR THIS?"

I pat my chest pocket. "Readier than you'll ever know. I made plans with Patrick to take a jeep from the estate and do some sightseeing, and we'll figure out the right place."

Our helicopter tour yesterday concentrated on the Na Pali coast, which isn't accessible by car. The stunning sea cliffs overlooking the ocean are pure paradise. There are great hikes to see the top of the cliffs, but probably too difficult for the sneakers we brought.

We want to take more up-close looks at a few spots that piqued our interest from our helicopter tour, so we head up the coast to Waimea Canyon State Park. I had planned for this to be the place, but unfortunately the fog rolled in, so it was difficult to see across the impressive gorge and canyon views. We could make out a few of the waterfalls in the distance, and it was beautiful, but it wasn't quite right.

"Papa, why are there so many chickens here running around?"

Greer looks at her travel guide. "According to the book, it says Hurricane Iniki in 1992 destroyed all the chicken coops, so they've run wild ever since."

"Oh, look at the beautiful hen. Red, blue, yellow, and black feathers. Wow! And look, she has, one, two, three,... six chicks."

I miss the turn for Wailua Falls, so we head to the other end of the road to put our feet in the sand at Hanalei Bay. The long scenic white-sand beach with mountain views is stunning. We squeeze a large blanket between the lobster-colored tourists and dip our toes into the water.

"The water is so warm here," Genevieve says.

"It certainly isn't our Northern California beach temps," Greer agrees. Turning to me, she asks, "Isn't this amazing?"

"I'm with my two favorite girls on a beach far away from the challenges of my vineyard. I'd agree." I pull both girls in for a family hug, and we enjoy the late afternoon sitting on the beach.

When it's time to leave, we stop at a local fruit stand on our way to our final stop, ordering fresh coconut, pineapple, and mangos and eating them roadside.

"Coconut always tastes better here in Hawaii," Greer says.

With pineapple juice dripping down my chin, I tell her, "I think this is even better here, too."

With a big sigh, Genevieve says, "I wish we could move here and not go back to the vineyard or your crazy job in San Francisco."

Greer nods. "Wouldn't that be fun? But you'd miss your friends."

Reluctantly Genevieve agrees. I'm in awe that Greer doesn't tell her that moving away would be silly or discount what she has to say. She treats her as an adult and offers a practical reason of why moving wouldn't work. I didn't think I could love her any more than I already do.

Finally, we head to our final destination for the day. If this isn't the place, then I'll have to figure out something else and soon.

When we arrive at Wailua Falls, I know this is it. The double waterfalls surrounded by lush greenery are perfect. This is the place I want to remember for the rest of my life. Our tour book tells us of a hike that will take us closer to the falls, and we all agree to wander. In my breast pocket is the engagement ring and my cell phone.

We all stand next to one another, admiring the beautiful flowing waterfall as the sun begins to set, casting a warm orange glow onto the water. Genevieve spots hikers who've gone down to the bottom of the falls. We take our photos, and I hand my cell phone to Genevieve, who snaps a few of us.

She looks at me and I nod. She reaches for Greer's hand. "Thank you for including me this week. It's been really fun. My friends are never going to believe that I was at Trey Arnault's wedding."

"I'm so glad you could come, and I'm glad you had fun."

"I know when we first met, I was a complete jerk. I just want you to know I really like you, and I see how happy you make my dad." She wipes a tear away and gives Greer a tight hug. My heart beats faster as I see the two women I love most get along.

Before Greer can say anything, I know it's my turn. "I know your work is important, and I never want to take that from you. I know we can figure out how to make it all work. You've become so important to both Genevieve and me and—" I get down on one knee while Genevieve holds her hand. "—because of you, we've learned to smile more, laugh regularly and dream often. We were wondering if you'd marry us and be part of our family."

She pulls us into a big hug, nodding and crying as she says, "Yes."

I grin, slipping the round-cut Tiffany diamond with adjoining pear-shaped stones on a platinum band on her finger. "I hope you like this. We can change it if you don't."

"I love it, and I love both of you so very much."

I'm the happiest man on earth.

A few words...

This book was a lot of fun to write. It was a little over a year ago that I sketched out this series. Eight books. Some of them were going to be more challenging than others, but I was so excited about Greer meeting a good guy. Her heart had been broken, and it's so easy for us to think we'll never find love, but I wanted to show that patience wins. But I loved so many of the secondary characters of this book. My favorites were Eve and her manic moments. What fun to just spew words and activities. Sophia came to me as I was writing—someone who felt the world had done her wrong. We all know that person, and sometimes it takes hitting rock bottom before they ever realize that it wasn't nearly as bad as they thought.

When I started this series, I sat down and talked to the voices in my head and out came the Venture Capitalist series demanded to be written first. I lived for many years in San Francisco and loved how close Napa was to San Francisco. Greer and Andy aren't based on anyone I know, but they are people I'd love to know. I did a lot of research on winemaking and how hard it would be to steal barrels. I came across an old article from early days that spoke of how the monks would move barrels around and thought it would make for a great plot line. I hope you enjoyed reading the book as much as I enjoyed writing it.

As an independent author, I rely on so many people to get my books to print. I'd never be able to truly do this on my own. Publishing takes a village—sorry Hillary. I have two hobbies—writing and reading. So when I'm not sitting in my car waiting for one of my boys to finish some kind of practice, I'm reading someone else's book or writing.

My amazing husband is my muse. He deserves a medal for all that he does for me. He really is my rock and truly the most supportive partner anyone could ever ask for. He is my alpha reader and loves more than just the steamy scenes. He has his opinions on who the mole is, but even he doesn't know. Despite being together for sixteen years, a girl still needs a few secrets. But, without his love and support, I'd never have taken the leap of faith to write these stories that are hidden in my head. Daniel, you are my happily ever after.

I have a wonderful group of friends. Some I went to school with, some who I've met through my professional life and some are writers that I've reached out to that kindly have offered me guidance. Gayle, Christie, Michelle, Nicole, Helene, Steven, Erin, Bree and Ivy, thank you for listen to me talk about my stories and pretend to enjoy the process as much as I do. (You aren't fooling me when you change the subject when I want to talk it out ;) You're all amazingly supportive, read all or parts of my books and cheered me on from the sidelines. Thank you all for being my posse. I love you all.

Aria Tran at Resplendent Media who does my amazing covers and Nadia who makes my paperback books insides look amazing. My words would be empty without your artistry.

A huge thank you to Mark Dawson and James Blatch at Self-Publishing Formula who helped show me how to get my books in front of all my readers.

A huge thank you goes to the girls over at Hottree Editing: Becky always gets my books first. Sometimes she shreds them and other times she is full of compliments. Kristin dives in and does the heavy lifting on my books. She goes through and line-edits and makes it so much smoother, while still leaving my words and intent. Donna makes the magic happen moving my book from one group to another, and her scheduling pushes me to stay on track. Barbara was my final eyes this go around. She was amazing and had caught a few good oops. And, no book would be complete without my beta readers: Sue and Michael. You all have helped make this book look professional, and error free. All of the errors in this back matter are mine and don't speak nearly to the help and guidance the girls (and Michael) give me. If you know of anyone looking to break into the world of self-publishing be sure to talk to Becky and Olivia—sending you all hugs for all you do for me.

I want to thank those of you who've taken the time to review my books. Reviews help those silly algorithms at Amazon find these stories. I love all for your kind words. It means so much to me.

And finally to all of my readers, without your support and encouragement, there would be no Ainsley St Claire. Thank you so much. I love getting to know you through e-mail, your reviews, sharing with me what you like and don't like; I do listen and adjust. Please tell your friends if you like my stories. Getting the word out is what allows me to keep writing.

Ainsley

How to find Ainsley

Thanks for reading *Venture Capitalist: Temptation.* I do hope you enjoyed Greer and Andy's story and reading the fourth book in the Venture Capitalist series. I appreciate your help in spreading the word, including telling a friend. Before you go, it would mean so much to me if you would take a few minutes to write a review and capture how you feel about what you've read so others may find my work. Reviews help readers find books. Please leave a review on your favorite book site.

Don't miss out on New Releases, Exclusive Giveaways and much more!

- Join Ainsley's **newsletter:**
  www.ainsleystclaire.com

- Like Ainsley St Claire on **Facebook:**
  https://www.facebook.com/
  ainsleystclaire/?notif_id=15136208
  09190446&notif_t=page_admin

- Join Ainsley's **reader group:**
  www.ainsleystclaire.com

- Follow Ainsley St Claire on **Twitter:**
  https://twitter.com/AinsleyStClaire

- Follow Ainsley St Claire on **Pinterest:**
  https://www.pinterest.ca/ainsleystclaire/

- Follow Ainsley St Claire on **Goodreads:**
  https://www.goodreads.com/author/show/
  16752271.Ainsley_St_Claire

- Follow Ainsley St Claire on **Bookbub:**
  https://www.bookbub.com/authors/
  ainsley-st-claire

- Visit Ainsley's **website** for her current booklist:
  www.ainsleystclaire.com

I love to hear from you directly, too. Please feel free to **email** me at ainsley@ainsleystclaire.com or check out my **website** www.ainsleystclaire.com for updates.

About Ainsley

Ainsley St Claire is a Contemporary Romance Author and Adventurer on a lifelong mission to craft sultry storylines and steamy love scenes that captivate her readers. To date, she is best known for her debut "naughty Nicholas Sparks" novel entitled "In A Perfect World".

An avid reader since the age of four, Ainsley's love of books knew no genre. After reading, came her love of writing, fully immersing herself in the colorful, impassioned world of contemporary romance

Ainsley's passion immediately shifted to a vocation when during a night of terrible insomnia, her first book came to her. Ultimately, this is what inspired her to take that next big step. The moment she wrote her first story, the rest was history.

Currently, Ainsley is in the midst of writing her Venture Capitalist series.

When she isn't being a bookworm or typing away her next story on her computer, Ainsley enjoys spending quality family time with her loved ones. She is happily married to her amazing soulmate and is a proud mother of two rambunctious boys. She is also a scotch aficionada and lover of good food (especially melt-in-your-mouth, velvety chocolate). Outside of books, family, and food, Ainsley is a professional sports spectator and an equally as terrible golfer and tennis player.

Made in the USA
Coppell, TX
21 November 2020

41822231R10157